The Flea Marketeer

STEPHEN V. ROBERTS

Outskirts Press, Inc.
Denver, Colorado

Outskirts Press, Inc.
http://www.outskirtspress.com

ISBN: 978-1-4327-6557-6

Outskirts Press and the "OP" logo are trademarks belonging to Outskirts Press, Inc.

PRINTED IN THE UNITED STATES OF AMERICA

Dedication

Dedicated to Arthur L. Roberts- International traveler, businessman, storyteller and teacher; a man more enriched by culture & life than anyone I could imagine. A man of humble beginnings and glorious pursuits, a man I'm proud to call my father.

Dedicated to Joyce H. Roberts- an Open spirit whose joy has always enriched our family and given the best foundation one could ask; the strength on which we unite and build- the woman who always believed in my success. A woman of humble beginnings and nourishing ways, a woman I'm proud to call my mother.

To my parents, whose lives through 59 years of marriage has given me compassion and means to make life a truly beautiful experience; To them, an eternal lifetime of thanks.

Your son, Stephen.

Great thanks to:

My lovely wife Kathleen and our wonderful children Brianna and Shane Roberts, the Connolly Clan (immediate & extended families), the Roberts Clan (immediate & extended families), and Family Vella

And the creative leaders I'm lucky enough to call friends: Jefferson Thomas-musician, Pietro Barbera-painter & sculptor, Donald Vaccino- painter, Professor Kenneth Sammond- PhD, Patricia Vass-painter & fashionista, Robyn Sassen- Artist & Journalist, Peta Kaplan- Painter & Innovator, Joe Vella-musician & technological genius

And the great institutions of:

Funk Thunder - music for another dimension - http://cdbaby.com/funkthunder3

Electro-Faustus - instruments of electronic frequency - http://www.electrofaustus.com/

MAY OUR IMAGINATIONS NEVER REST IN THE PURSUIT OF PURE HAPPINESS.

Prologue

The cab lurched to the curb of 6th Avenue and 47th Street. A shriveled little man adorned with a tweed hat and London Fog Raincoat scuttled into the dry compartment of the yellow car.

The driver spoke with a thick Pakistani accent, "Where to?"

"57th and Park."

The cabby hit the gas and zigzagged down the busy avenue. The radio filled silent airspace between lights, nothing Henry Hillerman understood.

Henry looked towards the rearview mirror and stared at the man's dark eyes; they dodged his glance. "Talkative one, aren't you?" he said under his breath.

The man grunted as the cab sped between other yellow streaks that filled the avenue. The droplets smacked the windshield and miraculously stopped when they hit Fifth Avenue. The car arrived in front of his apartment building minutes later.

"Six dollars and fifty cents," yelled the driver.

Henry pulled seven dollars from his money clip. "Keep the change," he said.

Henry opened the door and stepped into a deep puddle of water. "Goddamn potholes," he said. "Shit!" He stepped from the street and shook his wet shoe.

The cabby counted the money and in anger gunned the gas pedal. It hit the pothole and sent a shower of murky water over Henry's business clothes. Unfamiliar brazen words screamed from the cab's window- as the car pulled away.

Henry waved his fist, "You foreign prick! I ought ta!" He flipped the bird just in time to see the dark skinned man flip it back. Henry gasped, clutching his chest. The color drew from his face and beads of sweat layered the perimeter of his hairline. The doorman came to his aid.

"Are you OK, Mr. Hillerman?"

"Yea, I'm fine Donny, just a little pissed off. The city's cab companies hire the lousiest drivers and newest immigrants."

"Let me help you to the elevator. You don't look so good. Can I help you?"

Henry waved him off with his hand, "I ate something that's not agreeing with me. I'll be all right. Just need a good night rest," he mumbled.

"We all need a little of that. I'll get you the elevator."

Donny escorted Henry through the art deco brass doors of the car and went to the twelfth floor. "OK, Mr. Hillerman. We're here. Take care of yourself and rest up."

Henry focused, took a deep breath and responded in his normal voice, "Sure will. I'll see you at a six-thirty."

"You know I'll be here."

"Morning wouldn't be the same without you. Have a good evening."

The elevator doors shut and Henry tried to control the shake in his hand. He struggled to put his key through the small opening and then stumbled through the door. His body slammed backwards propelling it into the doorframe with a loud boom. The door locked behind him.

Intense pain stretched up his left arm and crept into his

chest, where his heart thumped louder than a bass drum. *It's too soon! A few months more, Lord! Please let me see it once more!* He fell on to his knees, and aimed himself at his cabinet safe. He struggled to crawl. The pain raced faster than he could move, circulating through his body. His eyes concentrated on the safe, his muscles spasmed. He fell forward on his chin. Seconds later, his body came to a halt. His eyes hollowed in disbelief; they stared at nothing but darkness.

Chapter 1
The Fleamarketeer

The sun seared the black T-shirt Randall Becks wore into his sweaty chest. He cupped his face and pushed his sticky hands against the front window of Sheephead Electronics to clear his vision from the sun. Clouds of gook slid against the high polished glass, but he quickly stabilized them to one spot which allowed him to see the small mercury thermometer nestled towards the back of the display case. It was in a miniature dust covered Swiss cottage souvenir, "Ninety-two degrees and only four hours into the day, God help us!"

He turned to face the street, stroked the thick black stubble on his jaw line, and spotted a torn *New York Times* lying in the trash. He looked cautiously side-to-side and when all other eyes were diverted, he snatched it without reservation. He snapped it open. *Wednesday September 6th. 1992, what's in store for me, today?* The light at University Place changed and he crossed the street.

He walked east beneath the shadows of soot-faced buildings on the street's north side. Jackhammers pounded the potholed street and kicked up bits of tar and cobblestone from the last century. These heat waves blew a mixture of sweat and

dirt down Stuyvesant. A slight breeze blew the stench of freshly baked tar and trash to his nose from the worksite close by.

He approached a condemned East Village apartment
building whose door was sealed with a four by eight piece of
plywood. It swung on an anchored commercial steel nail centered at the top of the doorway. He pried his fingers beneath
the half-inch board and moved the pine to one side. A candle
flickered from behind the red glass of an old railroad lantern
in the depths of the corridor. The drippings overflowed from a
small crevice between the glass and metal casing, which created
a large pile of multi-colored wax at the bottom. He smashed
a small stalagmite that formed on the floor with his foot, and
examined the one-inch wick that remained. He turned, reached
between the cracked rails of an antique staircase, grabbed another taper from an open-ended box wedged between, and lit
the new wick. He mashed it into the hot wax of the old, and
exhaled deeply on the molten mass to cool it. After a minute,
he shook the lantern slightly. *Like new.*

Every stair creaked under his weight. From the outside,
the building had been labeled "condemned", but Becks was
used to poor living. Step after step he rattled the encasement
until he reached the third floor. He pulled a ring laced with
keys from the front pocket of his tight blue jeans. Seven keys
released a series of deadbolts on a stained oak door. He walked
in, re-bolted the locks, turned to his left, and lifted a few strewn
papers from a tall plywood table anchored to the wall by heavy
bolts. He picked up a large felt marker and tucked it behind his
right ear. Each hard wood floorboard gave as he crossed the
room towards the light. The streaks of sun pierced the slats,
which extended across the length of the window. They fell to
the left side of his well-worn living room couch. He threw his
body onto it and every spring jarringly coiled as they struggled

to hold him. A plume of dust rose from the sinews of the pat-
terned wool. He nestled into the corner, opened the paper to
the classifieds, and scanned the auction page.

*Randall, you're on your game. See the small ads, the big ones get too
many. Too big a crowd, too little profit; too many people, too damn compet-
itive!* His finger slid down the paper. It stopped three quarters
of the way down at the name Henry Hillerman.

Auction
Thursday September 6th, 1992
Grames Warehouse 255 East 22nd St.
New York, NY

Large Victorian Cherry DR Table with 8 Chairs, One pair
of Victorian Marble TopSide Tables, Late 1800's Cherry
Hutch, Morris Chair with Carved Griffins, 19th Century
Grandfather clock, Victorian Armoire, Mahogany Slant
Front-Desk, Wurlitzer Spinet Piano w/Ivory Keys, Antique
Swiss Music box w/floral inlay, Victrola Phonograph,
French Brass Mantle clock, Neoclassical Bronze & Marble
Candelabra, Large Pair of Cloisonné Vases, 6 pc. Mahogany
BR set, 18th Century Violin, Cast-Iron Stagecoach Doorstop,
Antique German Cuckoo Clock, Degas Ballerina painting,
bird prints, Goebel & Hummel Figurines Royal Doulton
Toby Mugs, Limoges, Sterling Flatware Set, Bronze Lion
Bookends, Asst. Old Books, Depression glass, decorative
China & Porcelain, Cigarette Cards, WWII medals, pocket-
knives, Pocket watches, asst. 14k jewelry and Antique Quilts.
Terms: Cash or Check (w/ID) only. Geller & Associates

"Shit, I can walk to it from here!" He put a large star next
to the auction, and then put the paper down. He reached across

a rickety table for an open pack of Marlboro's and a pack of matches. He eyed the logo with fondness.

"The Pussy Cat Lounge, how utterly delicious." He smiled.

Randall slid one out, threw it between his lips, and lit it. He turned his head to look at the strips of plaster that fell in multiple columns from the hallway's ceiling. "How the fuck I'm I gonna get outta here? Think Randall, think!"

First, I get myself a Long John Silver Toby Mug. I pay $30.00 for it, and peddle it to Todor's Antiques for double or triple what I paid. He never shows at auctions and besides, he'll double his money at that cost! We both win and I get to buy my next meal. I just gotta remember to steal his paper from his stoop before he gets a chance to see it. By now, he must have noticed his Friday papers have disappeared for three weeks straight. He took a long drag on his cigarette. *I keep that damn shop running with all the stuff I get. For all the shit I know, I should own it. Why couldn't I be born with money?* He pushed his head back on to the soft cotton cushion. *Four years in this God damn place! If only I could get OUT!* He smashed his freshly lit cigarette in a white ashtray over the lean body of Seabiscuit that filled its center. He slammed himself back down, closed his eyes and in two minutes fell sound sleep.

A beautiful woman, scantily clad, walked towards him. He smiled. "Honey, would you pull the Viper into the garage? I think it's going to rain."

"Of course, you gorgeous man," Vera replied in a soft sensual voice. She kissed him, winked and sauntered to the garage.

He smiled with contentment.

Randall's body nestled into the couch beneath his dreamy skies. The skies mysteriously turned black, the clouds pierced the sky like a knife cutting through thick fog. He shifted.

"Vera? You've been in there an awfully long time! Where are you?" He jumped from his comfortable leather recliner and swung open the entrance to the garage. Randall's body trembled as he saw his girlfriend's body sway lifeless from the ceiling girders.

"Don't you do this to me! Don't you dare!" He raced into the garage, grabbed a machete from his tool bench, and hacked the rope with all his might. He threw the blade to the ground as he saw the last threads of the rope snap under her body weight. Her body slammed into his arms. He laid her quickly down and pulled the rope loose. He tossed her head back and performed mouth-to-mouth resuscitation. He pounded her listless chest in frustration. "Live dammit, live!"

Randall's body hurled itself to its side.

He bent down repeatedly, relentlessly. She remained still. He cradled her and as he did, the corner of a note fell from beneath her limp body. He pulled it out. He wept.

"Randall, I can't put you through this any more. I'm a coke addict and it's as much a part of me as you. I fought for years of my life and can't kick it. I can't bury my head in the sand. I know you tried. You did everything to free me of these chains, but I deceived you. Every hour you were gone she'd weasel her way back to me. I gave up running away, no matter how much you love me, I can't... and I won't bring you to this place. Fix by fix, I cheated, I stole, all the while your trust of waiting for me I destroyed. I can't face you or myself. You need to live and this you must- without me. I love you. Vera."

Garbled sounds rolled from Randall's mouth when suddenly his body jolted from its fetal position. He readjusted his eyes, forced awake by the recurring nightmare. Standing like a boxer who'd been hit in a combination of landed hooks, he wavered, covered in perspiration. His body went rigid.

"God damn you, Vera! Why wouldn't you listen to me? I loved you!" His fist hit the wall and a scab broke free from his scarred knuckles. It sent a small trickle of blood down his hand. *You weren't supposed to make the call! You were supposed to talk to me. You know I'll never find another woman the way I found you! When you died, you killed me too! I'll never touch love again, you hear? Never!* His heart palpitated.

"Let go of the past, Randall- the breakdown's done!" he yelled to himself. He plunked down on the couch and put his head in his hands. He plead, "Lord, I don't need much, just a ray of hope every so often. I don't think it's much too ask- just a smidge." He crouched over and looked at the floor. His eyes burned. In a pendulum of emotion, he stood up erratically and pointed at the ceiling. "Let this misery bury itself! I'm numero uno and that's all that matters!" He stormed over to a crayon stained painting nailed into an exposed beam: an abstract of misfits who walked Washington Square Park. He stroked the edge of the splintered wood. "Vera always told me, I was worth far more than you guys, even though I could see myself in your position." He rattled the wall with his open hand. "You'll never see me for what I am, like she did. You'll never see me cause when I buried her… I buried myself. I'm a loner; understand? A loner!!!"

Bury the past, man; bury the past. He bowed his head, walked to the bathroom sink where the plug kept a small pool of ripple less water, and splashed some lukewarm water on his face. He returned to the living room couch, took a deep breath, and regained his composure. He returned his mind to his daily agenda.

I've got to pick up some buys Thursday night at the auction, I'm in desperate need of merchandise "Most of my good stuff sold last weekend, so I'll need to work really hard for my sales this week. I gotta clear four hundred in profit between the three days." Randall lifted the corner of his couch. He shoved his hand beneath, poked it through a hole in the black felt lining, and felt a pouch stapled at the front. His hand clawed the stitches of material, searching for the zipper. He opened it and pulled a small wad of rubber-banded cash out, consisting of a series of twenties, tens, fives and plenty of ones. He counted eight hundred dollars. He took a twenty from the top and put the rest back.

"Man, I'm hungry. Suppose I should get a bite." He peered from his third floor window and looked over the construction equipment that took up half the street. He wedged it open and found the glorious scent of fresh bagels drift in from Jessie's Bagel Haven a block away. "I can't take it anymore!" He walked to the door, pulled out his keychain, and locked two of the seven locks, then slammed it behind him. Minutes later, he was in the bagel store. He looked at the half-empty refrigerator on the left, took a pint of Hershey's chocolate milk, got on a rapidly moving line, and requested a sun-dried tomato bagel. He watched the counter waiter lop a wad of cream cheese between the two halves. The waiter scribbled a number in crayon on the folded piece of wax paper that held the bagel, and returned it to him.

"Next," he shouted

Randall reached the register, ordered black coffee, and handed over the twenty. He got his change and walked out to the street, turned the corner and found a man he'd seen a dozen times before. His books were scattered across the sidewalk.

Randall looked at the chocolate milk then down at the

homeless man, "Hey, you look like you need a drink John Doe. I just got this. I think you need it more than me."

"Thanks, Joe," replied the man.

Randall sat down Indian-style next to him and leaned against the dark brown building, "You don't mind if I sit here with you, do you?"

The homeless man, a little shocked, stuttered, "Nnnn... nnnnno, not at all." He looked at him several times and spoke, "IIIII... IIIII....II got something for you." He reached into a small canvas sack next to his thigh and took out a book. "It.. it...itttt..sssssssss.. free for you."

"Diversification in Antiques: A Collector's Guide. Interesting. Thanks, Doe." Randall replied, "So what made you pick that book for me?"

"Well I, ...you're one of the fffffew people who talks to me. I see you're a bright young guy. Bright gggg..gggguys need books, and I thought this one was perfect for you." He sipped his chocolate milk.

"But how'd you know I liked antiques?" Randall asked.

"I see you luggggg lugggg lugggg all these beautiful things down the street at all hours of the day and night. I see mmm-mmmore than you realize."

"I guess you do," replied Randall. He put down his coffee and opened the antique book. He flipped through some pages and stopped. "Here's a chapter on making your investments work. Now this sounds interesting." He silently read the book mouthing every word that crossed his lips. Two minutes passed before he looked up and nodded. He closed the book, and then looked at his companion.

"Hey Doe, this chapter describes exactly what I do. It says diversifying attracts more people. Sometimes, you buy something and get only what you paid for it, but if that attracts others to look at it, and filters them off to get other things, then it's worth it. My strategy is if you buy one thing, say car parts, and a car convention comes to town, you don't make a penny. If you carry car parts, motorcycle parts, design materials and decals, your chances to sell something go up."

"I kkkknow that Joe, look at me. Books and magazines are easy to get, cost nothing, and are easy to carry, but I'mmmmm I'mmmmmm I'm not limited to that. I carry small toys and matchbox cars that I sell quick, sooo oooo oo" His mouth opened wide and paused in frustration. He breathed in deep, "When you're homeless, you gotta be light. You go where your ass ain't kicked and you get what ya can nnnnn nnnn, from who you can. Gotta run in a spot or a pinch; know what I mean? I use what little space I got to the fullest," he said.

"Part of the secret is being in the right place at the right time."

"Yea, I agree 100%. I always had a problem with that. I guess that's why I'm here today yhh yhhh yhhh." Doe laughed.

"The book says to know your market. I know personal paperwork sells best at mine. I don't know why, but there's this fascination with other people's lives. Mementos like old postcards, photographs, books, personal items, used stock certificates and other stuff like that. So naturally I look for em'. I put tags on the stuff immediately, so I don't under price it. If I don't price it in advance, I give it away. I always learn from my mistakes," said Randall.

"When you're as old as I, and you live half your life fuckkkkking up, you learn the hard way. I used to live for the horses; lost my wife, my house and my car on stupidduhhhh duhhity." He looked at Randall's soured face and quickly changed his tone, "but that's not important. I take risks too."

"I play it easy, unless I got money to play with. If I've got it, I'll gamble. I once bought an old Hebrew prayer box from a woman who told me her grandmother bought it overseas. She told me this big story and made me cough up fifty bucks for it. Didn't know shit about it, but I decided to take it. You know, I sold the damn thing for three hundred bucks!" He paused in thought. "Ya know it's about seeing the spark in their eyes, the desire."

"Yea, I guess." He sighed then bowed his head, "Hard for me to look into others eyes."

"Yea, I guess it's what you're used to. Can ya believe, I had no clue what it even said! Right place; right time. Strange world we live in," said Randall.

"No doubt," replied the old man.

Randall looked down at his imitation Rolex watch, "Well I'd better be on my way. Thanks for the book; can't wait to read it."

"I'll keep my eyes open fffffffor more," said the man.

"Later, John Doe."

"Later, Joe."

Randall picked up his bag and walked back home. When he entered his place, he placed his bagel and coffee on a stained particleboard table. Scattered chips and dents covered the face of the 1977 throw back placed on an angle to act as both an ottoman and a gathering surface. It scratched the floor in front of his couch. *I should rummage into the junk of my closet.* He slid open the wedged closet doors on wheels whose smooth rounded face had as many chips as his table. Every inch of space was jammed with hangers of clothes. He eyed neatly stacked boxes labeled "Miscellaneous" on the top shelf. He went to the kitchen, grabbed a partly varnished chair and hauled it to the closet. He stood on top, grabbed three boxes, and placed them next to the table. He went to the corner of his bedroom and grabbed an additional three boxes labeled "FM" for flea market, which he placed next to the miscellaneous ones.

He sat down, sipped his coffee and opened the first miscellaneous box. He gently unwrapped a baseball from its newspaper skin. He tossed it up and down in the air; and then gripped it tight. He took a pitcher's stance. His imagination lit with thousands of people who filled the stands. The crowds egged him on. Yankees, Yankees, Yankees, they chanted. *Here comes the pitch... he swings... it's high, it's going, it's going, and it's gone! Homerun! The Yankees win the series!* He opened his eyes and looked down at several signatures on the ball. "Damn, it feels good to touch something historical like that, some things are worth millions in your imagination."

He dug back into the newspaper-filled box and unwrapped ten sterling silver state spoons, each one inscribed on the bowl. "These are hot sellers. They're beautiful, but I can live without them." His fingers dug more rapidly into the box with each new find, like a child who's discovered a new toy, he could hardly contain his excitement. He pulled twelve pewter goblets from the box, held them to a battery powered Coleman lamp, and examined a hallmark beneath the lip of a cup. "I need to look this up." He went to a small makeshift bookcase nestled in the corner, and pulled out a book, "Hallmarks of the World, lets find these babies." He flipped though the yellowed pages until his finger rested on symbols, which resembled the ones in front of him. He compared the two carefully, "Made by Roberts & Co. in 1865. Says here, the manufacturing plant existed from 1860 to 1876. He pulled out a bright yellow pastel tag and wrote "Roberts & Co., 1865 Pewter Set $150. For that amount I'll give 'em up." He put another tag on a separate goblet with more specific details then re-wrapped them and put them carefully into the "FM" box.

He sorted through his miscellaneous boxes one by one until he gathered a small sampling of different items he'd lost interest in. He repacked what remained of his personal treasures into one tightly compacted box, which he returned to the top of the closet. *That should do it.*

"Auction night, here I come!"

Chapter 2
Auction Night

R andall adored auction night because it was his escape. It was the place he felt he'd had advantage over others because of his broad knowledge base. He knew value, and the fact he was such a fantastic salesman gave him a foot up. It allowed him to turn things quickly and gave him an edge over his competition. He jumped on opportunity and gambled. Life was a chess game. He looked for the checkmate move, to make a defeated person into a winning one. The ultimate move that would be the key to the shackles he lived in, the critical point at which tables turned and made him someone worthy of attention.

Randall lay on the floor, lifted the couch and took five-hundred dollars from the secret pouch to bid on various items at auction. He searched through a large paper stack on the right side of his kitchen for the New York Times. He picked it up and glanced at the starred ads. *My gut tells me to stick to the Hillerman auction.* He pulled his fingers through the bird nest of hair on top of his scalp and made his way to a cracked bathroom mirror. He gazed at his saggy cheeks. *No one will expect me to have enough money to place a big bid.* He nodded content with his look and stepped through his doorway. He whistled, then broke into song:

High on Henry
on the hill so high
found a man that once had died
Er he said once, Er he said twice
Henry Hill or man!

Randall sang his stanza over and over to memorize the man's name.

Although the weatherman broadcasted a night in the low eighties, Randall found it hot and humid. He placed both hands in the pockets of his jeans and strutted with dark sunglasses on. His head bobbed on his shoulders, as he took in the activity surrounding his walk. Kids ran and played, people yelled from high window ledges to friends, and youngsters played hopscotch. *If only I had no responsibilities again.*

Randall arrived for the auction preview, one hour prior to the auction. Smoke permeated the air and the smell of coffee lingered. A woman sat behind a small table on which she had a list of numbers and people who filled them.

"I need a number," Randall asked.

The woman went through her file. "Your name?"

"Randall Becks- 162 B Ave A."

She wrote down the information. "Thank you Mr. Becks. Your number is forty-two. Terms are cash or check, all settlements at the end of auction."

"Thank you."

Randall walked through the archway of a large cement warehouse. It was filled with metal fold up chairs lined in tight rows. The auctioneer's podium was on the stage to the right and there were draped tables at assorted heights throughout the auditorium. A majestic grandfather clock was at the front of the left side with paintings lining the back wall. People poked through boxes of loose goods.

An assortment of slick looking and poverty-stricken characters graced the platform. The crowd consisted of mostly unshaven men dressed in secondhand clothes. Many had the appearance of just waking up. If one couldn't see the dusk out the back window, they would have imagined it was the break of dawn.

Randall walked up the aisle towards a small stairway, which led on to the elevated platform. *Selection looks good, people look assorted, a few dealers, but not overwhelming. Trust your gut, Randall.* He walked to the seventh row, folded his paper, and threw it on a chair to reserve it.

Randall slid his number into the breast pocket of his checkered shirt, as he walked to the bathroom to brush his matted black hair. He lifted his concealed brush from beneath the waistline of his pants and pulled a small baggy of hair gel from his other chest pocket. He slapped some of it on and pasted down every strand of hair until he looked like Michael Douglas in Wall Street. He leaned into the mirror. *Buy, sell, buy, sell, intimidate.* "Now, focus kid. What you buy tonight, you peddle tomorrow. Like it or lump it, you gotta to double your money. You can do it," he whispered to himself. He clapped his hands, turned, and howled like a lone wolf. People curiously looked on, as he made his way back into the crowded room.

He aggressively walked to the front stage and immediately spotted a few things he liked. He scribbled small notes to himself on the minimum and maximum bids. The auctioneer's associates paced the stage to help answer questions. In front of the auctioneer's stand was a glass case, which included some jewelry kept under lock and key.

"Excuse me," Randall said.

"How can I help you?" asked the associate.

"I'd like to see a white gold chain you have in the jewelry case over here," he asked. Both men walked over to the jewelry case and the associate pulled out a key ring. He put a key in and withdrew the necklace, locking the case behind. "What's your question?"

"Do you know the carat and the weight of this piece?"

The associate pulled a loupe from his pocket, and carefully searched the inside of the clasp, "it's stamped .750, which is 18k." He walked behind the auctioneers' stand to a small digital scale and tossed the necklace on it. He watched the numbers scan like an automatic lottery machine. "It weighs 83 grams. I hope that helps"

Randall wrote the details in his notebook. "It does, just another couple of quick questions. I saw your Planters peanut jar at the top of the stage. It didn't have the top. Is it missing?"

"It is. We received it without the lid."

"Ok, and lastly, there's a side cabinet with a number on it and a box of paperwork on top. Are they being sold together or as a lot?" asked Randall.

"No, each one will be sold individually."

Randall nodded his head in agreement, "thanks, that's all the questions I had." He walked back from the stage to take one last look. *I like that cabinet. Could use something like that for the house.* The lights flickered

"Please return to your seats, our auction today will start in ten minutes," said the auctioneer.

The remaining people on stage made their way back to their chairs. Randall scribbled fifteen items in his book to bid on as he returned to his seat. He looked them over and debated the price range of each. He sketched bids that ranged from ten dollars to one hundred dollars for each. The auctioneer approached the podium, "we'd like to start our auction today with the sale of the Henry Hillerman Estate. There's some magnificent jewelry along with furnishings and wonderful antiques." He covered the microphone with his hand, "Rod, what do you have over there, Victorian candlesticks? Bring them here," said the auctioneer.

The auctioneer watched Rod hold up the candlesticks. The man maneuvered his way through the merchandise as he reached the podium. "These gorgeous Victorian candlesticks are hallmarked with a picture of Queen Victoria. Of course you know that means they're no later than 1890. They're forged from genuine sterling silver and total two hundred and fifty grams each, un-weighted. Who'll give me two hundred, two hundred, two hundred? No? How about one-fifty, one-fifty? One hundred?"

"Yep!" yelled one of the spotters to numerous hands that sprouted in the air.

I wish I studied those candlesticks more closely. His hand flashed to the air, time after time, as he watched the price climb and flying hands dwindle. *Three others want this thing! How high will they go?*

"Two hundred, two hundred," replied the auctioneer. Three hands continued their bid war.

It's too early, stick to the plan and for God's sake, don't get carried away! You have only five hundred bucks! "Damn these people," Randall said to himself. He took a deep breath, exhaled, "alright, I'm here for the duration."

"Sold for three hundred and fifty to the man with the black pipe! What's your number, sir?"

"Sixty-two!"

The auctioneer put his head down and scribbled the winning bid in his notebook.

Randall watched the box lots come to the front and sat on the edge of his seat eager to see what came to the block. For the next forty-five minutes, his arm flexed fast and furious to compete for dominance. The items he bought were small, easy to carry items: an old gold necklace, a Dutch whisky bottle in the shape of an old bearded man, and a cast iron penny bank with a magician who pulled a rabbit from his hat when a coin was deposited. He chose his items, carefully screening their size and occasionally passing his maximum bid.

As the time passed by, the auction slowed its pace. Randall watched with excitement. *Look at all these people packing it up! I love this opportunity!* As the end of the auction approached, the auctioneers found an undiscovered lot stashed beneath a table. Randall overheard the auctioneer say as he covered the microphone, "I should have put these on earlier." Randall was alert as ever to the change of people in and out of the auction, when he noticed him. A man about five foot ten, 180-pounds, lanky and in his forties. He had a pen behind his ear and a checkered cap slightly slanted on his head.

"It's that son of a bitch!" Randall said under his breath. "So they're gonna rig this auction with a plant. Disgusting! That motherfucker's gonna boost bids outta my range. He'd better not fuck me over again like he did at Oceanside Auction. I'll make his world miserable." His eyes bulged. "You scammed me once out of a Victrola Phonograph, but not again."

He watched the man take a seat in a back row to the far side of the warehouse. He resumed his attention to the next item. Randall saw an auctioneer's assistant struggle to push a highly polished mahogany end table with wheels to the podium. The strain on a man's face was apparent. The auctioneer whispered to the man and returned to his microphone.

"Here we have a fine example of early Americana. It's an antique safe hidden within an end table. I bet half of you neglected to see it was a miniature vault. They just told me, I had no clue! The unfortunate problem is the combination is lost. It's a fine piece of craftsmanship. Who'll give me a hundred, one hundred dollars? How about seventy-five, fifty?" said the auctioneer, "at that price you could drill it and still make money!"

"I'll give you thirty-five for it," said the man from the back row.

"Forty" shouted Randall.

"Forty-five."

"One minute," shouted Randall, "This auction is rigged! He's a plant!"

"What?" said the auctioneer. He looked confused.

"He's a plant to raise bids and screw us out of our money!" Randall screamed, "Here I'm biddin on this piece of furniture and he's pushin up the prices so you get more! He's done it at other auctions, I've seen him! He did it to me at Oceanside Auction, but I'll be damned if he's gonna do it here!"

A gasp came from the rest of the bidders. They turned to face Randall in disbelief. Worry filled their faces, and then anger quickly filled the room. Many turned to the auctioneer when Randall's bidding opponent exited hastily.

"Ladies and gentleman, I can assure you we do not use plants here!" said the auctioneer in a reassuring tone. Convincingly he continued, "If that man came here, it was of his own will and if he bid for it, it was because he wanted to buy something. Now, you all know we're a reputable firm," he paused, "I'll honor your last bid Mr.?"

"Mr. Becks," said Randall.

"Do I hear any more bids?" asked the auctioneer with haste, "Sold to Mr. Becks, number forty-two for an incredible price of forty dollars." He covered the mike, "I hope he gets a hernia movin the thing."

After Randall identified the man from the back row, many people got up and walked out in distaste. From that point on there was no riff-raff. He stayed a little longer then collected his G.I. gun sack of small items and checked out his number. He paid his owed money and counted his change. *Ten dollars to boot!* He was directed through the back door to collect his safe. He looked at the safe, and put his bag on top. He went to push it and gasped. His smile disintegrated. *What have I gotten into! How the hell am I gonna get this home?*

Randall wheeled the heavy safe out the backdoor and on to the street, "Oh my God! What did I do?!" he shouted, "Thirteen blocks! I'm never gonna make it! Where's fucking Superman when you need him? I'll die movin this!"

He pushed the piece of furniture over the cracks on the pavement. As the street steeped downhill, it picked up momentum. It lasted for the first six blocks, and was relatively easy. He jumped in front of the safe several times to slow it down. The next nine blocks were slightly inclined and crueler on him. He found a broken two-by-four near a doorway, picked it up and used it as a brake. The sidewalk down this stretch of the city contained trees whose roots over time pushed up the concrete, and was in general, poorly maintained. It'd gone uneven in many spots. Time after time, he'd hit a break in the concrete and crack his ribs by a dead stop. At one point, he stepped back.

I ought to leave this monstrosity here! He stopped and looked down in exhaustion. *Why'd you invest so much time in this thing? You know investment is part time, sweat and hard work. This mother better pay off!* He took a deep breath. *Now, get your ass movin!*

When he rolled the safe into his place, it was midnight. He couldn't have been happier. He shoved it into the corner and sat down. "God Dammit. I can't believe I gotta be up at five. That mother fucker is NEVER movin again. The next squatter will be stuck with it, my compliments." He felt his muscles tighten. He rubbed his aching joints, walked back to his room, laid on his bed, and fell asleep.

Chapter 3
The Market

J ohnny Rascal arrived at Hunklemann flea market on the corner of First Ave and 13th Street. He walked through the gates of a cage-like pen, large enough to fit a car. It was the only breach to a twelve-foot high barbed wire topped fence. He looked up.

Why on earth would they have barbed wire here, if they're gonna have an opening large enough for a truck? Bunch of idiots!

At 4:00 am it was a dank dreary place with broken tables, graffiti lined brick walls, and little else. Not many circulated this time of the morning; it was too late for the night partier and too early for the mind-set corporate executive. Moneymakers like Rascal, a hybrid of the two, used all their senses to detect even the slightest irregularity on the barren landscape before 5 am- when morning security arrived. Only at that time did vendors safely flow in due to the surrounding elements- the thieves, the ruffians, the gangs and the dark alleys in which bodies had been known to be found. Those who lurked the street this early usually had nothing but trouble in mind.

His flashlight waved back and forth in the darkness as it lit his path. He pushed his shopping cart inside the parameter of the fence and made his way to the back of the lot when he heard the splatter of what sounded like rain. His flashlight scanned the ground and noticed a trickling stream, which flowed down the uneven pavement. He winced at the smell of urine, as he quickly flashed his light on the back of a man, huddled in a corner of a building.

"Oh, sorry," Rascal said.

"Huh?" The man's swaying head came to rest on Johnny.

"Didn't mean ta disturb ya."

The man snorted, "thought you were a cop. No where to go and ya know, lots ta drink…"

"Yea, I know how it is."

The man shook, pulled up his zipper, "I'll be on my way."

"Yea… later." Johnny replied. *You son of a bitch.*

The man bumped into him as he tried to keep himself erect and walk. Johnny pushed him and he staggered to the side. "Next time, use a bottle! God damn stink."

The man groaned and bowled himself through the open cage. Johnny waved his head. *Goddamn drunks.*

He returned to his piled cart and pushed it to a green canopied table labeled 'Reserved'. He pulled a canvas bag along with a small bag of birdseed out, threw them on the table, stepped back and studied the weathered structure. There were adjoining four-by-four wood posts, attached to the vendor's table that held hardy green beams at their top made from two by sixes. Johnny walked around to the back of the stall. He leaned in and noticed a small carving on the post, which read 'Randall's Table'.

Johnny grabbed the post and pulled himself up. He stood in the middle, stuck his head through the center and looked over the weathered timber at the height of the frame. He shook one of the supports, nodded his head in approval, and then snickered. He crouched down, ripped open the birdseed bag and grabbed a handful, stood up carefully and laced a fine line of food with precision into a small routed crevice at the rear of the stall. He returned to the ground and assumed Randall's position behind the table. "Pleasure to meet you today, I'm Randall and I'm going to sell you something expensive." He waved his hands impersonating his friend.

"Beautiful day, isn't it?" He leaned his weight on the post and watched for birdseed to cascade down. *Nothing.* He leaned forward on both his hands gently shaking the table. "Not an ounce of seed. This is gonna work!"

Johnny reached into his canvas bag and pulled out a large mortar & pestle and some rubber gloves, which he placed on the table. He retrieved a large box of E-Lax from his pocket, ripped it open and poured the tablets into the mortar. He ground the tablets into a fine dust. When he completed this task, he slipped on the gloves, and poured the dust into the birdseed bag, manipulating the two together to make sure the birdseed was coated. He jumped back on to the table and with the steadiness of a pool shark's hand, laid thick lines of the concoction along the beams.

Within the course of ten minutes, he finished the last touches, hopped down and brushed the table of any evidence that remained. He checked his watch, "Five am, time to set up, sit and wait." He walked to the adjacent table and slit the tape of his first box.

Randall walked through the gate at five forty-five with a cup of coffee in his hand.

"Top of the mornin' to you! How's me best friend, today?" Johnny asked with an Irish brogue.

Randall looked at him suspiciously, "what are you up to, Johnny? You're way too happy."

"Had a wonderful day, yesterday! Business was grand, weather was fine, so I thought I'd get here nice and early. You know what they say about the worm!"

"Uh, huh," Randall stood silent. He stared at him cautiously. "What are you up to?"

"What, I can't be happy?"

"No, you can't."

"You're growin paranoid with age, Randall."

"You're telling me you have nothing in store for me, joker?"

"No way, man. I couldn't do anything to my best friend. You know I'm not that kinda guy!" he said sarcastically, "I just feel like beaming." His hands protectively crossed his chest.

"Did you get laid?

Johnny paused, "is it that obvious?"

"I don't know who would wanta sleep with you, ya ugly bastard. How many drinks ya buy her?"

"Why da ya think she'd have to be drunk, anyway?"

"Look at ya!"

"You shit."

"Well," he paused, "that's as good a reason as any. Can't remember the last time I got some, too many complications with sex," Randall replied.

"Yea, love."

-but we're here for business- survival." Randall looked to the sky. "Looks like it's gonna be a beautiful day."

"That's what we're expectin' and I have the feelin' it's gonna be one hell of a day."

"Excellent," replied Randall. "Now, let me get on with my work."

"You got it!"

Johnny looked to the sunrise over the rooftops, but caught

a glimpse of three pigeons who gathered on the ledge of the building next door. Each bird sidestepped back and forth along the stone as if they were catching up on a day worth of gossip. They're heads bopped up and down and they cooed amongst themselves.

Randall laid a crisp white sheet over his table and then positioned a box of merchandise directly in front of his feet. It was labeled with a large FM and 5 stars symbolizing its value in the one to five star system: Five being best. He reached his hands into the shreds of torn newspaper.

"Ya got any sports stuff?"

"Save that stuff myself," Randall replied. He chose his words carefully, "but plenty of interesting things- old things, odd things, antiques."

He removed each item slowly from its black and white protection, enticing the dealers. They gathered like vultures in anticipation, each on their toes to react quickly to the revealed wares. He unpacked a chipped Coronation plate with Queen Elizabeth on its face, a Limoges cup and saucer with flowers, an African thumb piano, a railroad fob and a bag of 1950's match books which were picked up and handed between several dealers. They moved closer to the table. Randall found the first of several ink stained towels and exposed an old middle-eastern urn; he placed it on the table. A man with a scraggly brown beard grabbed it.

"Hey, how much is this thing?"

"There's a price on it," said Randall.

"No, there's not," he said. "What the hell is it?"

Randall grabbed the urn from the man and searched it for the pastel colored label. "I know damn well there was a tag on it when I put it out. The thing's seventy-five." He placed it back on the table.

The bearded man raised a cupped hand to his face when Randall looked down. He saw his suspicious behavior through the corner of his eye and shot him a quick look. He grabbed the man's fist and pulled it down to the table. He forced it open.

"Don't suppose you saw this fifty dollar price tag, right guy? Get the hell outta here! I'm not sellin' you anything from here in! No matter what you look at!" He waved his hand at the crowd, "Ya hear that? Anyone caught pullin' off tags, switching tags, or stealing, is banned from my table. I'll beat the shit out of anyone caught stealin'. Comprende?" he said harshly.

"Yea, yea," one of the dealers said in dismissal.

"What's the best you'll take on this old pocket watch, pal?"

"It's a fourteen karat casing and priced at fifty bucks, but it needs a little work," said Randall.

"I'll give ya ten bucks for it. It's no good if it doesn't work."

"Give me a break! You know if that thing worked, it'd be worth two to three hundred bucks! Even not working, it goes for twice what I'm asking," Randall said bitterly.

The dealer frowned, "but it's no good to me, if it's not working."

-then leave it. I heard you repair watches. Parts couldn't cost more than a couple of bucks," Randall replied.

The dealer looked down, smirked and stifled his laugh. Another person turned to Randall, "you got him there."

"It's fifty or nothing," said Randall.

"Ok, tough guy," he reluctantly pocketed the watch and pulled out two twenty dollar bills. He handed them to him, "forty, cash in hand."

The man went to walk away, and Randall paused. Irritated, he yelled, "I'm missing a ten, sir!"

The dealer stopped, looked directly at Randall and stared for what amounted to five seconds. He erratically pulled out his wallet, grabbed a ten, crumpled it up and threw it at Randall. "Punk."

"Thank you," Randall added sarcastically.

The haggling went on with many of the dealers, as each treasure was pulled from the box. Some attempted to get behind the table and beat their competition to the punch, but were quickly shuffled off, each empty box being stored beneath the display. Everyone low balled Randall's prices, which was to be expected. Some he graciously accepted, but others he downright refused. After about twenty minutes, the burst of activity died down. The dealers retreated to their own tables with their newly bought purchases, some that made their way back to the selling table with prices twice of that paid at Randall's booth. The sun was out and when Randall finished his fifth box. He took a breath and looked over the table from his spot.

"Had a nice little run there," shouted Johnny Rascal from across the aisle.

"Yea, it was good. I like havin' a bunch of 'em around, gets cutthroat. They're more likely to snap it up when they're in bunches like that."

"How'd you do?" asked Johnny.

He counted a folded stack of cash, "not bad, but I'm not gonna jinx myself." He returned it to his pocket. "I wanta get the passersby. I need to make a profit today."

"I suppose that's a good thing," said Johnny, "means you're at least sellin' stuff."

"Like I said, I'm doin' all right. Keep your fingers crossed," Randall replied.

A stately woman in her mid-sixties approached Randall's table. Her white hair was tied into a bun at the back of her head, not a loose hair out of place. She looked oddly placed in a market like this, but in New York, you had all kinds. Every seller masked their humble surroundings with artificial smiles. As she passed, Randall noticed a large gold charm of the Austrian flag which hung from an omega necklace around her neck. His eyes fixed on it.

"From out of town, Miss?" Randall asked.

"Vy yes, young man. How did you know?"

He looked her over, gently took her hand and stroked it. "You have this je-ne-sais-quoi and your accent's gorgeous."

She giggled, "you're sharming aren't you?"

"I like to make people feel at home. My guess is you're from Austria."

Johnny focused on the crowd of pigeons, which went from three to about thirty over the course of an hour. He watched a single bird fly from the building to a bracket above Randall's head. It perched itself unnoticed by Becks, who was in the depths of conversation; undoubtedly a scout on a mission.

The woman winked at Randall. "You're indeed right, I'm Austrian." She picked up a large bowl of purple Depression glass and fondled it. "This bowl reminds me of one my mother kept in Austria. She used to serve punch to all the neighborhood children in it. It brings fond memories."

"That bowl is very unique. I bought it from an Englishman's estate sale. I understand he immigrated here in the 1960's. From what I know, he traveled extensively through Europe, including Austria, Switzerland and Germany. I'd imagine he picked it up somewhere in that vicinity. I'm sure an expert could tell you its origin. Unfortunately, I never got that far. I purchased it for its sheer beauty. I never saw anything like it, it's extraordinary."

Johnny found it hard to contain his laughter. He listened to the pigeon coos, which grew louder, as if one was alerting his friends. Two more pigeons arrived above Randall's table.

Randall looked at them. He gently shook the post. They repositioned themselves.

"Please excuse these street birds. They're all over New York and bold as hell. They're an annoyance, but there's no escaping the damn things."

Johnny's laugh suddenly ripped out hysterically. Randall shot him a look and he went rigid. He pretended to sweep dust from items on his table.

"We have zees zings too. Very tame. Never mind." She returned her look to the bowl. "You're right, it's gorgeous. How much do you want for it?" she asked.

"I was looking for two hundred and fifty dollars, but because you like it for sentimental reasons, I'll knock off twenty-five."

She shot back, "Would you take two hundred?"

Randall put his hand on his chin and scratched it. He watched her reaction. *Not a flinch.* "I don't know. I'm hardly making a thing on it. I'll tell ya what, if you buy it, I'll throw in this Royal Doulton cup and saucer set, which was purchased from the same sale. You can have tea while you study your crystal punch tureen. I priced the tea cup set at fifty."

All at once, about twenty-five pigeons descended in a wave that mirrored the movie "White Squall". They landed and pecked furiously at the birdseed. The horrified woman stepped back and cradled the Depression glass. Randall grabbed a support and shook it violently to try and rid the table of the flying rats. Birdseed fell everywhere, as the pigeons feasted.

The sight of all of the birds fiendishly pecking the top of Randall's stall dropped Johnny to his knees in laughter. The laxative had an instantaneous affect on the birds and crap fell everywhere: over the merchandise, the table, and Randall. Everyone stopped to see the sight unfold. Randall swept an opening on the table, jumped on to it in one leap, yelled loudly, and smacked the pigeons from their perches. His eyes followed the lines of his stall, carefully examining what remained. *JOHNNY!* He turned in horror to his friend's table.

Johnny's nose was buried in his hands. Everyone was repulsed. Men hunched over in bellyaches from their exuberant laughter. Women cowered with nausea as well as his stately customer.

Disgusted by the sight of the table, the merchandise, and Randall's shirt, the woman gently put the glass back on the table. She held her nose and let out an "ugh".

"Maybe next time, young man." She waved her hand back and forth quickly to avoid any scent, which might cross her way. She walked on.

Randall looked at his table saturated in bird shit. His rage exploded as he leapt from the tabletop hitting the pavement. Johnny sprinted from his table like Flash Gordon and flew down the aisle; Randall's outstretched hands only inches from his shirt. They ran out the gate and for a block until Randall stumbled on a piece of cracked pavement. Outmatched, Randall vowed revenge, "Damn you, Quick Johnny! You cost me two hundred bucks!" He spun around and walked back towards his stall. He threw up his hands and screamed, "Dickhead!"

As he passed Johnny's stall, he grabbed a couple of red satin bed sheets Johnny was selling. Johnny watched in the distance while Randall took them to his stall.

"Come on Randall, it was a joke!"

Randall ignored his pleas and slowly wiped the droppings from his table and merchandise. He did it methodically. Johnny watched with horror, as Randall made sure every inch of the sheets were covered. He threw them back to Johnny's table.

"You piece of shit! MOTHER FUCKIN ASSHOLE!!!!" Randall's primal scream echoed between the buildings. He inhaled deeply. "Fucker," he said under his breath as he looked at his table. He cleaned his merchandise from his table and reached underneath to pull out another tablecloth. He walked the stained white sheet to a neighboring garbage can and threw it in.

Johnny snickered, "match that my friend!"

Randall stood there speechless. *Fuckin prankster!* "You better watch the rest of the day if ya know what's good for ya!"

Chapter 4
The Heckler

"The Heckler," roared from the aisle's end. His deep baritone laugh pierced the surrounding voices through the marketplace. Randall looked at him surprised by his response. He approached Johnny, who took refuge at a nearby stand.

"Johnny- that was piss! I think Randall nailed it when he called ya Quick Johnny. If you could have seen yourself running from Randall...man." He slapped his palm to his thigh. "No photo could have captured that look on your face, or for that matter, his. You look like you were running for dear life."

"I was!"

"I think we got ourselves a nickname for ya."

Johnny panted, "he looked like he was gonna kill me! Better to let him cool off than hang and be killed!"

The Heckler shook his head and continued to laugh.

An angry voice came from a few stalls down, "Shut the fuck up, Harry!"

"What??" The Heckler's face reddened with anger. He pushed his way forward towards Randall's stall. Threatened by his appearance, people stood aside and gawked at Randall for having the balls to say such a thing. Harry's 6'3" 300lb tattooed frame towered over Randall's. His dyed jet-black hair was tied in a ponytail; his dark aviator sunglasses hid his eyes. The black leather vest revealed his heavily muscled arms.

Harry leaned over, "I'm not sure if I heard you right, smart guy. Wanta' run that by me again?" He spread his arms across Randall's table and leaned down on his fists. Blood veins popped in his rippled biceps. They throbbed beneath his body weight.

"You got some sort of stick up your ass? Why don't you go back to your stall and grab some hopeless little fuck you can sell those Harley parts to!"

Randall and the Heckler stood eye to eye. The Heckler's breath was long and steady. His expressionless face, like an expert poker player with a royal flush, was still.

"You know I could destroy you with my pinky, don't you?" He removed his sunglasses and exposed his albino pupils. The miniscule veins in the white of his eyes were lit a hair-raising red. "I just came here from Chrome Amnesia, with a lot of drinks under my belt and I'm not in the mood to be thrown in jail for hittin' someone not worthy of my punch."

"Harry, snap outta it, it's me Randall. You on something?" He smacked his arm a few times.

The Heckler shook his head, "what the... shit Randall. I'm sorry, man."

"It's not like we've been strangers the past five years. Sometimes I think you're on another planet."

Harry leaned over, "Don't you EVER wise up to me in front of these guys. Friend or foe, I gotta reputation to keep and if I gotta knock your block off, I will. The pecking order's gotta stay in line. People talk and when you break people's legs for a livin', the last thing you need is someone with a pair of balls. Got it?" Harry whispered.

Randall whispered, "Harry, I've watched over you since parole. Believe me, it wasn't a picnic. Not many could take bein your counselor."

"Yea, the half way house ain't exactly a five star hotel."

"You should know by now my lips are sealed. No conversation in these ears goes out through this mouth. If you don't know me by now, you'll never know me."

"Kid, I trust you with my life," Harry said. He tightened his fist and held it out. Randall punched it. "We're good."

Harry turned to walk. "Harry, come here." Randall shouted.

The man backed up. His eyebrows rose.

"A little closer."

Harry moved his head within earshot of Randall's voice.

Randall spoke softly, "Who was that woman you told me bout a few years back?"

"More than a few years, kid. Jessica Lovitska, why do you ask?"

"I thought about something you said regarding sacrifice and I was thinkin about the things we do," Randall paused, "Was she worth the time you did?"

"Every minute, guy. She was beyond beautiful, thoughtful and warm. The kind of woman you only find in dreams- the package."

Randall thought about his recurring nightmare, "-and you never found her?"

-Never after Sing Sing. Can't say I blame her. She saw a side of me I didn't know I had. When I came out of the blackout, a knife was in my hand, and four policemen were holding me down. I was drenched in blood." He took a breath then paused, "What would you do?"

"Don't know… probably the same. I don't think it's a

hopeless cause. If I was you, I'd still look for her. Many years have passed."

"Yea, but it's a big city and I don't know. If she felt anything for me, she would have come forward when I went to court, right?"

"Ya never know circumstances, pal."

"Just the same, what's done is done, and we carry on."

"Yeah- now, you'd better get some coffee before you lose your head again," said Randall.

"Suppose you're right." He stood up straight, winked at Randall and his voice rose, "next time you speak to me like that, I'm gonna make you eat through a straw!" He about faced to a crowd of people whose faces looked at him curiously. He waved his hands to the surrounding people, "What the fuck are you lookin at? Get back to your business." He pushed someone who stood too close.

Randall lowered himself below the edge of the table to hide his smile. He put on his act, and reemerged with an expression of fear. Johnny ran over.

"You ok?"

"Of course, I am. You know Harry as well as I, he puts on a show. Sure, he'll beat the piss outta ya, but I've known him a long time. He's not gonna be public with it, unless he absolutely needs ta. I don't doubt he'd kick the shit out of me, but he'd do it in private. We're friends; you know what he's like."

"Yea. I'll never forget when you first took his table. It was like today, only then I thought he was much less disciplined. He was gonna send ya to the hospital. When I look back on it now, I laugh. It's almost as funny as today's prank."

"Nothing's as funny as today's prank, Johnny." He held his hand out to shake and when Johnny went to grab it, Randall pulled it away and slicked back his hair.

"You really out did yourself, but you know how paybacks go."

"Yea, they're returned twice as hard. My eye'll be on ya." Johnny paused, "hey, one last question."

"Yea?"

"How did you calm Harry that day?"

"You mean after he jacked me up?"

"Yea, his face turned blue with fury. He could barely control the shake in his arms. For Christ's sake, he had you by the throat!" Johnny said.

"Well, I used to be a Parole Officer. I knew this inmate named Larry Pickford, one of the biggest and meanest motherfuckers in Sing Sing. He was convicted of murder and sentenced to death, but after 15 years of red tape, they find out through new DNA testing, that he never committed his crime. They released him into my custody to help him adjust to the outside. Help him get back to normality."

"Yeah," Johnny said, "and..."

"As I helped him, he helped me understand the power system behind bars. He tossed me a big tip towards the end; told me if I'm in a jam with an ex-con; tell them before they have a chance to beat me, "the Preacher will get ya.""

"Who's the Preacher?" asked Johnny.

"Pickford's nickname, because on his walk to the electric chair, the lights flickered. He saw it as a sign from God, and wouldn't ya know it, there was an operating problem with the chair. The juice wouldn't stream through. They postponed it, and bang, he gets a pardon. He began to Preach- thus the Preacher."

"I see."

"As much as he preached about the goodness of God, he was respected and founded the greatest prison information network ever. It extended beyond prison walls, reached mythical proportions. Prisoner's knew him everywhere."

"Back to the story, so what happened?" Johnny asked. He leaned further across the table.

"So when I hung there by my throat, I saw the web tattoos on his elbows. I told him that the preacher was gonna get him if he did me wrong," said Randall.

"Harry, knew him?"

"Personally, they shared floor C in the pen."

"I never saw Harry back down from anyone, but when he put you down, brushed off your jacket and let you keep his table, I practically keeled over!" replied Johnny.

"You weren't the only one," Randall said, "one of the vendors took me aside and told me never come back. He thought I'd end up in the swamps of Jersey."

Johnny looked at Randall, "I'm pretty goddamn glad you didn't end up marsh meat. I'd only pull that joke on you. If you weren't here, this whole thing couldn't have happened. Laughter's the body of soul and since the laughs on you; you cured a lot of today's woes." He pushed his shoulder, "Cheers to your good health."

"Don't try and cool me down, Quickster. I'm gonna have vengeance."

"Till death do us part," said Johnny. He walked back to his stall and stood above an assortment of silk and satin sheets, Asian incense, hash pipes, and discretely hidden sex videos. "Wake up, everyone! We've got a beautiful day!"

Randall raised the coffee cup from the floor. He held it closely and examined the rim, surveyed the cup, sniffed the stuff, and shook his head. *Not worth the risk.* He took it to the trash and threw it. When he returned, he stretched his eyelids back with his fingers until only the white showed. He scratched his night shadow and cracked his knuckles.

"Let the games begin!" he yelled.

Randall stood at his stall and 'people watched'; one of his favorite pastimes. He studied a mole on the head of an olive complexioned bald man as he bent over to look at his goods, the slender figure of a young woman just old enough to pass for eighteen, a brunette who's facial scar went from her mouth to the middle of her cheek, an awkward man cross dressed in stiletto heals who was still learning to walk and two old men whose forearms held naval tattoos worn into their skin, they smoked fat cigars. It was a menagerie of interest- one he took in and processed in his own way.

Up the aisle, a heavyset man carried a cup of "Lou's Coffee", supplied by Lou, a strangely named Middle-eastern pushcart vendor with a heavy Arab accent. The man walked with his girlfriend, a petite brunette with graying hair and a rose tattoo on her shoulder. The man slowed to a stop in front of Randall's table. The woman stood behind him and got distracted by the goods on Johnny's table. She meandered over as the man perused Randall's treasures.

"Good morning!" Randall said, "Fine morning isn't it?"

His permanent frown, deeply carved with wrinkles, looked up annoyed. With all seriousness he spoke, "How can you say it's a fine morning? Who are you to tell me, it's a fine morning?"

Randall looked at his worn face, and then locked eyes with the man. He'd dealt with guys like him before; know it alls who can't accept other opinions, prisoners who fought to stay alive and learned to react before they thought. Time and time again, he took the shit, but this morning already started on a bad note. He leaned across an opening between his materials and countered, "What's your problem? Misread the imaginary sign on my chest that says I'm here to take your shit?"

The customer leaped at Randall with his fist held tightly. With lightening quick reflexes Randall, caught the man's fist before it jammed his cheek. The woman grabbed her boyfriend's arm, "Rocky, come 'ere- check out these silk panties." She pulled him away.

The man gritted his teeth. "I should knock ya in that fresh mouth of yours and if my woman wasn't here, I would. You should feel lucky, pal."

"Lucky like what, a dog in heat?" Randall said sarcastically, "if you were any more handsome I might hump your leg. Why don't you come back and meet me later."

The disgusted man shot him a repulsive look. He pulled his girlfriend close and shook his head. "Queer!" he yelled. Guided by his girlfriend, he turned his head to examine Johnny's stuff.

If this is any sign of what the day is shaping up to be, I'm in for a doozy. He rubbed his right hand up his cheek and to his temple, and then laughed. He heard the Heckler a few stalls down.

"The day keeps getting better and better!" he shouted at Randall. "You, my friend, are a poet and comedian!"

"Is it me? Do I look like I'm lookin for trouble today?"

"It's all over your face, friend."

"So, you like that last comment?" Randall asked. "Imagine if I was wearin a dress!"

"Oh baby! If you're clean shaved and wearing a dress you could be a damn pretty woman," said Harry. His eyes studied Randall's unsteady gestures.

Uncomfortable, Randall shifted his body, "Ok, Harry enough. I think you've passed the line of comfort and civility. Back off freak!"

"You're so damn gullible!" Harry said with a laugh, "piss off."

"Your mother was gullible," he said sarcastically. He watched the Heckler's face turn sour, until he threw up his fists in a boxer's stance. Randall waved his hand towards Harry. "Bring it on…"

The Heckler shook his head. "Why do I bother?"

Randall pulled a loud speaker from beneath his table and aimed it towards the other end of the market, "Extra, extra read all about it! Fine wine's a simple thing to get, but you gotta be a fool to make the rules, to make the real deal flow. Nothin but art here. You can call it trash, you can call it treasure, and if you're smart, it'll add to your pleasure. Come on by, please say hi. My name is Randall 'the big man' Becks. Plenty for sale, something for everyone!" He put the speaker down and gazed at the crowd that approached his stall. *I have some medicine for you, my sweets. Something a little tasty which will add to your ecstasy and if you take it just right, you'll own something from Randall tonight. God, give me some cash.…*

He faced the first customer in a dense crowd of people, attracted by his calls, "The price on that's sixty, sir. It's a Depression glass flower vase. The fine details are in the vibrant colors, especially the orange marigolds and blue lilacs. In the early days, glass wasn't perfect like it is today. If you hold it to the sun, you can see bubbles in the glass itself. These imperfections were inevitable and it was the art of the glass blower, to limit their defects. The coloring was even more difficult," said Randall. "Now, look at the edge of the leaves and how sharp they are. Someone must have put his or her heart and soul into it. It's gorgeous."

"I wasn't really shopping for a vase, but they're my wife's favorite colors. She loves beautiful things, but can't stand places like this. She'd never be caught dead in a flea market. Her birthday's tomorrow and I was thinking of buying her a dozen red roses. They might look ideal in this vase."

"What you should do is buy her white roses. A vase like this stands alone as a piece of art, I mean, where on earth can you buy something as beautiful as this? Certainly, red roses are traditional and pretty, but common. Everyone gives red roses. They're probably not right to put in this, but I guarantee if you put white roses in this, she'd be knocked out. They'd make it pop!" Randall exclaimed. "I wish I could tell you more on the history of it. If it could talk it'd tell you many a romantic story I'm sure, but you know what's amazing?"

"What's that?" asked the man.

"It's not necessarily the actual item that you give, but it's the thought behind its presentation. The idea itself is art. When I think about it, I see the future filled with beautiful flowers in vases like this. I'll always refer back to this moment and you filling that vase with a dozen white roses for your wife. Its romance at it's best."

"Yea, it's perfect. Here's sixty. Thanks for the spiel; you'll be my romantic advisor. Lord knows, I could use one! You have a bag?" I don't want to accidentally crack it."

"Certainly." He wrapped the old vase carefully in a wad of newspaper when out of the corner of his eye; he spotted a hunched woman who squinted at a brass doorknocker on the right side of the table. He barked, "Ma'am, I'll give you a deal on that knocker. I've had it in my inventory for sometime. It's marked at twenty-five, but I'll let you have it for fifteen. You look like a smart shopper."

"Preposterous! Even at fifteen dollars it's expensive," she scowled.

"Lady, you don't understand. The knocker's special. It has a lifetime warranty for the finish. You look for it in any store and it'll cost you three times the amount I'm asking for it."

"What's your absolute best price," she emphasized.

"I'm tellin'ya, fifteen is the best price."

"You're never going to sell that piece of junk."

"Lady, get outta here, I don't need you to waste my time. If you think I'm gonna to sell it to you, after your foul comments, you're crazy."

"I still wouldn't take it if you offered it to me for eight dollars," she said.

In frustration, Randall turned and faced the customer who purchased the flower vase. He picked up the knocker, "sir, would ya like a brass door knocker to go with your vase? You've stood here and listened to us. I'll give ya a special price for being the nicest customer today. Do you have a brass knocker on your door at home?"

"No," he replied.

"Wait a minute," the woman said. She felt humiliated.

Randall ignored her, "I've got an idea. Mount the door-knocker early tomorrow morning before your wife wakes, stand outside with your dozen roses and wake her up with it. What da ya think?"

"I'll take it for fifteen, sir," the women pleaded.

Again, Randall ignored her and watched the gentleman carefully consider his pitch. "Sir, I'll give it to you for five."

The man hastily replied, "you have a sale!"

"Asshole, you can't do that!" cussed the woman.

He turned to her and pointed at her face, "this is my business, not yours. You can't make demands on me. If I want to give it to someone, that's my prerogative. So next time, you're negotiating with someone over something, try not to be such a bitch, and maybe you'll get what you want. Don't demean me, because I'm far more intelligent then you think, plus I can be a really nasty prick. Good day."

The woman's face scowled after the man placed the brown

handled bag by his side. Appalled by Randall's behavior, she stormed off in a huff. The man continued to look.

"You made short change of her," he said.

"I deal with people all the time. I'm used to negotiation, but when someone takes a real attitude with me, it pisses me off. I gotta bite my tongue sometimes cause I really need the money, but today's different. I have a little cushion to lean on, so I can speak my mind. She's a regular and we all know she's a penny pincher. It's sad to say, many of us give in to her nasty bitterness, given our situation. She probably figures we all need the money, and have to bite our lips when she asks for the cheapest price. We gotta make a living, right?"

"Yea." said the man.

"I don't ask for sympathy, but gimme a little respect."

"I'm glad you said something," the gentleman softly said. He looked into Randall's eyes, "You're not the only one who feels that way. Have a good day and take care of yourself."

"You too." said Randall. He reached out for a handshake and took the man's burly hand into his. The man's look was sincere. *Should be more people like this in the world. If only some had the compassion this guy does, we'd live in a better place.*

Randall looked over the head of a short woman who leaned on a cane in front of him. "Good morning, dear lady." She was slightly bent over with a small hump on her shoulder. The bifocals which had slid down her nose, hung from a beaded chain draped behind her neck. She held the edge of the table and stretched as best she could to look at a bronze knife towards the back of his table. He picked up the knife, "Not thinking of killing your husband are you?" Randall said sarcastically. She giggled. He pointed at it, "This marvelous Islamic dagger and bronze holder are studded with pieces of jade and agate. They're only in the best daggers. Something's written in Arabic, but I don't know what it says. If I did, I'd probably get a lot more than I'm asking. For now, I'd be better off telling you it was Ali Baba's."

"You're funny," said the woman in an English accent, "do you have any Wedgwood?"

"I'm afraid I don't, but I do have a wonderful piece of English Stoneware." He pointed at a large blue and white glazed pitcher. "This is an extraordinary piece of pottery. You can see the Union Jack and English coat of arms on the bottom." He turned the piece upside down and faced it towards her. "I don't know much about the piece, so I'm asking only a hundred for it."

"That seems a little high, considering you don't know much about it."

"I'm practically giving it away at that price. I've seen comparable stoneware not near this quality, asking double the price. As you understand, I need to put food on my plate," he paused in thought and continued, "but since you're my prettiest customer of the day, I'll knock another ten off the price. For you, and only you, I'll make it ninety."

"Well, it does sound better, but, that's still too high for me to take a chance on. Maybe I'll give it better consideration at sixty, toots." She turned her head slightly and winked, like a young schoolgirl.

Randall faced her and spoke softly, "sixty is practically what I paid for it. It's an outrage to ask me to do that." He shrugged his shoulders, "If I have anymore customers like you this morning, I'm gonna need a tin cup and organ grinder monkey. Please don't make me humiliate myself. I get enough of that from the guys here." He grinned reassuring her that his protest was in jest. "I'll tell you what. You look like a nice lady." he whispered.

He went to the outside of his table and put his arm around her shoulder, "If you give me eighty in small bills, and deposit them in the waste paper basket over there, you have a deal."

"Are you implying that it's stolen?" she said with a shock.

"No, it's not stolen! I'm just having a little fun with you."

"I hope so."

"I see you're a tough one. Hmmm... I know... for seventy-five, I'll give you the stoneware and a dance."

"What kind of dance?"

"You'll have to pay me seventy-five to find out."

The woman looked at Randall. He winked and watched her pull her purse from her pocketbook.

"You drive a hard bargain, sir. You know I'm only giving you the seventy-five dollars to find out the type of dance you're going to give me."

"I know, so I'll be especially creative. I want you as a repeat customer."

"You'll get it if you're good."

"I'll wrap the pitcher for you. You got a great bargain," said Randall. *Now, what kind of dance can I do to make this queen come back to see me again. Especially creative dance. Johnny must have a tape he can blare for me.* "Johnny! Blare a tape for me. I made a deal with this woman that included a dance on my table."

Johnny searched his cassette tapes then came across a tape on his table by David Rose & his Orchestra- "The Stripper".

"I got one perfect for ya, Randall!" You're customer will love it!" Johnny put the tape in and blasted it.

"Johnny!"

Johnny crossed his arms and ignored him.

I should have known not to ask that guy for music to dance to. Guess I'm in short demand. "Here it goes lady, the best for your money," he said. He grabbed the posts of his table and slowly stepped between his merchandise carefully placing his feet. He gyrated his hips in time to the stripper music. His hands caressed his biceps, then triceps, up and down his torso. His tightly cut T-shirt hugged his body and he slowly stripped it off to reveal six pack abs. People hooted and clapped as they came from up and down the aisle. With one last gyration of his hips, he hopped off the table, looked at Johnny and swiped his finger across his throat. Johnny turned off the player. "That's the show everyone!"

"Hey come on, a little more," said a short ragged woman, "I got a dollar!"

"I'll second that dollar," said a girl with multiple piercing.

"Get back to business," said a fellow vendor from behind him. "I don't need this shit."

Randall turned around, then back again. "You heard the man, ladies. Business is business." He returned his look to his customer.

"My," said the woman. "I was getting ready to shove some dollars in your pants. That's the best seventy-five, I've spent in awhile."

"Why thank you!"

"You're quite an entertainer. Let me know if you get any Wedgwood, I'll be the first to shop from you."

"You can also thank my partner in crime over there, Johnny maestro. It wasn't the dance I had in mind, but obviously he needed a good laugh, as he always does."

A girl in a tight spandex shirt stepped forward; her hair was dyed the same color and her eyes were layered in heavy eye shadow. She had an earring through her eyebrow and a hoop, which jetted from her lower lip along with a line of hoops, which went up both ears. She picked up a steel dog leash that was wound up in a ball.

"How much is this?"

"Couple bucks."

"I'll take it," she said. "It'll be good for the raves." She reached into her steel studded purse, pulled out two dollars, and gave it to Randall. She heard a hoot from Johnny's stall, turned to him and gave him a sinister smile. Johnny studied her fishnet stockings.

"That guy kills me," Johnny shouted.

"If you played me that music, I'd have killed you," the woman said. She tucked the chain into her pocketbook.

"Whatda ya gonna do with that?"

She went over to his table and leaned over. She motioned him closer. When Johnny moved his face close to listen to her words, she suddenly slapped him across the cheek. "Wouldn't you like to know?"

He shook his head, "I think I'm in love!"

She laughed, "nice stuff, but you're too old for me. I'd kill you."

"You're probably right."

"Another satisfied customer!" Randall yelled.

The more Randall yelled, the more people gathered in frenzy. They butted against each other, shoulder to shoulder, "How much? How much? How much?"

"Twenty-five, sixty, one hundred and forty two!"

"A hundred and forty two? What the hell kinda price is that!"

"It just sorta sounded good with twenty-five and sixty. Make it a hundred." He looked down the aisle and yelled, "Come one, come all to the stall that never quits. A place where you can find the odd, the art, and antiquities with hands- tick-tock goes the clock when you come by, and before you know it, I'll have to say goodbye. It's my aim to make you smile today," he yelled.

Randall's electric personality scored more sales, one after the other, all for being himself. A joyful mood spread multiplies and others simply came to see what was going on. He wheeled, dealed, and most of all, joked. Johnny watched in awe.

He turned to face his single customer, "Can I help you with something?"

"Just looking," said the stranger. The mustached man passed swiftly by.

Johnny sighed. He pulled out a cigarette, took a puff, tossed it down and ground his foot into it. "God damn cigarettes."

Chapter 5
The Opening

Randall arrived home at six o'clock with his boxes, put them neatly away and returned downstairs. He went to the piece of furniture he'd purchased the night before and bent down to eye it for any damage he may have caused during its move. "You're a recurring nightmare!" He said, "but you do look good! Well, my friend I didn't invest my money in you to think how pretty you'd look in my corner. I have to know what treasure you're hiding from me in the depths of your steel. I have plenty of tools and a stethoscope to crack ya. Dynamite's out of the question, since I value my cockroach-infested apartment. If I adjust the stethoscope near the dial, the click may just be loud enough for me to detect, but first, I gotta get you to my room."

Randall hurled the stairs, opened his locked door, went underneath the kitchen sink and pulled out a heavy nylon rope and mover's blanket. He galloped down the stairs, wrapped the furniture in the blanket, and tied it securely with the rope. He bent at the knees and lifted with all his might till he stood straight, gasping as he got it to chest level. He held it tightly as each foot hit a stair one after another like a forklift with weight enough to tumble it over. Floor after floor, he avoided the weak points. His breath was heavy, his arms were rigid, and his legs hurt. Every landing he'd unload the heavy safe on to the floor. Every stop, he thought about not picking it back up, but he was determined, until he finally reached his apartment. He opened the door and pushed it in next to his couch, where he fell. He rested for a few minutes, went to the bathroom and grabbed a stethoscope from an old medical bag he kept below the sink.

Randall listened carefully as he worked the combination in a 3-2-1 sequence. He worked hours to open the safe with a series of different combinations until his impatience boiled over. "Screw this!" he screamed. His feet thundered across the floor to the closet where he kept an immense sledgehammer. He quickly pulled it out.

"If you think you're gonna outlive me, you must be joking!" he shouted. He said these words as he swung the sledgehammer over his shoulder and slammed it heavily into the dial. It knocked the dial clear across the room. Beneath the dial he saw a mechanism. He bent down, studied it, and tried to manipulate it. He grabbed the screwdriver and pounded it into the mechanism with relative ease. He picked up industrial grade pliers and twisted the screwdriver back and forth, until it "popped". The force threw him off balance and sent him ass first to the floor. He landed with a loud thud. He stroked his bloodshot eyes, and watched the safe open slowly. He crawled to the safe.

"What do we have here?"

The air inside had a stale smell, like an old clothing filled closet. An aroma of mothballs wafted past Randall's nose. *Mmmm, the smell gives me goose bumps. Most of my most memorable valuables were discovered hidden in places with this smell.* He bit his bottom lip then his tongue, to keep his nervous laugh from escaping.

A stack of papers was strewn across the bottom of the safe. He stuck his hand in and grabbed the first 8 1/2 x 11 paper. "Henry Emmanuel Hillerman born at Mount Cherry Medical Practice, December 4th, 1926 Brooklyn, New York." He thumbed the finish on the paper, "The calligraphy and engravings on this are fantastic." He set the birth certificate to one side and picked up another. "Henry Emmanuel Hillerman here by takes Lena Louise Schwartz in holy matrimony, City Hall, Manhattan July 6th, 1951." He stacked it on the last document. "Lena Louise Hillerman born September 16th, 1930- died April 22nd. 1990. Sixty years old, poor thing, that's so young to die."

He picked up two rubber banded bundles of paper, one of photographs and the other yellowed envelopes. He fingered the photos with empathy. "Henry and his wife at the entrance of the Empire State Building." Randall flipped over another picture titled, 'first car'. "A Studebaker. He looks so proud leaning on the hood with his arms crossed. A smile ear to ear." Another photo was simply titled 'Lena'. *Bathing cap, two piece form fitting bathing suit with frills, flowing hair- Wow, was she a beauty in her day!* He looked closer at the print on the pier in the background. *Pier #9 Coney Island.* "What a smile, now this is joy." Randall looked across his room at a solitary photograph, tacked to the wall." He stood up and walked over to it. His felt the crisp corner. "You were once a beauty weren't you Vera, long before you were taken from me?" He leaned over with his palm against the wall and compared the two photographs. "You have the same smile as Ms. Lena Louise. Vera… Lena… Vera….. Lena." He took out the tack and stuck it through the bottom of the bathing beauty so it was above his girlfriend. He walked over to his large table, which stood like an elephant's hoof in the center of his room. He pulled open a drawer and extracted a sturdy manila envelope. He pulled out her death certificate. He pulled out her death certificate. "Oh, Vera- April 22nd 1987- wait a minute." He went back to Lena's death certificate next to the safe. He looked at them with a stare. "April 22nd, 1987! You both died the same day! What are the chances?" He paused in thought, and continued, "same smile, similar names- maybe it's a sign." He took Lena's death certificate and placed it in the envelope with Vera's, returned it to the drawer and sat back at the safe.

Randall reached back into it and pulled a sealed black envelope out, the portrait of a 2-year-old glued to the front. He flipped it over and opened it. *Desmond Hillerman born 1953, died 1955, fuckin death certificates.* He turned it back and studied the child's picture. *Such a happy little guy...*He shook his head clearly disturbed, and put down the picture. *Goddamn tragedy.* He put the envelope face down on his 'looked through' pile. His fingers stretched across the steel of the bottom shelf and pulled out a small box, which contained 50 shares of Edison Power & Electric, 50 shares of Bell Laboratories and 25 shares of Xerox stock.

When he reached the second shelf, his fingers grasped another thick rubber banded paper bag. He lifted it slightly to ease the contents out. *What could it be?* He pulled off the rubber bands enough to reach into the bag and feel a stack of crisp cotton-fiber bills. He pulled out a stack of twenty-dollar bills. "Jackpot!" he exclaimed. He jumped up and wiggled himself around the room with excitement. "Money for the business, money for the food! Food glorious food!" He swung his right hand out and arched his left, then waltzed through the room. The bills rubbed through the palm of his left hand. He threw himself into his seat and proceeded to count the cash. "Five thousand dollars! Whoo hoo! His hands trembled. "Christ, what do I do first?" His life started to flash. "I need a cigarette. Yea, that would calm my nerves." He lit up a cigarette and took the first drag deep into his chest holding it like fresh Colombian grass.

He fingered the cash not once but three times in disbelief. *The shelf seemed difficult to lift. Maybe there's something in the back I missed.* He leaned on his oak table and peered into the safe.

He approached the mound of steel, pulled up his right sleeve and slipped his hand into the narrow passage of the top shelf. He gripped a blue box wedged halfway into the safe. Randall's fingers gripped it like a dentist extracting a rotten tooth.

"Fancy box, beautiful lock, must be something valuable." He carefully slid the lock to the side, took a deep breath, and lifted the lid. The satin lined bangle box held a black velvet pouch pulled tight by a black rope.

Randall wiggled his finger inside and pulled the bag open.

"Damn, a large chandelier crystal! And I got myself worked up over this damn thing!" he said walking closer to the light to examine it. "Looks like the bottom of an expensive lamp. Probably a priceless memory, an old ballroom- somewhere him and his wife danced when they were kids."

The light bounced from the facets of the crystal. It cast reflections of a rainbow on the wall. "Damn this dull side destroys the value, I'm sure. Looks like the chandelier must have held it from here. Would be beautiful if it was fully cut; someone saved a buck. I suppose if it was perched high above a ballroom floor, no one would know the difference. Must have some value; maybe it's valuable European rock crystal. I'll check it out down on 47th. Street tomorrow."

He sat down at the table to sort his finds one more time before he retired for the evening. "So many people fall by the wayside when the world passes by. They get stuck in their old ways, doing little to change their future…My God! That's what I've done!" he said to himself. He spoke as he looked through the dilapidated ceiling. "Henry Hillerman, you'll get the respect you deserve."

Randall walked to his bed and threw himself belly first toward his pillow. He landed in a soft thud, as his body bounced off the old spring mattress. He turned himself over, put his hands behind his head and leaned back. He sighed, and then yawned.

I think it's time to grow up. No more life in the fast lane. I need to set goals, make myself a nest egg. I won't be able to party on the street as a 60-year-old man. I want to move forward for once, and not backward like I've done my whole life. I need to start an antiques business. Maybe this is my wake up call. He looked at the two photos on the distant wall. *Vera, Lena, smiles, same day of the same year. It's gotta be a sign. Someone up there's finally looking out for me.*

Randall shut his eyes and fell asleep. His body tossed and turned, as his brain overflowed with life's new master plan. *'Welcome to Randall's Antique Oasis- your secret brownstone in down-town Manhattan- built to serve your needs.'* His eyes darted back and forth in an excited frenzy. He lay for hours in a light sleep, until 5 am, when he finally fell into a deep one. Light pierced the makeshift curtains at 10 am and woke him.

He dragged himself out of bed for his morning dose of coffee. His temples pounded as his head searched in vain for the caffeine that kept his body alive. His hair stood at all angles. He exited the bedroom, got to the kitchen counter, and stared at the coffeepot. "Hey Mother Hubbard anything left in my cubbard?" He opened the kitchen cabinet, "rice crispy treats, coffee and Crunch Berries- breakfast of champions. Been awhile since these cabinets have seen food." He went to a tiny refrigerator powered by a car battery, "a few cans of beer, milk, bread, some left over pizza and a bag full of fresh carrots." He took one out and chewed it.

What happened to that sub-personality in charge of cooking? You know you were a famous chef in a past life. It's too bad that damn Mexican restaurant wouldn't take you off the deep fryer to prove your point. Six months was too long at that damn place. He opened a floor level cabinet. "The non-stick pan is now a stick pan. New pans are in order, so I'm going on a major shopping venture. It's been too long since I've had a decent meal and I think I can afford it now. " His voice echoed off the barren walls, "I'm going shopping!"

He lifted the couch, smiled at the feel of his secret stash, and then thumbed a couple of bills. The couch thudded as it hit the ground. He had $200.00 in his hand. Randall broke into song, "Yap Yap, you know you talk too much." A smile lit his face, as he recalled the day he met Keith Richards, at Tower Records signing autographs. He laughed with giddy joy and sauntered to the mirror, where he pulled out a comb like Arthur Fonzerelli and slicked back his hair. He returned to a drawer in a cabinet, overstuffed with clipped coupons- he grabbed a handful and shoved them in his pocket.

He picked up the keys from atop the safe and looked around the place. "This could be the last time, this could be the last time, maybe the last time I don't know… oh no," he sang, as he stood inside the door frame. He spotted the black velvet pouch. "Ah!" he said as he started walking to it, "Na, maybe later." He left it there on the desk as he exited his apartment.

The supermarket was two blocks away and with every step

he salivated more. His hand fingered the coupons he collected from useless papers discarded by commuters. "These should help me save a little money, especially for those tough months when food's hard to come by. I can't be frivolous with these new riches." He stopped at the shopping carts and pulled out the first. He bent down and spun the wheels. "Well lubricated, this should do."

When he entered the supermarket, he gazed at the ripened fruit, "irresistible." He gently squeezed the oranges looking for the most succulent of the bunch. A beautiful woman passed in a form-fitting tank top. He squeezed the oranges harder, "Mmmm, tits." She quickly turned to him and caught him red-handed. He laughed, "Oops. Uhhhh- hello." She scowled at him and stormed off. *You idiot.*

Randall looked strangely out of place in the supermarket. He slowly walked the aisles, leaning the top half of his body over the chromed steel baby seat. The tips of his toes guided the metal cage back and forth from one side to the next. Awkward, he popped up the empty carriage when he leaned in with all of his weight. It crashed back to the ground and fellow shoppers looked at him. He smiled and corrected his bent stance as he turned the corner. He stopped in the spice aisle and compared prices. He used his restaurant knowledge to pick up some cinnamon, coriander, basil, and parsley. He tossed them into his basket.

"The international aisle, I'll vacation through my cuisine," he said to himself.

As he slowly walked down the aisle, a woman entered from the opposite direction. She wore a sweat suit with her thick black hair tied back in a sweatband. She eyed Randall sorting through the Chinese section of the aisle. She stopped to watch him, and then dodged his eye when he glanced her way. She turned at the end of the aisle, and peeked around the corner.

"Tonight, I'm going to make a meal so good that all of China will want to come over; A little of this, a dash of that. I hope I'm not too far out of practice. It's been months since I've really cooked," he said to himself. He considered all the products, compared prices, matched coupons and simply enjoyed himself.

The woman disappeared for ten seconds at the end of the column of food, then quickly reappeared and rapidly pushed her cart down the aisle. As it approached Randall, the sound of the off centered wheels made him turn his head. She pulled the cart back to a slow push, like a jockey pulling back her reins. She stopped almost diagonally from him, and looked at various foods on the top shelf.

Randall turned and looked at her. She smiled. *Am I paranoid or is she following me? She's probably a store detective making sure I don't steal anything. Is attractive though- olive complexion, blonde hair- bet she'd be hot in a nice slinky dress. Maybe I can strike up a conversation or something. What is she looking at?*

"Do you think you can help me?" asked the woman.

"Why, uhhhh sure."

"I need to get that, but I can't reach it." She pointed at a long slender bottle out of reach.

"You mean that?" asked Randall, "it's a strange looking bottle." He stood on his toes and grabbed the bottle. He read the label. "According to the bottle this is Tunisian Orange Olive Oil- extra virgin. You must be a cook."

"I dabble."

Those eyes! She's got the most incredible olive green eyes. He tapped the bottle in his palm, then tore himself away and unclenched his teeth to simply talk, "You know some people may think you have other intentions with this."

"What do you mean by that?" she said with an attitude.

Shocked by the boldness and misinterpretation of his own comment, Randall recovered quickly, "what I mean to say is, no one knows better than you on how to satisfy your hunger. I'd suggest you use first cold pressed extra virgin olive oil for your recipe. It'll make everything taste wonderful."

"Is that so? My name is Milly, Milly Van Lowe," she said. She held out her hand.

He took her hand, and returned the handshake. "Randall, Randall Becks."

"I suppose olive oil would give me the utmost satisfaction, although I couldn't claim it to be extra virgin," she said, with a strong emphasis on satisfaction.

"Wow, is it getting hot in here, or is it just me?" He repositioned his feet.

"No, it's getting hot in here," she said with a twinkle in her eye. "I see you're in the middle of a major shopping trip, and I don't want to disturb you. I presume you're from around here?"

His brain scattered, *could this be true?*

"Yes, I live pretty close. I do most of my shopping here and it's strange I haven't seen you before."

"I've just moved here from Brooklyn. The commute to work was too far, so I decided to move closer. Now, I can avoid the subway altogether. I can reach work in about 15 minutes by walking, instead of almost forty-five minutes in a congested train car. You wouldn't think it could take that long to commute from across the river, right?"

"My God, that's insane! I'm glad you decided to move; otherwise I might not have been so lucky today. Would you like to meet for drinks later, then I could show you around. I know some places that'll make you feel miles outside of the city," he said.

"Good, I need some R & R. The pressure of moving has been a little much lately. Let me write my phone number and address on the back of my business card," she said. She leaned over and began writing away while Randall's eyes moved up and down her body. She finished, winked and said, "Give me a call, later." Her slinky hips shook back and forth down the tile floor away from him.

"Definitely," he said smiling. He watched her curvy body turn at the end of the aisle, and then returned to his shopping cart whistling. He eyed her handwriting. *Angelic and almost as beautiful as her face; Milly Van Lowe- Director of Interior Design- Renaissance d'Italia, Inc.* It was stamped with a fine embossed gold logo. *Impressive card.* Then the fear struck him like a bolt of lightening. *This is a woman of class and who am I? I like being a no one and living life in the "undisturbed lane". She'd never want someone like me; it's like Aphrodite asking Oscar the Grouch on a date. Even though I can speak to anyone, I couldn't lie about these feelings. I'd probably have to change conversation topics often or ignore them. God forbid she asks me for my job description! I'd be left in a "no win" situation.* He paused momentarily in thought. *Fuck it! The goddamn woman intrigues me. I'll call her this evening and be myself. If we get along great, if not- who needs her!*

"I've gotta eat soon or I'll starve to death and there'll be no need to see that woman," he said to himself. He picked up a jar of honey from the shelf, and then licked his chops. *Yes! Crispy orange chicken lathered in honey! My God, that could be as good as an orgasm!* He sighed and his mind refocused on his shopping.

As the cashier rang up the bill his foot tapped. It totaled $194.63, the most he'd spent in a long time. He handed over the two hundred-dollar bills and placed the last bag in the cart.

He walked towards the exit and past a few people depositing their shopping carts at the exit. A large sign was posted above them, "Shopping carts prohibited outside the store". *Now, how in the hell am I gonna carry all these bags two blocks?* He turned his head and looked around. *I'm sure they won't mind if I borrowed it. It's only a felony if you don't return it. Two blocks at a quick sprint with a shopping cart and I'll be in the clear.* Again, he looked behind him, then in front. *No policeman in sight.* He pushed the cart outside the door and ran.

Randall reached the first corner before the security person from the grocery store ran out in pursuit of him. "Hey, get back here!" he yelled. Randall sprinted along the crosswalk with the vibrating steel cart in front. He dodged between people like an erratic pinball shooting through a machine. "Breakin the law, breaking the law," he sang as he manipulated the cart. The voice of authority became distant, but he didn't want to risk being caught. When he turned the second corner, he dodged into an abandoned shed behind his building. It was covered in overgrown weeds. His breath came in small puffs and sweat rolled off his face. "Success!" He surveyed his bags, "Not one can of soup missing!" he said as he panted. He grabbed the two bags and made his way around to the front. He wedged the tip of his toe into the bottom of the board and pushed it aside, using his whole body to fall into the place. He climbed the stairs to the third floor.

He put the groceries on the ground, unbolted the door and opened it. He brought the food in and unloaded the bags into their respective spots. When he finished, he stood back to glance at his full cabinets. "What a difference to have choice!" He rubbed his stomach, "but nothing's better or quicker than a no nonsense ham and cheese sandwich on a hard roll."

He pulled Milly's card from his wallet and smelled it. A rose scent whiffed pass his nose, "Wow, she didn't look like a high fluting executive, more like a Greenpeace worker or Peace Corps woman. If she hadn't given me this card, I'd never have known. She seemed so down to earth." He looked around his place and rolled his head on his limbering shoulders, "She'd have a stroke if she entered this place. An interior designer… yikes. I'll have to keep her away from here for awhile and feel her out," he said, then giggled at the words he muttered. "I'd better watch what I say too."

He sat at the table and cradled the sandwich with two hands as he took large bites. He saw the velvet pouch at the center of the table. It was hidden between the salt and pepper shakers. He shifted the sandwich into one hand like a professional basketball player who palms a ball. He pulled the pouch close to him by the small rope at its top. He reached in it, spread his fingers, and then grabbed the large crystal in his free hand. He held the stone while biting his sandwich. He placed the crystal on the wood table and knocked it side to side with his index finger.

Randall wound up a finger blast that sent the crystal flying for the edge of the other side of the table. His eyes widened, he dropped his sandwich, and his whole world moved in slow motion. He immediately pushed the table with his free hand, spilling both shakers and tumbling the napkin holder. His legs sprung from a seated position, launching his whole body in the direction of the stone. It approached the floor with lightening quick velocity and Randall's fingertips stretched to grab the crystal only inches from the ground. His body smashed the wooden floor like a rock thrown from a 10-story building. His head bounced off his left biceps.

"Arrrrrrrgggggghhhhh," he said imitating the sound of

a crowd. "Oh man, I think I hurt myself. What a save!" He struggled to a standing position, rubbed his ribs and started to laugh. *That was one for America's Funniest Home Videos.*

He threw the crystal up in the air and caught it. "Time to watch a little TV. Back you go," he said as he placed the translucent stone back in its pouch. He returned it to the center of the table, turned on TV, and adjusted the rabbit ears to tune in channel 7. He moved the foil wrapped antenna from left to right. *God damn static! If it wasn't for the news I'd trash this thing.* "It's 5:30pm and Eyewitness News is on." He turned up the volume.

"Now for our top story, Bala Bala Diamonds of East 47th. St. has kindly donated a flawless 5-carat diamond to the Marty Lyons Foundation for terminally ill children. It's to be auctioned by the charity for urgently needed money. Eyewitness news caught up with owner Paul Striker to discuss his generosity, "Mr. Striker, why have you donated such a precious stone to the foundation? I understand diamonds of this size are rarely flawless," asked the reporter.

"That's true, but I recently had a conversation with a woman who worked for the foundation. She told me of a 7-year-old child with cancer who had a dream to visit Disney World before he died. The foundation had granted his wish to go to there with his family, so they flew down and the child lived his dream. He died tragically on the return journey. At that point, it occurred to me that a flawless diamond represents absolute purity and is very much like the soul of a child. So I felt this diamond could do much more for the foundation than occupy a place in my case. I donated it to a worthwhile cause."

"You're a remarkable man, Mr. Striker. To see people like you give so much for so little in return, makes it even more incredible. You're an inspiration to New Yorkers everywhere.

We'd like everyone to know that the Marty Lyons Foundation accepts donations at the following number. Please dial 1-212-977-9474 and please be patient. Your donation could make the difference in a child's life. This is Alicia Moran with Eyewitness News."

Randall nodded his head, "What a fantastic story. I wouldn't mind going to that auction for curiosity's sake, I'd love to know how much that diamond would raise for charity. If only I could treat that guy to a beer." He looked down at his hands, "that reminds me, my hand's empty." *I'll get a beer then call Milly. Ahhh, but maybe I should wait, I can't show her how anxious I am. I don't want to appear desperate.* He went to the refrigerator, grabbed a Milwaukee Light and pulled the tab open. He went back to his comfortable couch and put his feet up to drink his beer. "We need more people like that in the world."

Randall picked up the phone. "Well, on second thought…" He dialed the phone number from Milly's card. The phone rang four times before it was answered, "Hello?"

"Milly?"

"Yes, this is Milly."

"Milly, this is Randall Becks. I met you in the supermarket today. I hope I'm not disturbing you."

"Not in the least, I was hoping you'd call."

"What are you doing this evening?" asked Randall.

"You're a straight shooter, aren't you? No small talk, just straight to the point." She giggled, "I like that. I'm not doing anything tonight, how about you?"

"Nothing. I was hoping you'd like to go out for a few drinks. I know a few places around town. What type of place do you like?" asked Randall.

"I have to warn you, I'm unusual. I'm not the soft, quiet, comfortable type of woman. I like places where you never know what might happen from one minute to the next; a place where the rhythm of music never stops your feet. I like to shake it up."

"Interesting," he said.

"What do you like Randall?"

"The same. You couldn't have put my thoughts better. Have you ever been to the Limelight?"

"No."

"Then the Limelight will be our stop for tonight. If you enjoy chaos, atmosphere, and the most unusual people in Manhattan, it's the place to be. I enjoy the company of what other people may call 'Freaks'. What da ya think?"

Milly replied, "I've always wanted to go there, but was never lucky enough. I have the feeling I'm in for an interesting night. What time should we leave?"

"I'd like to get to the club about 11pm, so I can meet you at your place say 10:30pm? The Limelight is on 20th and 6th. How long does it take to get there from your place by subway?"

"Subway?" Milly asked, "you great romancer," she said sarcastically.

"Ok, ok. We'll go for the gusto and take a cab."

"By cab it'll take about 10 minutes. My place is 511 52nd Street near 3rd Ave. My apartment is on the 10th floor, number 1014. So, I'll expect you at 10:30?" she asked.

"Definitely, I look forward to seeing you," said Randall, "By the way, I suggest you wear black."

"I planned on it," replied Milly. "See you then."

Randall hung up the phone. *I think I need a black velvet overcoat, to add some class to the evening. Nino's usually carries stylish and reasonably priced stuff.* He passed the black velvet pouch on the table. *I need a jacket the exact color as this velvet. I'll take this with me as a sample.*

"Got a date with a lady, a lady all covered in pearls, she is all covered with diamond rings, needles and collars and fancy things. No, I don't think it goes like that." Bugs bunny would be disgusted. *It'll be faster to jog down the fire escape.* When he reached the ground floor, he exited the building. He jogged down the next few blocks until he reached Windward cemetery. He looked through the gates at a plant hung from a single shepherd's needle, and then searched the cemetery wall for a loose stone. He found one, put it in his pocket, and then proceeded inside. He walked through the grounds with his head bowed until he reached her plot. The Shepherd's needle was the only marker on the grave with the exception of the small round stones Randall deposited on every visit. These surrounded her plot.

Randall pulled the stone from his pocket, knelt down and put it along the border. "I know it's been awhile since I visited you, Vera. You never leave my mind, but there's a reason I came here today. I'm attracted to another woman. We have a first date." He rubbed his face and repositioned himself in a cross legged seat. "I want you to know there's no one I loved more in this world than you, nor will there ever be. I've never been able to get past your suicide. The pain's somewhat subsided and I feel I can stand on my own two feet again. I've learned to accept your absence here and although I'll never be the same, I know I must carry on. Certainly you must understand and I hope as you look on from your cloudy bank, you'll agree?"

Randall looked through the cemetery and saw a yellow swallowtail butterfly flying in the wind towards him. It landed on the flowers hung from the shepherd's needle. "It's the same butterfly as your tattoo, Vera. Thank you. If there's such a thing as reincarnation, I bet that's you." He stood up and looked down its beautiful yellow and black wings. He raised his finger and put it close to it before it flew away. *Just like you- never let me get too close.* He stroked the ground, then said, "God bless." He stood up and left the cemetery.

Randall walked up to 6th. Ave till he reached Nino's at 34th Street; one of many clothing outlets that littered the area. He entered and a salesman pounced on him.

"Ah my friend, how come you wait so long to visit me again? It must be six months! You should really come visit Abdul more often. I have a thousand things a good-looking man like you could wear, some irresistible to women. Trust me I know."

"Abdul, didn't you take all my cash last time?"

The salesman pointed at himself, "How could you forget this face?"

Randall slapped his cheek gently a couple of times and said, "I'm looking for a black velvet jacket," he pulled the pouch from inside his pocket, "with the same material as this. Show me whatcha got."

The salesman felt the black pouch, "plenty of things, plenty of things." He shuffled Randall to the back of the store until he came to a rack with velvet attire side by side in the colors of the rainbow. "What do you think of that for selection?"

"Not bad." Randall felt the soft plush jackets. "How much do these run?"

"You're in luck. The black is on sale today for $99.99. I think you'd look very dapper in it," he said. "Are you going to wear it everyday?"

"No, I'm meeting a special woman tonight and I want to impress her."

"That'll definitely work; I have a whole outfit that'll make you the King of New York. We'll put this aside for you." He shoved Randall over to the shirts where he isolated a sheer black shirt with black and silver buttons. He went over to a pants rack and pulled out a pair of matching pants. "You try these on and if you don't like them, we'll give you your money back. Dressing rooms there." He pointed towards the back.

"Ok." Randall said. He took the ensemble to the dressing room, and then looked at the clothes in the mirror. *Man, these are class threads. I've gotta keep my cool.* He put them on and stepped out to look in the three dimensional mirror. He saw himself through his periphery vision from all angles.

Excited by the fit, he kept a stone face and asked, "How much?"

The salesman studied him, without delay he said, "two hundred and twenty -five, everything included."

"Two hundred and twenty-five! That's too much. I'm going for an evening on the town. I may never wear these again. I'll give ya one hundred and fifty."

"Your girlfriend will be at your mercy wearing that outfit. Isn't that worth the money itself?"

Randall's expression didn't flinch. He looked back at the outfit. *Shit, he's right. It makes a statement and it's definitely worth that much, but I didn't plan on spending that. I'll have to get more money from home for the evening.* "I'll tell you what. I'll give you $150.00 and the stone I have in this velvet pouch; it could be worth thousands." Randall pulled it out and showed it to the salesman.

The salesman picked it up, looked at it in the light, "that's some lousy crystal. I wouldn't give you $5.00 for it. You expect me to come down $75.00 for some lousy crystal? No can do. I'll give you the set for two hundred."

"You know you could be making a big mistake by not trading for the crystal."

"You could be making a mistake by trying to sell me the

crystal. What do ya got on you, guy?" said the salesman.

Randall stopped for a minute and repeated the thought in his head, *A worthless crystal wouldn't have been kept in that big safe if it were worthless. I should check it out first.* He showed the clerk the money in his wallet, "I have $175.00 in my wallet, look," the clerk looked into his wallet, "but if you sell me this outfit for the amount I have here, I'll be sure to tell everyone where I got it. I'll even tell them to see you. You work on commission, right?"

"Yea."

"So that means if just 2 people come here to buy the same suit after seeing me wear it, you'll be that much richer. Sometimes, you gotta sacrifice a little to gain a little. Besides, look how long I've been here. I just stepped through the door. If I leave in the next 5 minutes, you can boast how good ya are to the other guys. What kinda excellent salesman sells someone in a matter of 15 minutes?"

"You put up a good argument, my friend. $175.00 it is. Cash. It's tough when one bargainer meets another, but I think your bullshit smells better. I learn from this. You send people to see me."

"I will," said Randall.

The salesman took him to the register and rang him up. He put the outfit in a chic black plastic carry bag, which Randall flung over his shoulder.

"Give me your card, so I can tell people who to see," Randall said. The salesman handed it to him, "Abdul Estabi." He nodded his head. "Thanks Abdul, I'll be back."

"You better, with ten of your friends!"

Randall left the store whistling. He walked home, retreated to his bedroom, and laid the outfit on his bed. He looked at his watch, "Eight-thirty, an hour to spare." He walked to his window, edged it up between the planks and peered over the avenue at a dirty old brick building. He watched the faces change- nameless people from old to young, from saggy to blue, from white to black, from drug free to those on smack: He was completely absorbed. The next time he looked at his watch it was nine-thirty. He got up, went to his bed, changed and left the apartment.

Chapter 6
A Date

R andall arrived at Milly's at ten forty-five. He rang the buzzer to 1014 on an electronic board at the front door and waited with his ear to the speaker.

"Who is it?"

"The Good Humor man."

"You make deliveries this late?"

"It's not late, the nights just beginning," he said. The buzz of the buildings front door made him grab its handle. He opened the door and proceeded inside a small lobby. The floor was lined with black marble, and in the center was a beautiful Asian rug. A greeting desk was to the right of three elevator doors.

"Can I help you?"

"I'm here to see Milly Van Lowe on the tenth floor. She just buzzed me in."

"Fine, you need to sign in."

"Thanks." Randall took a pen and wrote his name in a small book, which was filled with visitors. He hopped on an elevator, pushed the 10th floor button. He listened to the soft sound of jazz, which filled the space from a round speaker mounted at the top center of the ceiling. The doors opened. Milly stood half out of her door on the right side of the hall. She was dressed in a black velvet skirt with a black lacy shawl hung over her shoulders. Her long black boots started from her knee and fell down around her sultry calves until they stopped at a three-inch heel. Her blonde hair contrasted with her olive complexion, and made her deep green eyes radiate. Randall's eyes were fixed.

"You think this is good for the club?" asked Milly. Randall stared blankly. She snapped her fingers, "earth to Randall, are you home?"

Randall shook his head, "sorry, I uh. I… I'm speechless. You look incredible."

"Thanks. Can I get you a drink before we go?" asked Milly. "Come in."

Randall stepped through the door and his jaw dropped. *I can't believe this place, the furniture, the artwork, and the fireplace. If I have a drink, I'll fall apart. It's too early. Keep your shit together!* "No, I'll wait till we get to the Limelight."

"You sure?" Milly asked. She turned and walked towards a bottle of Johnny Walker Black next to a crystal decanter on a white marble bar. Her shapely hips swung side to side, like a willow blown in the breeze. When she reached it, she took the top of the Scotch bottle and rubbed it with her fingertips.

Randall controlled his internal screams. *Fuck, fuck, fuck. I'm sooooooo outclassed. We gotta get outta here.* He took a deep breath, "not now, perhaps a nightcap later. We'll have to wait twice as long to simply get in the place if we don't get going soon. That's not a problem is it?"

"Not in the least." She went to her closet and pulled out a translucent trench coat. It was a gossamer cocoon layered over her black clothes. "Ready when you are."

"Let's go," he said, as he motioned her through the door. He watched her slender curves move. *Smooth.* They reached the curb and Randall waved down a cab. He opened the door for Milly, followed her in, and slammed the door shut. "20th and Sixth," he said to the cabby. He sat back next to Milly and stared toward the end of her boot. He traced her outline, up her leg, to her thigh and as his eyes crept closer to her short skirt; his peripheral vision caught her looking at him. He cleared his throat.

She turned to him and winked, "Don't worry, Randall. I don't mind."

"So, how is it someone like you would see a plain and simple Joe, like me?"

"Call it intuition. I was attracted to you when I first saw you," said Milly. "So this place sounds exciting. What can I expect?"

"Well, the club's built in an old church that dates from the mid 1800's. It's very Goth and the stained glass is awesome. There are nooks and crannies everywhere, with a giant disco ball that hangs from the center. It has a crucifix mounted on it. The feeling's strange when you're walking around, like you're doing something sinful. The founders of the church must be turning in their graves," said Randall. "The second floor overlooks the first and when a band plays there, it's like they're playing to you. You'll love it."

"I can't wait," she said. "What time's the place close?"

"I think 4 am."

"I turn into a pumpkin after two."

"So I'll make sure to get you home before then."

She laughed, "You have a great sense of humor. I hope you use that in your work!"

He turned his head and whispered to himself, "more than you know."

She got closer. "I'm sorry I didn't hear you."

"It was nothing."

"So, what do you do?" she asked.

Randall skirted the question, "it's not important. I get by, and that's what life's about, gettin by."

"You must have aspirations though? There must be something you want out of life," she asked.

I want you. He paused. "I'm sure I'll know what it is when it hits me. I'd like to write a book about life and how to live, but who has the time?"

"You've gotta make the time. If you've got something to say, you say it. Life's not forever," she said.

"You're right," he said, then looked out the window.

"The Limelight," said the cabby.

Randall turned to Milly and whispered, "wait here." She looked astonished as he shuffled out his door and ran around to open hers. She put her delicate foot outside the cab, held Randall's hand and pulled herself from her seat.

"Thank you," she said. She smiled.

"How much cabby?"

"That'll be $6.85," he said.

Randall gave the driver a ten. "Keep the change."

"Thanks, chief," replied the cabbie. The taxi took off.

Milly surveyed the old stone building from its curb. She stared at the steeple when Randall joined her. "What an interesting place. I can't believe they'd make an old church into a club like this. Prior to the industrial revolution I'd imagine it stood isolated in this decrepit cemetery with old knotty trees and deep nightly mists. It's so Goth."

"That's what makes it so great. At least, the line's not too long. I've seen it an hour easy." Randall said. "Let's take our place."

Milly walked with Randall to the end of the line. They stood next to each other. Randall put his hands in his pockets and rocked on his heals to and fro. He whistled.

"Do you want to hear something funny?" she asked.

"What's that?"

"I can't whistle."

"Noooo. I don't believe you."

She puckered her lips and blew through them, the sound of air passed. He laughed.

"I'll teach you," he said. "First put the tip of your tongue on the back of your bottom teeth, elevate your tongue in an arc, pucker your lips in the shape of an O, tighten them and blow."

She watched him, listened and tried. "Whewwwww… nothing but air. Is this what you do for fun?"

"No, but it does keep me entertained. I used to be an avid partier, but I've mellowed with age. I think it's important to tap into the creative side. I find these notions of inspiration after I've been to museums or intimate music events. So, I guess you'll have to classify me as a 'strange guy'."

Milly watched his mouth form every word. "Who's your favorite painter?" she asked.

"Van Gogh. It's not just his use of color and the mastery of his art, but it's his story. Look at Starry Night… it was painted when he was in an asylum. All the craziness around him; battling his own demons, and bringing forth something absolutely amazing- making the best out of the worst situation. Everyone has a story, and I know what someone like him can provide to an ailing soul. Consider all the years he painted without a single painting sold, or consider his mental illness. It's a tragic reality. Now, a single painting sells for more than most of us make in a lifetime. To me that is inspiration."

"Yes, he is but you must consider his brush with Gauguin, two fantastic painters whose paths cross, whose influence on each other is legendary. It's Van Gogh who cuts off his ear in shame after a critical argument. It's the epitome of his career. When you look at how his brush manipulated the thick paint, you can tell every stroke was painted from his soul," replied Milly.

Randall stepped back and gazed at her, "have I met you in a past life?"

"Perhaps. All this passion in the arts, we must have been lovers."

"Or artists," replied Randall. His arm pulled her in and he looked deeply into her eyes. "Did you ever think two people could be meant for each other?"

Milly looked into his, "absolutely."

"That'll be $15.00 each," said the bouncer.

Randall ripped himself from her stare. He pulled out the money and paid the man. "That went so quickly."

"Too quickly."

"Never mind, I'm excited to show you the place." He grabbed her hand and pulled her behind him into the dimly lit corridor crowded with people. They waited patiently and took minute steps until they came to the entrance of the enormous ballroom. She looked at the disco ball hung from the ceiling. It spun ever so slowly, light cast from every mirror across the club.

"Fabulous."

The club was already filled with people and the techno rhythms were deafening. Randall escorted her to the back bar, where they squeezed into a small open space. "What do ya want to drink?" yelled Randall.

"A martini would be nice."

"One martini it is," he replied. He faced the bartender, "I'll take two martinis."

"You're having one too?" she asked.

"Planned on it all evening," Randall replied. "Do you read minds or something?"

"If only I could, life would be so much easier. How was I to know you would order a martini? I'm perceptive, maybe extra sensitive to others. But that shocked me. I thought you might be more of a Jack Daniels kinda guy."

"I like that too, but not tonight. I save that for the boys."

The bartender returned with two martinis'. Randall handed him a twenty, "keep the change."

"Thanks," replied the bartender.

Randall returned his looked to Milly, "so how do you perceive me?"

"Well, I see you as highly intelligent, sensitive but not to a fault, organized and most of all- mysterious. There's something about you I can't put my finger on, but I plan to find that out in time," she said.

"Are you looking at me as some kind of science project?"

"No, I'm looking at you, for what you are," she said.

"And you think you know?" he replied.

"I told you I'm impressionable and deep, with the understanding of a poet."

"I see. I like that."

"Good." She winked. "So, how'd you find out about this place?"

"A friend of mine told me he saw a band called Fishbone here. Are you familiar with them?" he asked.

"Party at ground zero-

-waca doo, waca doo, waca doo. Yea," said Randall. "You're shocking, a surprise in every word." He went to the edge of the dance floor and waved to her. "Come on."

"I'm not ready. I need another 6 drinks."

"Who needs drinks? People here don't know if you've had one or ten, besides no one here knows you. Be yourself and dance like the freaks." Randall said. He swung his head up and down and wriggled his hips.

Milly laughed, "are you a part-time comedian?"

"Full time, just no one's discovered me yet."

Milly roared.

Randall grabbed her free hand and dragged her on to the dance floor. He spun like a gyrating top around her. Every moment he smiled, she returned them effortlessly. People pointed at the couple and smiled, their heads bopping to the music. Absorbed into the moment, Milly was thoroughly entertained. The music thumped and their bodies imitated ocean waves as they crashed the dance floor. As tides rolled in, and pounded the beaches, they rolled out and before they knew, hours had passed.

"Not all things matter," Randall said to her, "like time".

Milly twisted and contorted herself in a wild dance around Randall. "Randall?"

"Yes?"

"I need a drink," she said, then grabbed his hand and pulled him away towards the bar.

"Hey! What if I'm not ready?"

"If I'm ready, you're ready."

"Not gonna argue that," Randall replied. "I love this place! Those primitive rhythms make your body explode with groove. You're the goddess of groove, lady."

"Shut up," she said with a good-natured chuckle.

The bar was hidden beneath a crowd of people. The couple stood three people out from the bar, when Milly looked at Randall.

"Do you think this wait is worth the hassle? I can barely hear you!" she yelled.

"I don't know. It might be better to get some coffee in some place quieter or sit back and observe. There's a place upstairs in the center of the club, which offers seats, but I'm not sure if we could find any. We still need to tour the place, follow me." Randall grabbed her hand and pulled her through the club until he reached a door in the corner of the place. They entered a dark passage and climbed a set of circular steps past a line of stained glass windows, until they reached the second floor lounge. They stared below at the dance floor.

"Amazing, isn't it?" asked Randall.

"When I die, I want to be buried here," she exclaimed.

Randall snickered. "You have plenty of time before that, besides, how would it look a 90-year-old grandmother getting buried in the hippest place in 1990's New York?"

"I think it'd be cool," she said.

Randall stopped to think, "You're right. I can't think of a better way to be buried."

A skinny pale man with contrasting black hair bumped into Randall. His body was thrust against Milly.

Randall turned to look and found the man's face full of piercings including one through the bridge of his nose.

"Hey," Randall whispered.

The man stopped momentarily, growled and continued on his path through the sea of people. He led a crowd of at least ten others, each one bumping into them as they made their way through.

"It is crowded," Milly said.

"Maybe we should leave here and get a cup of coffee. What do ya say?"

"What time is it?" she asked.

"Jesus Christ, its 2:30! I've gotta get home. My pumpkin will turn into a car, if I'm not home in time."

"Don't you mean that backwards?" she asked.

He turned around and faced his back towards her. He repeated the same phrase. She pushed his body forward. "We should go."

They left the club, hopped in a cab, and went to Milly's neighborhood where they drifted into a 24-hour coffee shop, sat down and ordered decaffeinated cappuccinos. The lights quivered. A busboy stopped at a vacant table next to them with a grey bucket and tossed clanking dishes into it, along with used napkins and water glasses. The white Formica tabletops were topped with a small jukebox by the window which took quarters.

"You're something else, Randall Becks."

"As long as I'm not something, I'll be ok."

"What do you mean by that?"

"Well, with being something there comes responsibility. I have no need for additional responsibility at this point."

"Are you burdened with a lot of responsibility, now?"

He stuttered, "uh.. well... no. I've just had some stuff happen," his expression soured.

She looked at him with empathy, "are you ok? I didn't mean to bring anything up."

"No, no, it's ok. It's just that it still seems fresh," he replied.

"You're very secretive, but that's ok." She grabbed his hand and caressed it with her other. "What's still fresh?"

His eyes tried to avoid her piercing stare, until he couldn't any longer. "I was crushed in a relationship four years ago. My fiancée died unexpectedly."

"My God, I'm sorry. What happened?"

"She had a depression problem and a cocaine habit she couldn't kick. I was working two jobs which kept me busy and when she bottomed out, I wasn't there. She overdosed on purpose to save me. At least that's what she thought- she was saving me," he said. "I never thought she'd hit that low and do it," he paused, "and I blame myself for not being able to save her." He turned to look out the window.

She looked at him with the confession of this weight and stroked his hand. "I'm truly sorry."

He raised the arm of his jacket and quickly rubbed it over his water filled eyes, his mouth muttered, "This jacket's bothering me. I think I gotta take it back tomorrow and have it adjusted. Feels like it's riding on my back." He looked down at the wet sleeve, forced a smile and then switched gears. "Wonderful coffee, do you come here often?"

Her eyes penetrated his imaginary front, so she lightened the conversation, "on occasion. There's a fantastic pizzeria around the corner from here. I swear they make the best pizza in New York." She continued to stroke his hand.

"I love pizza," he said.

"We'll have to go there another day, maybe next week."

"Why not tomorrow?" Randall asked.

She smiled, "why not tomorrow, I'd like that." They both smiled and sipped their coffee under the white florescent lights. Randall flipped the song lists on the jukebox, "Would you like to hear some music?"

"I think we've heard enough for this evening. My ears are ringing."

"It's not that good anyway, mostly country music." He watched her have the final sip of her coffee. "I think we should call it an evening. I've got to be up early."

"Really? It's Sunday, you should sleep in."

"My body wakes me at ungodly times, no matter what time I get to sleep. Shall we?" asked Randall.

"Certainly," she replied.

Randall and Milly left the coffeehouse and walked hand in hand to her home. They approached her door, "would you like that nightcap we talked about earlier?"

I should go in, I should go in. He looked at his watch and his expression dropped. "Milly, you're the most incredible woman I've met in a long time. Can I get a rain check on that nightcap?"

She frowned, "please" she said in a soft baby like voice.

"I can't. Maybe, tomorrow, unless that's too soon," he said.

"I'll accept that," she said. "Goodnight, Randall Becks." Their bodies closed in on each other. Randall's hands touched her cheeks softly and pulled her lips to his and as they embraced one another, he pulled apart to speak.

"Shhhh," her index finger went to his lips, "Goodnight Randall Becks," she said in the sultriest tone Randall ever heard. She turned away, climbed the steps to her apartment building, blew a kiss, typed in her code and closed the door behind.

Randall stood dumbfounded. He walked away in a daze, when he broke into song:

Milly, Milly, my heart's found Milly,

Milly, Milly Van Lowe.

Milly, Milly can't you see you're with me

The sweetest, my dream Van Lowe.

Randall repeated the words over and over again as he walked home. He stumbled in at 4 am, slept for an hour then woke up for the flea market.

Chapter 7
The Irrepressible Dream

It was early Sunday morning and although he was accustomed to early morning work at the flea market, the blood filled Randall's eyes. Every muscle in his body ached and his hour sleep was barely enough to keep him coherent. He had set the timer on his coffeepot and filled a thermos with its contents, before he dragged his carcass to his reserved table at the market.

"Good morning, you conniving bastard," said Johnny in a good-natured tone.

"Nothing good about it," said Randall. "Still selling the same ole shit?"

"Na, tired of fighting these no good penny pinchers. These people have no appreciation for value, so I'm gonna sell these original lobby cards I picked up this week. I framed 'em myself with $5.00 frames and each of the cards was $3.00. I'm selling em for $25.00 a piece to blow 'em out. I know this market's a hit or miss, but I figure it's worth a shot. I put some other things on my table too, as a precaution."

Nodding his head, "Impressive Johnny, impressive. So who'd you steal these cards from, an old woman?"

"Your grandmother. She gave em up without a fight, kinda like the way she gave herself to me."

"Don't mess with me today, you twisted freak." He punched his friend's arm.

"So really, what da ya think?"

"I think they're beautiful, price is right, but I don't know if ya have a shot here. They're not for this type of market. I don't think people can reason the value out. Besides, not everyone appreciates artistic integrity like you."

"I had to try something new and these came around at the right time. If I sell only three, I'll make my money back and then it's all profit. With the crowds that come through here, that should be easy."

"Yea, but its overcast today. We might get rain and if that happens, you might as well go home." Randall said.

"Don't ever say I'm not prepared! I have a tarp to cover my merchandise."

"Ok, Eagle scout!" Randall ripped.

"Bastard," Johnny retorted, "whatda ya think I'm a permanent child?"

"Sometimes I wonder!" he said. "Hey, you should see the hottie I met yesterday while food shopping."

"I hope she didn't see you stockpiling pork & bean cans again. I bet you have a closet full of em," joked Johnny.

"Yes, I mean no. No, I don't have a closet full of beans, yes I met her at the supermarket."

"So you've resorted to pick up women in a supermarket, you're pitiful."

"She approached me," Randall said.

"You're full of it. I suppose you went out with her last night too." He moved his head closer in interest.

"Yea. Got home at 3:00 am."

"You serious? If you are, why the hell aren't you still in her bed? You know she'll never forgive you for this," Johnny spoke with astonishment.

"We didn't sleep together, Johnny."

"You're tellin me the opportunity was there, and you didn't hoist the flag? I should knock your head in!"

"It's too soon. I'm playing hard to get."

Johnny gasped, "Randall, get back to your table. You disgust me!"

"You ever been with someone who made ya break out in a sweat, become a mumbling fool, a blithering idiot? I don't know what I said to her, especially after I looked into her eyes. It all came out like mumbo jumbo."

"I can't listen to this sensitive bullshit. You need a therapist for that, not me. Embarrass yourself no more!"

Harry the Heckler strutted over to join the two, "what's up guys?"

"I gotta go Randall, I got a customer. Tell Harry about your new woman," he said. He turned to Harry, "Can you believe this crazy motherfucker blows the chance of a lifetime to come here! Would you knock some sense into him?"

"See ya, Johnny," replied Randall and Harry in unison.

"Is it wrong not to sleep with a woman if the invitation is there?" asked Randall.

"Na, but I think you're stupid if you don't and you have the invite. Unless of course, you want to fall in love with her." he replied. "You don't want that do you?"

"Hard to say," Randall replied. "I think I could. She feels like a missing puzzle piece. Something I've been without for some time."

Harry looked around and leaned in, "Randall, this is for your ears only and goes no further, got me?"

"To a tee, Harry."

"Years ago when I met Jessica Lovitska, my gang hung out at a bar called Rigid Frau and she came in there one day with some other biker chicks. We got to hangin together, but every time I was around her, I was speechless. So one day, we decide to meet away from our gangs," said Harry, "we went to local watering hole, but a rival gang, The Urchins, came in and started to harass her in front of me. I pushed the leader and told him to give us some respect. As I turned to sit down, he caught me with a right hook. Stunned, I shook my head, and then blacked out. Before I knew it the cops hauled me out that night in handcuffs. It was the last time I ever saw her," said Harry in a melancholy tone.

"Jessica Lovitska, huh?"

"Yea, I'll remember the name forever. Not soon after that, I was put in the slammer for first degree manslaughter. Till this day, I don't remember a thing. The police found his blood all over me."

"I can't imagine," said Randall, "have you ever tried to look for her? I can't see her disappearing without a trace."

"Randall, that's a night I'd rather forget. She must have seen everything, and the carnage I caused."

"But you protected her. Doesn't that count for anything?"

"I suppose," Harry said, "that was years ago. You're the only one besides a former cell mate I've told. I'm not gonna dwell on it, but I don't think there will ever be a woman in my life like her again." He smashed his finger against Randall's chest. "Take my advice, listen to your insides. Sometimes they know better."

"Thanks pal," said Randall. "I better get back to business."

"You do that buddy. Later."

Randall realigned his focus and concentrated on a middle-aged man sorting through a shoebox of postcards. "Those postcards are only .50 cents each; there's all kinds in there, most from the 1930's. I'll give ya a deal if ya take a bunch. If you need something, just ask."

"Do you have any ship postcards?"

"Not sure if I do," said Randall. I purchased the lot at once and took out the ones I wanted. Take a look, there's still some good one's in there."

The man returned to sorting through the stack.

A young blonde boy with his hair flattened on one side, asked from below the table top, "What's that, Mister?" He pointed to a small ink tarnished bottle.

Randall looked at the mother who smiled, then crouched beside her son. He smiled back and returned, "That's an old inkwell from the 1800's. It's made of glass. You can even see some dried ink on the inside. Let me teach ya something." Randall searched his moneybox and found an old pencil. He grabbed both ends and broke it over the edge of the table. He took the eraser end and found a flat piece of rusty metal on the ground, which he stuck in the eraser to form an oblong triangle. It looked like a crude calligraphy pen. "Back in the old days, people never had pens. They used to take what looked like a little sword, dip it in ink, then write with it." Randall picked up his Bic pen. "You see all the stuff in this pen. That's the ink. Today, pens hold it. In yesteryears they didn't." Randall took the crude pencil and dipped it in the jar, demonstrating the use of it. "Isn't that neat?"

The boy looked at his mother in question. "It's true, dear. The man's telling you the truth." She turned her head to Randall, "How much is it?"

"Kid, do you have a show and tell at your school?"

"Sure do," he said with enthusiasm.

"Would you like to show all the kids how people used to write?" asked Randall.

"Well..."

Randall winked at the mother. "I'll tell ya what. If you promise me you'll take the inkwell to school for show and tell, I'll give your Mom my cost on the bottle. And... and...your Mom will have you to thank for such a good price," he paused, "it's only cause I can see you're a good guy."

"Ok, I promise."

Randall looked at the woman, "Five dollars, I was asking twenty."

She looked at him with doubt, "You sure it's ok?"

"Yea, there's a lesson in it, but make sure he takes it to show and tell. Not enough kids learn history nowadays."

"That's sweet," she said. "You're a good man."

"That's what they say." He gave her a wink.

She smiled and took her son's hand. "Don't forget what I told you! Show and tell!" Randall stuck his thumb up. The boy turned back and stuck his thumb back in response. *He's just like me as a kid!*

"Hey guy, what da ya want for the stack of postcards?"

"Well, I don't know. I haven't counted, must be at least 150. At .50 each that would normally be $75.00, how's $60.00 sound?"

"I think $50.00 sounds better," the man said.

"Man, why's everyone gotta bust my nuts around here? How's about $60.00?"

"You're shrewd, maybe I'll give you $52.00 cause I know the extra $2 will buy you some gum to chew. It's great for stress ya know."

"You're a funny guy. Ok, Ok, $55.00 and that's my final

offer. I'm only givin that to you cause you made me think of gum," said Randall.

"Deal, but not one cent more!"

"You got it."

He tried desperately to watch the handled items and the tags strung through them. Some fell in the feeding frenzy; others were switched from more expensive items to cheaper ones. Randall rapped off prices, disregarding the tag, many right on key. He knew his inventory.

"You want the Uncle Sam bank, you gotta pay $20.00"

"How bout I give you a buck for it, like the tag says?"

"Don't give me that bullshit, I saw you switch the tag. It was $20.00"

"$20's highway robbery. You can't get $20.00 for that," said the customer with razor attitude.

Randall said, "To you, it'll be $20.00." The man held on to it for the next 10 seconds while his eyes perused the other goods on Randall's table. He put it down for a few seconds, and another dealer snatched it up.

"How much for this?"

"For you, $10.00," said Randall.

"What da ya mean, $10.00! You told me $20.00," shouted the previous handler.

"It was $20.00 for you. It's $10.00 for him."

"You can't do that!"

"Says who? You give me attitude; it costs you an extra ten bucks. Maybe if you'd get off that pedestal you're on, it'd cost you $10.00 also. But you're an arrogant prick, so I worked it into the price."

The man bit his tongue and watched the dealer fondle it in his hand. "So, you gonna take it?" asked the man between gritted teeth.

"Not sure, I'm thinkin on it."

The man hovered over the dealer's shoulder. When the dealer moved closer to the table, so did the man. Randall watched closely. Clearly undecided, the dealer took one last look, when Randall interrupted, "sir, if you want the Uncle Sam bank, it'll cost you $5.00."

"Sold," said the dealer.

The man behind the dealer went berserk. "You arrogant, mother. Who the hell da you think you are?" He reached across the table for Randall's shirt when he felt a large hand on his shoulder. He turned to see the intertwined tattoos on Harry's hand.

"Can I help ya?" asked Harry with his deep baritone voice.

"This jerk just yanked my chain over something I really wanted. Sold it really cheap to piss me off. He deserves a good sock in the mouth."

"Only one who's gonna get knocked in the head is you, if you don't get the hell outta here. In fact, if I see you again in this flea market, I'll make sure they carry ya off on a stretcher. He's a good friend of mine and if he's upset, I'm upset. So be gone." Harry pushed him away from the table.

"Fine!" The man shriveled under Harry's piercing eyes, as he quickly walked away.

"Thanks, Harry."

"Keep your nose clean, champ." Harry said walking back to his table

A quiet moment came and Randall flipped over his watch, "1:00? Unbelievable!" He reached in his pocket, grabbed his folded bills, and counted them below the table line until he reached $452.00. *What the hell did I sell?*

"Hey, prick!" Johnny shouted, "Your ugly face is scarin' off the customers again."

Randall walked over to his stall. "How ya doin?"

"Not good, my friend, not good. I sold only one still so far, and I think that was luck. A Frank Sinatra fan bought my only Sinatra lobby card. I'm gonna lose my shirt here today. I thought they'd sell so well," said Johnny. "Guess that's life for ya."

"It's not so bad. Think of it as a learned experience."

"I got no time or money for a learned experience!"

"Do any of us?"

"Guess you're right," said Johnny, "I'm frustrated."

"I know. We've all been there. What time you gonna wrap it up?"

"At this pace, early. I have better things to do then sweat my balls off here. Probably three," said Johnny.

"Do you wanta come by later for the game? Dallas versus Giants, should be good," asked Randall.

"I'll let ya know before I leave. You live close by, right?"

"Right round the corner," said Randall, "but if Milly calls, I'm kickin ya out. I mean you're pretty and everything, but she's HOT."

Johnny raised his voice in a high pitch, "Jeez, thanks so much for your wonderful comments," imitating Randall's earlier impression, "You're so kind!"

Randall punched his arm, and then headed back for his table. *Coke, Coke, Coke, the world for more Coke.* He turned to his fellow dealer, "scuse me friend, could you watch my stand while I run to grab a soda and pee? I'm hittin that point."

"I hear ya- I usually wait until the bladder is downright hurtin before I go. End up limpin to the nearest port-a-pottie."

"I try not to wait that long. Never know what the line will be. Don't worry though, I'll be fast. Can I buy ya a drink?"

"Na, that's ok. You could watch the table when it's my turn."

"Fair enough," Randall replied. "I'll be fast."

Randall ran down the aisle to the toilet, and then stopped at a yellow van mounted on center blocks which had a built in kitchen. He purchased two Coke's and a Taylor ham sandwich. He rushed back to his table. His friend looked down at his watch.

"Five minutes, not bad!"

"Don't like to leave my stuff and miss potential sales."

"No doubt."

"Just let me know when ya need to run. It's tough when you're on your own."

"Yea, I'll need ya soon. Thanks."

Randall sipped his Coke and caffeinated himself through the day until 3:00pm. His eyes were blurry and he hadn't seen a sale in over an hour.

"Fellas, I gotta go. I'm gonna pass out. I think most of the crowd's grown tired of shoppin. All we're gettin is a bunch of lookers now."

"Agreed," said Johnny. "How'd you do?"

"Pretty good, considering; made about $650.00. Not many sales, but good ones."

"That's what counts. I made about $200.00, but as usual, the day was a good laugh."

Harry came over, "Johnny, did you see this guy," he pointed at Randall, "and how he eyed the old women? It was scary."

"Yea, you know it's been a long time since he got a little. I can't believe he didn't get some last night. Damn guy must be desperate by now," said Johnny.

"There's somethin about a gray-haired woman that really turns me on," Randall said with a straight face. They both looked to him for a cracked smile, but saw none. They looked at each in uncertainty, "Gullible fools. I'll see ya later. Maybe I'll be lucky and get another date tonight," he said. *If only they knew.*

"Good luck," they said in unison.

"You owe me a beer," said Harry.

"No, you owe me a beer," said Johnny.

Randall left them to argue over who owed each other beers. *I'm gonna call Milly and ask her out for dinner and a movie. She's too classy to wear these rags for. I gotta get something new.*

Randall pulled his hand truck past an empty parking lot, where a person sat on a hydrant. Entirely satisfied with his day, he greeted the man, "Afternoon, friend."

The man simply turned his head, and nodded at him quizzically. Randall quickly passed by with a skip. He rolled his cart on until he reached his place, entered through the board awkwardly like he did every weekend. He gasped as he stood at the base of the stairs, and then proceeded. Step by step he pulled his cart and struggled up the three flights until he reached home. He unloaded his cart and placed the boxes in the corner of his living room- the only place they'd fit. He rushed to his bedroom, picked up his velvet jacket to take for adjustments in it's Nino's bag, returned to the middle of his table, where he opened a white envelope and tucked away $450 for a new outfit. He saw the velvet pouch on the table. *Might as well kill two birds with one stone.* He picked up the pouch and walked out the door. *Maybe I can unload this for even more money today.* He walked 36 blocks uptown to 47th St.

Where do I begin? One block of densely populated jewelers. His eyes were attracted to a large neon light sign that read Atari Gems. He walked into the medium sized store and wandered through the cases of gold and diamond jewelry. *Look at the size of those diamonds! They got everything here!*

"Can I help you sir? I saw you looking at our diamonds, could I show you one?"

"No thanks. I saw you buy and sell here."

"We do. Are you interested in selling something?"

"I have something I'm trying to find out more about it. I'm interested in selling it, but only at the right price," Randall said. He reached into his pocket and pulled out the velvet pouch.

"What is it?" asked the man.

"I was hoping you could tell me." He emptied the stone into his own palm.

The salesman eyes burst open and his forehead wrinkled in astonishment. "Could I see that?"

"Sure," said Randall. He threw the stone to the salesman.

The salesman's body clenched and with his hands open, he caught the stone with the tenderness of powder to a baby's bottom. Immediately, a sweat broke above the man's lip. He rubbed one of his palms against his pant leg and exhaled deeply. He took a loop from his pocket and turned the stone over as he analyzed it. Randall watched the man carefully, as he stepped over to the counter and put it under a lamp. His hands trembled.

Boy, that guy's nervous. You'd think he was holdin a diamond or something; he's shaking like a leaf.

The salesman lifted his head, "Would you excuse me a moment. I'd like to get the owner's opinion on what we could give you."

"Sure," Randall replied.

Randall watched the salesman go inside a small windowed office to speak with another man. He saw them huddle together, but only heard whispers from the door. He strained to listen and heard, "are you sure he doesn't know what it is". The salesman glanced back at Randall with a smile, realizing it was louder than the other conversation.

Boy, if that doesn't look like a forced smile! Look this way, please.
The boss got up calmly from his seat and turned to his partner
then to the window; perfectly visible to Randall- he read the
man's lips. *"Let me do the talking - keep your mouth shut."*

A moment later the door opened and a man emerged followed by the salesman, "Good afternoon, sir. My name's Sid
Barchetti, I own and manage Atari gem. I understand you're
interested in selling your stone."

"Only at the right price," said Randall.

"I understand." Barchetti took the stone and placed it on a
velvet pad in front of the men. "Do you know what you have
here?"

"I think so," said Randall with an exaggeration.

"Well," Barchetti's eyes looked dead into Randall's, "What
you have here is an exceptional piece of rock crystal that's partly cut. It's mined in certain areas outside the United States, but
also mined here. The one you have here is an exceptional quality and quite valuable for a crystal. It hasn't reached its full value
because it's only partially cut, but when the stone's fully cut its
worth much more. We have our own cutters in New York and
overseas, so we could finish the stone and make a little money
from it. I'm willing to make you a handsome offer."

"So how much is it to cut?" asked Randall.

The manager's eyes looked at his ratty shirt then followed
his body down to the blue jeans he wore, "much more then
you could afford, my friend."

Randall's heart palpitated, but he bit his lip and maintained
his cool. "How much does it cost for cutting?" he retorted.

Barchetti's eyes again looked him over. "$1500 to $2000
dollars" he said confidently.

Randall picked it up, looked it over and placed it in his
hand. "How much would you give me for the stone?"

"I'll make you an offer of $1000.00," said Barchetti.

One thousand dollars!! I can't believe it; my luck keeps gettin better and better. Randall suddenly looked around alarmed. He saw the man at the entrance speaking to a man outside whose back faced the window and two others whose faces he saw. The men were fixed on what the salesman said. He watched them nod their heads up and down with him. The man whose back faced the window disappeared to the right and the others remained.

"Ehm," said the manager. He cleared his throat loudly, trying to refocus Randall's attention.

Randall's head shot back. "A thousand dollars you say, or $1500 to $2000 to get it cut."

"Yes."

The salesman reentered the store and took his place back in the office, but not before he shot Randall an underhanded look. He disappeared as he sat down.

Somethin's not right here. He'll give me $1000 for the stone or it'll cost me $1500 to $2000 to get cut. That means for him to make a profit he'd have to double it's cost. He'd have a cost of say $3000.00 which means his net would have to be $6000. I should get much more for the stone. It must be worth more. "So it'll cost me $1500 to get it cut?"

"More in the neighborhood of $2000, could even be more" he retorted.

First he says $1500 to $2000 then he says it'll be $2000 or more? I don't trust this guy. Randall spit out without thinking, "I want to get it cut."

Barchetti's face dropped like a brick. He recomposed himself instantaneously, "For you to get it cut, it'll cost you a 20% down payment on $2000, or $400, do you have it?"

Randall said with a bluff, "of course I do." Barchetti's eye quivered ever so slightly. *He's nervous, I got him nervous. I think the stone's worth a lot more. I gotta check it out further.*

"Excuse me," said Barchetti. His brows lifted. "What was your name?"

"Randall."

"Yes, Randall. I have to see if I have a buyer for that kind of item, I need a moment." Barchetti, took a quick walk to his office and reunited with the salesman. He sat down. Randall could see neither man. He kept his eyes on the window and saw Barchetti's hands fly up several times from a seated position. He stood up with his employee and straightened his tie.

Composed and a fine actor, I must say! Randall thought.

Barchetti returned. I currently have no buyers available for such a stone. Fine rock crystal's not a popular substance, I think that $1000.00 is more than fair for your stone; however, I'll give you $2000 because I'd like to add it to my own collection.

Two thousand dollars!! Oh my god! This can't be happening. There's somethin wrong here. No one doubles their bid unless they have leeway to do so. This is a con. I gotta get out of here. Randall stood still, his expression one of deep thought. "I'm gonna consider your offer Mr. Barchetti, but I need time to think about it," said Randall. He looked at his watch, "I really should go."

"Ah, but my friend, you just got here. Please have some coffee with me. I have a freshly brewed pot in my office."

"I really must go, but I'll definitely give your offer serious consideration." Randall walked to the door.

"Alright, alright, I'll give you $2500 for your gem."

Gem? He hadn't told me it was a gem. Is rock crystal a gem? "Thanks, but like I said, I really must go." His hand reached the doorknob and pulled it open.

In desperation Barchetti shouted, "Three thousand."

Randall stopped momentarily, but didn't look back. He exited hastily and saw the two strangers who spoke silently to the salesman minutes earlier across the street. He turned back to the window of the store in time to see a nod from Sid Barchetti. Randall raised his right hand and rubbed his neck from side to side. *$3000 from $1000, in the course of 15 minutes, they should have hooked me for less than three, way less than three. I'd have been happy with $100. Obviously there's something to this stone, or gem, or whatever the hell it is.* He walked towards Sixth Avenue, passing several jewelry shops and a line of Brinks trucks. He lifted his head in time to see a large sign.

"Bala Bala Diamonds, that's the place I saw on the news! They donated a 5-carat diamond to the Make a Wish foundation. They've gotta be honest and reliable," he said.

Randall entered the store.

The two men from the other side of the street crossed, one took a position with his back to the window and the other opened the door and followed Becks in. A grey haired man approached Randall, "Can I help you, sir?"

"Didn't I see you on the news?" Randall inquired.

"Yes, that was me, Paul Striker at your service."

"It was a beautiful thing you did- that donation. There should be more people like you in the world."

"Thank you, but really it was nothing, now; what can I do for you?" Stiker's eyes surveyed the man who followed him in, then the window.

"I have a gem I wanted to find out about. I'm interested in selling it and I've already been given an offer. I'm not sure if the price is in the ballpark or not."

"Can I see it?" asked the jeweler. Cautiously, he looked behind Randall, then back.

"Certainly." Randall dumped the stone from its velvet sack into his own coarse hand. *He seems awfully preoccupied with the man that followed me in. He's got most of this guy's attention.* Randall turned slowly and recognized his assailant as one of the men that spoke with the salesman from Atari Gems. The man resumed his position looking through the cases. Randall leaned into Striker and whispered, "do you know this guy?"

"What?" said the owner, a bit shaken. "No, no. Let's look at that stone of yours." Randall placed the gem in his hand. He cupped it with care,

"Gggggeeeeeeeeezzzhhhhhh." he said. He took out the loop and eyed the stone, practically dropping it. His head quickly resumed its position to the man who followed Randall in. The store owner leaned down to Randall's level and whispered.

"Do you know Henry Hillerman?"

"Why yes, uh, how did you know?"

"He cut this stone. You're in serious danger, now listen carefully. Hang on to this with your life until we can talk privately. The man who followed you in is after you. It's critical you lose him. I know you may not trust me, but I'm not gonna ask for your phone number. Here's mine, it's a cellular. When you lose him and you know you're not followed- call. I'll meet you 7 pm tonight at Columbus Circle beneath the Titan monument. I have extremely good news and extremely bad news, but here's not the place to discuss it." He finished whispering, his voice climbed, "Over here we have our sapphires and emeralds; I think your girlfriend would like this one." Striker put his fingers in the case and snatched a bracelet.

Randall stood dumbfounded. He whispered, "can't you tell me more?"

"It's beautiful isn't it?" he said with a loud voice. Again, he whispered, "keep it down. In time. Henry was a good friend of mine, that's all you need to know. Now get outta here. You look agile enough to lose those guys. Whatever you do, hang on to that stone!" His voice returned to normal, "Well, I'm sorry we don't have what you're looking for. Have a great day!" said the jeweler. The stranger rubbed his ear and eyed Randall.

Randall waved with a smile. *How can I ditch these guys?* He looked out the window. *The subway's right out the door. I'll spring for the subway, run down to the platform and return on the other side of 47th Street. At a full sprint, I'll be able to make the 8th Avenue subway at 42nd, hopefully before them. If I can't shake em, I'll have to go dodge in and out of some restaurants, maybe through the park- yea, the park. Anyone could get lost in Central Park. I'll call Milly later to cancel the evening. I hope she doesn't feel jilted. Whatever this is I can't get her involved in it.*

Randall exited the door and watched the two men closely pursue him. He bolted down the subway steps, hit the bottom platform, and jumped the turnstile. He gained a few seconds on the men, but when he reached the tracks, he found a dead end. He heard the roar of one of the trains' approach and in a screaming leap, he flung his body quickly in front of the on coming train with just enough time to clear the rails. The train mowed down his garment bag after it slipped from his hand.

Both men stood in shock, as they watched the subway train barely miss him. "Tim, I'll go back to the street! Try to keep your eye on him through the windows!" He shouted, and then scurried out of the station. Tim tried to see him through the windows of the stopped train. People poured from its doors, but he saw Randall scoot up onto the opposite platform- he paced impatiently. The thug who desperately tried to watch him, heard the roar of another train approach on Randall's side in the opposite direction. He jumped from the platform to retrieve the dirty garment bag. He saw the light of a coming train and retreated to the platform from which jumped.

Above ground, the other man yelled as he was almost hit by an on coming car. "God dammit!" He sprinted across the street and battled a sea of people who gushed out of the subway. He watched for Randall's face to appear from the center of the stairs.

Randall watched the on coming train. *Come on baby! Faster!* His head dodged frantically left and right. *He'll be down the platform any minute!* The downtown F train arrived, the doors opened, he hopped on and walked through several cars. The other thug ran down and watched the doors of the train shut from the stairs.

Randall sat in the car. *My clothes, my new clothes. I can't believe I dropped em. $150, down the toilet.* He grabbed the pouch, which sat securely in his pocket and held on to it tight. *You'd better be worth the trouble I'm going through, little gem of mine!*

The two men reunited on the street. "Sid's not gonna be happy, Gino."

"Look Tim, we tried. He gave us the slip, but at least we got his bag. It gives us a starting point. Now let's get back to Atari's and get this over with."

"Yea, let's do it," replied Tim. The two men walked back to Atari's. They hesitantly pushed open the door.

"Where is he?" Barchetti yelled.

"He got away, but we got this." said Gino. He pulled from behind his back the fancy bag with Nino's imprinted on it.

"Ok, at least that's a start. Where'd he go directly after here?"

"He went to Bala Bala Diamonds and spoke with Paul Striker. Showed him the stone, and left shortly after. I couldn't hear a word they said," said Gino.

"Paul Striker of Bala Bala Diamonds. He's on our books, in fact, I believe he's overdue a month. I'll collect it, personally," said Sid Barchetti. "We've gotta find the kid before he learns too much about the stone. Go to Nino's and see what you can find out. I want an address for this guy, yesterday. If you don't get him, your families are gonna pay," said Barchetti.

"Yes, sir," replied the men. They left.

Sid Barchetti put on his Versace suede overcoat. He reached into his top desk drawer for a pair of heavy brass knuckles, which he pocketed in his overcoat. *I hope you're prepared for my offer, Paul Striker, because it's your unlucky day.* He strolled down 47th until he reached Bala Bala Diamonds. He opened the door to find Paul Striker in the midst of showing a one-carat cocktail ring.

Oh, Christ! Barchetti never pays personal visits. "Excuse me miss, I must tend to a small problem. Please look around and enjoy. If there's anything we can help you with please let my assistant know. Thanks," he said to the smiling patron. She meandered around the cases, as Striker went to greet Barchetti.

"Good afternoon, Mr. Barchetti. How are you?"

Barchetti leaned over the counter; "You know why I'm here, don't you?"

"I know I'm a month late, but I should clear the money by week end. I'm sorry, things have been tough."

"Protection is tougher," said Barchetti, "but that's not why I'm here. The kid that came here earlier is why I'm here. I'm sure you know he stopped to see me first. I gave him a good offer for the stone, but he didn't take it. He came down here, saw you, and disappeared a few minutes later. I think you know something, Striker."

Striker leaned forward, "I know he saw you, which is precisely why he exited so promptly. I didn't tell him what he had, because I knew it would only come back to haunt me. I washed my hands of the whole situation and told him to give your offer serious consideration. I told him it'd probably be the best he can get. I'm sure he knew he was being followed though, he seemed edgy and when he left here, he practically ran out the door. You'd think he'd stolen something."

Barchetti whispered, "Listen to me carefully, Striker. If I find you had anything to do with his running off, I'll hurt you and your family business. Badly. You don't want that do you?"

"Of course not, but I'm tellin you; he wasn't happy at the fact I couldn't help him with the stone. He left immediately and where he is, I don't know." Striker said, looking Barchetti directly in the eyes. They stared at each other for seconds in silence. Barchetti heard the bell on the door ring as the only woman in the store exited. He surveyed the store, gripped his brass knuckles tightly and threw Striker an undercut into his ribs. Striker fell to the floor in pain. "Next time, you pay on time, or you won't be so lucky." Barchetti quickly pocketed the weapon. "Have a nice day." he said, then exited the store.

Gino and Tim exited the subway at 34th St. carrying the garment bag. Five minutes later they arrived at Nino's.

A salesman greeted them, "My friends, welcome to Nino's."

"Thanks!' exclaimed Gino. "We're hoping you could help us. A recent customer of ours left this bag at our shop. He was looking at diamonds for his girlfriend and we wanted to return it to him, because customer service is what we pride ourselves in."

"Diamonds, huh? I should have known not to trust that guy. Bet he had plenty more money on him, I can't believe he looked at diamonds. He paid me only $150.00 for those clothes and he has the nerve to leave it at your place!" said the salesman.

"So you helped him?" asked the Gino.

"Yes, the name's Abdul."

"Do you have his address?"

"No, I'm afraid I don't, he paid cash," Abdul stopped to think, "maybe I have his name on file from a few months ago. He came in and bought a bunch of things. I tend to keep customer cards on people with large purchases. Hang on," said Abdul.

Randall stroked his hair as he sat on the F train thinking. *I can't believe I gotta call off my date with Milly. It's insane! How do I know to even trust this guy, he could shyster me like the first.* He sat and looked at the reflection of his face in the window as the subway turned through the dark barren tunnels. *Well, my gut instinct told me to trust him, and that's usually the best. Those guys were definitely after me and if I'm in danger, he could be too.* He watched the sign appear for Delancey St. *Maybe I should get Harry to come with me, I don't need the trouble.* He stood up and exited the car.

When he arrived home, he phoned the interior designer.

"Hello, Milly?"

"Yes?"

"It's Randall. How are you?"

"I'm well. I'm looking forward to tonight, any idea on what movie we'll see?" she asked.

"It's about tonight, I had an emergency and I can't make it," he said.

"Is everything all right?"

"Yea, it's one of my friends. He's in a bit of trouble and needs a hand. Can we do it tomorrow?"

"I'd love to do it tomorrow. Anytime is wonderful, the sooner the better."

"Can I call you in the morning then?"

"It needs to be before 8:30 am, because I have to work."

"Good. I'll talk to you after 8:00 am," he said.

"I can't wait," she said

Randall hung up the phone and danced. *The sooner the better, the sooner the better.* He jiggled his ass back and forth, shaking his leg. *I look forward to talking to you too. Yes I do.* Randall went to the window, "It's great to be alive!"

"Piss off!" came a response from a stone doorway.

He pointed to the homeless man, "I love you too!" He shut the window in time to stop the flying fruit thrown from his dirty hands.

"Now, what can I wear tomorrow?" he said to himself. He went to his closet, reached his hands between two outfits and pushed outward on the packed clothes to see them. *A black collared dress shirt, black jeans, a checkered vest to break things up and a slick black coat. Yea, something totally mod for the artist. Who says ya can't be stylish with old clothes?* He pulled the four items from their hangers and tried them on. He went to the mirror. *I'll lay these out for tomorrow night, and get back to business.*

"She should love this."

After Milly Van Lowe hung up the phone she laid her head down on her pillow, her left cheek felt the comfort of the down which filled it. She placed her hands together like a prayer position beneath her pillow. *How can I get this feeling so fast? I only just met him. You know you're too sensitive, and too forward too fast! You don't want to scare him off.* She sighed and looked at the red tasseled lampshade on her side table. She grabbed the bronze ball attached to a chain and pulled it. The light went out.

Randall walked from his bed and was struck by a heart pounding panic. *The stone! Where'd I put it?* He ran to the living room table and found the black pouch. He quickly grabbed it and felt for the stone. "Three thousand dollars, who'd a thought? No wonder why Hillerman kept it in the safe. I never would have guessed he cut stones either. I'd better call Harry."

Randall picked up the phone.

"Hello?"

"Harry, Randall."

"What's doing, chief?"

"I ran into a snag getting an appraisal on a stone I bought. Two thugs followed me from one jeweler to another then chased me down after leaving. The last jeweler wanted to meet me at Columbus Circle at 7:00 tonight. Could you give me a lift and watch from a distance, just in case?"

"Sounds serious."

"I wouldn't ask you if it wasn't."

"Not a problem. What time do ya want me to pick you up?" asked Harry.

"How about 6:30 pm?"

"I'll wait for you downstairs."

"Thanks, Harry."

"It's alright. Did you talk to your honey?"

"Yea, we were supposed to get together tonight, but I'm gonna meet her tomorrow instead."

"Take care of her."

"I will," Randall replied. He hung up the phone, too paranoid to exit his apartment. He watched the minutes tick away.

Chapter 8
The Tag

The three tiered mirror, the focal point of the garment shop, stood adjacent to the counter. The tailor stitched a French cuff on the lower right pant leg of a customer while Gino paced the floor patiently waiting for Abdul to reappear. A musty smell radiated through the garment shop and the heat left the men with beads of sweat on their foreheads. The tailor took long pins from his mouth as he quietly adjusted the hem. Abdul stepped through the open doorway of a tiny back office.

"Sorry boys. I didn't find the information you were lookin' for. If you leave your name and number I can call you if he comes back or phones. Our name is written all over the bag, so he may think a Good Samaritan will return it. You never know."

"My name is Gino, I'll give you my cellular number. Contact me, especially if you get his name, address, and phone number. Make sure he doesn't know, because my boss was going to surprise him with a special deal for his girlfriend."

"What's your last name, Gino?"

"It's not important. Call me anytime."

"Thanks. Remember; come back when you have time to shop. We're here to satisfy any need," said Abdul.

"Thanks." The men exited Nino's and Gino turned to his partner. "You know where we have to go, right?"

"Where?"

"We need to watch Striker. Let's get there, before they close for the day."

They hailed a cab, hopped in and made it to 47th before 5pm.

Tim barreled into Atari's, "Sid, we couldn't find any address on the guy from Nino's, we told them to call us if he inquires about his lost clothes. In the meantime, we're gonna follow Striker."

"Where's Gino?"

"We split up. He's running surveillance on Bala Bala Diamonds."

"Now, you're doing something right. I spoke with Striker earlier today about the conversation with this guy and his overdue protection money. He claimed he said nothing. Said he didn't want to be involved. I threatened him not once, but twice and he stuck to his story. Bala Bala Diamonds is too important to him. Three generations in the same place might want to make you keep status quo. Take my brother Bill, for an additional set of eyes. He's at Brilliance Book Fair across the street" said Barchetti. "Stay in touch with me by cellular."

"Ok, boss." He hustled to the bookstore and searched its aisles. He found Bill Barchetti perusing the firearms section.

"I just spoke with your brother and he wants you to help us follow Paul Striker. We tried tracking down this Randall character, but couldn't find anything on him, so we're gonna follow Striker. We hope he's gonna meet him later."

"Striker's on our blacklist, right? We can get his home address from the book."

"What if he doesn't go home and goes directly to meet this guy? It'll be a useless cause," said Tim.

"Good point. You and Gino watch his moves from a distance. Nod at him when he exits. I only had a quick glance at him from the window of Atari's earlier." Bill looked down at his watch. "They should be closing momentarily. I'll try and stay close to him. Let me close in on Striker. You guys let him see you, that way he'll try and ditch ya. We'll let him think he did, all the while I'll be right with him. He won't have a clue. I'll call you when I see him get comfortable and you come back. Got it?"

"Yea, I'll let him know the plan."

"We split right here. As far as I'm concerned, I've never seen you before in my life. Hopefully if they meet, the guy will have the stone on him. Be cautious and wait to hear from me."

Bill Barchetti exited the book fair, crossed 47th, street and walked in the direction of Sixth Ave. Tim exited ten seconds later and walked down the same side of the street until he rejoined Gino at the corner. It was directly across from Bala Bala Diamonds.

"Gino, anything happen?"

"They've been packing up goods from the front window. I'm glad you're back." He saw Bill Barchetti lean on a corner building. "What's Bill doing over there?"

"Since Striker's never seen Bill, Sid wanted him to tag along. Bill had a plan to follow him from a distance. We let Striker spot us, then ditch us, and Bill takes over."

"I don't know. If Sid catches wind of us losing him twice, he'll beat the shit out of us," said Gino.

"We won't lose him, trust me. Bill will contact us by cellular when he knows where the rendezvous is. So, if he sees us, don't panic. Just make sure Bill's close by. Got it?"

"Got it," said Gino.

Armed guards stood at the back of several Brinks' cars, as gems were carried from the local jewelers and transported into the safety of the bulletproof walls. The brown spotted sidewalk was lined with dealers who stood and chatted outside their windows. An occasional police car patrolled the street, while everything seemed to be orderly. Faces meshed into each other. Tim and Gino disappeared within a sea of faces as they patiently watched from their position. A half an hour passed when they saw Bala Bala's employees leave for the day.

"The owner will probably be another fifteen minutes," Gino said. "The alarm and safes need to be set."

Tim looked at his watch and nodded in agreement.

Sure enough, 15 minutes later, they saw Paul Striker leave the building. He closed the door, pulled down the steel gate and locked it with a key. He stood in front of his store and carefully surveyed the people all around the area. Gino and Tim bowed their heads and shuffled through some people until they were behind a Brink's truck. They watched through a corner of the windshield. Striker's head slowly turned and searched the terrain and saw nothing out of the ordinary. At ease, he limped towards the subway system holding his side. As he stepped through the entrance he saw the two thugs through his peripheral vision disappear through the glass of the armored car.

Chapter 9
Cautious Suspicions

Henry walked downstairs to the street, continued three blocks east to the Marble Corridor and walked through the entrance.

"Henry!" shouted Maury from across the bar, "Damn good to see you!"

"Maury, are you buttering me up for a good tip?" shouted Henry, "If you are it's working."

"You want the usual?"

"You know I do. Why do you bother asking?"

"I'm a polite guy. God forbid I serve you incorrectly. You'll endlessly chastise me." He leaned over the bar and winked. "What's new in your life, Henry?"

"I just had an incredible dinner at Gio's. I must have put on three pounds in baby fat."

"You mean you fit three pounds of food in that skinny little body of yours? You must have rolled here!"

"I left the skateboard outside."

He laughed. "Come here, Henry." The bartender

hunched over, "The bear looks at the rabbit and says 'Do you have a problem with shit sticking to your fur?' The rabbit says 'no'." Henry sipped his drink. Maury picked up his head and looked around, "So the bear wipes his ass with the rabbit."

Henry's laugh drew the martini from his mouth through his nose, curling the hairs in his nostrils. He quickly grabbed a bar napkin and held it across. Between his agony and his laughter, he let out a deep breath. "You kill me… I know you hear the best of them. Had to be why I came here tonight. Today was one of those damn stressful days. Kinda like years ago… you know, 'the incident'.

"You mean the twenty-eight carat diamond?"

"Exactly. I reached a time in my life when I felt I could conquer anything. I was convinced I knew exactly where to hit this diamond, and Ubi, the owner - my boss, told me to beware of being too much of a hot shot. When I brought down the chisel and shattered the thing, I damn near had heart failure. Many people had substantial bets on me making 20 carats out of it, and I fucked up. I was convinced Ubi was going to fire me, but surprisingly he took it in stride. He let me keep my job." Henry paused. "The fact is you need to keep the goodness of life in your heart and accept horrible things do happen. It's the acceptance of that which clears your conscious."

"I buy that, but do you think that'll make me a better man?"

"You wait another six months and the goodness of life will find you." He leaned over the bar and waved Maury closer. He put his bar rag down and leaned in. "Two years ago, only three years after I lost my wife, I took a trip to the Rockies. It was one I prepared to take for a long period of time, but never allowed myself a chance to. Doctor said it was dicey because of my heart. I didn't care, figured I'd die out there. What did I need to live for anyway? The love of my life was dead. On the fourth day, I found her."

"What did you find?"

"Well, I found my nest egg and I'll leave it at that." Henry leaned back in his chair.

"God dammit! Why do you do this to me?"

"Cause I love ya, buddy." He sipped his martini. "It's made me realize that regardless of your age you have the right to dream. Occasionally, you might even be pleasantly surprised. Things happen for a reason. In six months I'm gonna come here and give you the biggest tip you've ever gotten."

"Sure, Henry," he said dismissingly.

"I'm not bluffing, for God sakes, I'm a jeweler! How many jewelers do you know who aren't trustworthy?"

"Ok, ok, I'll give you that. So ya think I'm worth my weight in gold?"

"Yea, I think you are. You're one of the good ones. Cheers to you. Have a drink on me?"

"Na, I have plenty of the night to go. I'm glad we can at least talk." Maury said. "How have you been dealing with Mrs. Hillerman's death? Hanging in?"

"It's been tough. When you're married fifty years, and lose a great sparring partner, a piece of you is lost. When I found my nest egg, everything was clear- there was a future. I had a reason to live again and something to give the world. I'm going to make my baby pure perfection, a piece of artwork that'll out live my name and me. It was like my wife guided me to it and she was there the moment I found it." He took a sip of his martini. "Promised myself I'd buy her the biggest tombstone in the cemetery, so I stay focused on my mission."

"That's great," he said, "Can I get you another?"

"Just one more then I head home."

Maury mixed another and brought it to him, then returned to scores of other customers. Henry stirred a toothpick in his drink until he sank it into the soft skin of the ripened olive. He picked it up and gobbled it down. He stared at the bar top with a blank stare, and then quickly swigged the remains of his drink. He stood up unsteadily.

"Goodnight, Maury, I'll see ya next week."

"Right, Henry. Be safe."

———— ‹‹◊›› ————

God dammit, it's the numskulls from earlier. I have to dodge them. I'll pretend they're invisible. Striker trotted down the steps of the subway for the downtown E, he carefully watched the men from a distance. He boarded it to 34th St. Penn Station. He watched their faces appear through the window of the connecting car. *I feel confident they have no clue I know of them.* Striker exited at 34th. Street. He followed the crowd through the terminal making quick erratic movements to try and lose himself in the crowd. After a few minutes he stopped, leaned himself up against a wall, until he spotted them dodge into a small deli. He continued past the numerous small kiosks until he reached the platform of the Southbound 3 train. He patiently waited to board, glanced around until he found them sitting on one of the wood benches which lined the platform. When the 3 train came, he boarded and they followed one car down. Striker took this to Christopher Street and exited once again. *Lord knows I can't run with this bruised rib, so I'll just have to be bright. I have enough distance to lose them, so I'll do it this time.*

Striker quickly glanced at the men, and boarded the 3 again, in the opposite direction.

"What the hell's this guy doing?" asked Tim.

"He knows we're on him. He's trying to throw us off the trail. We'll stay with him for now."

They're still with me, now, for the Kit and Caboodle. Let's see if this works. The men again followed him onto the train, taking the car in back of his. Striker sat down on a seat next to the door. Both men peeked through the window of the next car and dodged their heads back. At that moment, Striker heard the blare that accompanies the closing of the subway doors. He moved like lightening and hurled himself off the train before the doors shut. He stood motionless in front of the subway as the cars slowly made their way out. He watched the men's expressions warp with his presence on the platform. Gino plastered himself against the window as Tim shook his head. Striker waved at the moving car as it passed. *Thank you James Bond.*

He walked up the stairs of the #3, searched for the #2 uptown and went to the platform. He hadn't noticed Bill Barchetti close behind. His muscles relaxed and the Northbound 2 arrived moments later. He boarded the train and took it to Columbus Circle. The time was 6:45.

At the same time Striker arrived, Randall was travelling on Harry's Harley to the same place. Randall sat comfortably on the back of his Motorhead.

"Harry! Can't you quiet this thing down?" yelled Randall above the roar of the engine.

"You gotta speak up buddy. I can't hear you!"

"Can't you quiet this thing down!"

"Sorry?!"

"Forget it!" *How the fuck can he think when he rides this thing!*

I can't believe he has any hearing left at all. I think my brain's going to vibrate out my ear. Randall watched the buildings move quickly by. *If only I had this motorcycle, without the noise. Heaven!*

"Randall, I'm gonna turn down 54th towards 9th Ave. and come around. I'll drop you at 61st Street. You can walk down from there and I'll watch from a distance. If anything happens, I'll get you immediately. Since Columbus is right on the park, we can make a quick exit if necessary. Make sure when you walk, walk uptown so you pass me by. Ok?"

"Sounds good," Randall said. Harry dropped him behind the enormous globe at Gulf & Western Building. "I'll see you later."

"Don't worry, pal. I'll be right here," said Harry.

Randall walked towards Columbus circle.

Bill Barchetti picked up his cell phone, "Boys, this is Bill. It looks like we've ended up in Columbus circle. Hop in a cab and get over here immediately. Striker's beneath the monument with a gold woman on top. My phone will vibrate if you call. I have a good feeling. That Randall guy'll have the pouch if he meets Striker. So get here quick, but be discreet!"

"On our way," said Gino.

Randall approached the circle with caution. He eyed the Christopher Columbus monument at the center of the circle. *I feel a million eyes watching me since I found the value of this thing. I should approach Paul Striker from the park, that way I'm not double-crossed.* Randall followed one of the footpaths that led around the back of the monument.

Paul Striker sat at a bench and watched cars circle around the monument. *I hope this kid shows for his own sake. He probably*

*won't believe me when I tell him he's sitting with the world's largest dia-
mond. I wonder why Henry never told me about it. The sly devil probably
wanted to take all the glory from cutting it himself. He must have died
before he had a chance to finish it.* He looked to the heavens. *If only
you'd given a shit about what you ate, smoked, or drank! You always
knew how to live, Henry. You'll get the credit you deserve, sure as my name
is Paul Striker.*

Barchetti's men leaned forward on the black leather seat of
the taxi and noticed the green line of traffic lights down the
avenue.

"Tim, another 5 blocks and we're there. We should get off
a block before and run over, so he doesn't see us," said Gino.

"I think you're right. Cabby, let us off at 59th St., before
the circle," shouted Tim.

The cabby nodded his head in agreement and pulled the
cab over to let them off.

Randall cautiously approached Striker patiently sitting beneath the monument. Striker recognized him instantly and rose
quickly.

"Mr. Striker? I hope you can greet me with good news,"
Randall said.

"You made sure you weren't followed, right?"

"Yes, no one followed. I don't want to discuss this in the
open. Maybe we can walk along Central Park West towards the
Museum of Natural History. How do I know to trust you?"
asked Randall.

"I think you've seen one too many versions of COPS. I'm a
jeweler, who loans out millions in diamonds, besides, I'm not just
helping you. I'm helping my friend, Henry. Did you know him?"
asked Striker. They began to walk up Central Park West together.

"I'm sorry to say I didn't. I went to his estate sale and picked up some things. The stone was the byproduct of a safe I purchased. I broke into it after hours of work and there it was," said Randall.

"I'll be damned. What else did you find in the safe?" Striker asked.

"Some other things, mostly paperwork."

"What a shame. His death took most of us by shock. He was kinda of like George Burns. You always expected him to be around forever. He'd exit his work, light up a huge cigar and puff away. He'd always say hello to his fellow jewelers," said Striker. "About five years ago when he lost his wife of fifty years, he found himself alone. We no longer heard his joyous laughter. He clammed up, stopped skipping with enthusiasm and just moped around, like he lost part of himself. We all felt sorry for the guy. He depended more on work than ever. We urged him to take a trip a few years later when things didn't seem to change in his mood. He returned and something changed. He was his old self- he changed." Striker took a breath. "Ubi Cancade, his employer, had to sell off Henry's goods to finance his funeral. He collected donations from many of the jewelers in the district to help with the funeral arrangements." He paused in thought, "that rascal."

"He sounds like a fabulous guy, but who was he? What'd he do?"

"He was a diamond cutter-"

"A diamond cutter! You mean-

"Take it easy, kid," said Striker, "let me see the stone."

Randall pulled the velvet pouch from his pocket.

Bill Barchetti closed in on the men, watching Paul Striker pour the stone from its housing. *He's got the pouch. I can't believe it. There's*

no one watching, Striker's got to die. It has to be smooth, with no loose ends.
Barchetti crept within ten feet of them and pulled out his revolver
when he heard a thundering noise from the street. A large Harley
Davidson was dodging through four lanes of traffic.

Randall turned around as the revolver fired.

A bullet struck Striker in the center of the back. He clutched
the stone and pouch, as he fell forward. Randall caught him before he hit the ground. Blood poured from his back.

The motorcycle jumped the curb at full speed as it fired
towards Barchetti. Harry clothes-lined the man before he had a
clear shot. His body flew ten feet through the air and when he
hit the ground, he was unconscious. The intimidating biker distracted Gino and Tim, who had come up close behind. They
pulled their guns to protect their boss.

Randall grabbed the stone from the hands of Paul Striker
and ran uptown. Gino and Tim shot at Harry, pistols capped
with silencers as he fled the scene. His motorcycle burst
through an opening in the brick wall. He zig-zagged over the
grass, as both of them tried to hit the biker.

Gino quickly pocketed his gun, "Thief!" he yelled. "Get
him, that man's a thief!"

A few passersby saw Randall run with the pouch and saw
the motionless man still on the concrete. Like a contagious disease, the masses emulated Gino, "Thief, get him!" they yelled.

Harry redirected his Harley back at Randall who sprinted
down the sidewalk. He gave it full throttle and pulled along
side of his friend.

"Suppose you were in a little trouble, weren't you?" asked
Harry.

"Guess a little more than I expected," said Randall. Randall
boarded the bike and they both took off to 9th Ave. and returned downtown.

Chapter 10
Wanted~ Alive or Dead

"Harry, I'm not sure we did the right thing. We didn't look good leaving the scene of the crime the way we did."

"We had no choice, Randall. Those guys would have gunned us down in cold blood. I agree it didn't look good, but with my rap sheet and the way you live, we would've been thrown to the dogs, no questions asked. Unfortunately, I got a habit of being in the wrong place at the wrong time. Besides, the police wouldn't have let you keep that stone; it would've been kept as evidence."

"Turn on the news, I bet it's all over it."

Harry turned on the TV. "Tonight on the 10:00 news, a breaking story in Central Park as a man is shot, stay tuned," said the television broadcaster.

"I told ya! Oh, Jesus. Don't you think we could simply tell the truth?" Randall asked innocently.

"We could, but it doesn't make a difference if you have no one to collaborate your story. If Striker survives the gunshot, we gotta chance. He knows what happened and he knows what's going on. The shooters framed us." Harry said. "Do you know who they were?"

"I caught a glimpse of the first shooter before you knocked him clear through the park, but I didn't recognize him," Randall said. He went silent in thought, then spoke up, "Before Striker was shot, he told me the original owner of the stone, Henry Hillerman, was a diamond cutter. I attended the guy's estate auction, do you think-

"Let me see that thing," said Harry. Randall tossed him the stone. Harry caught it and cradled it in both hands. "No, way. Couldn't be. Look at the fucking size of it! It'd be better in a baseball case. Let's assume Hillerman has this multi million-dollar diamond. Someone would have to know about it, or would have claimed it."

"Not necessarily. Amongst the paperwork in the safe was a brochure to some gem fields in Colorado. If the guy cut diamonds all his life, wouldn't he know what to look for in rough form? Someone like you and I wouldn't have a clue, but this guy would. Maybe he got lucky. Would make sense, no?" asked Randall.

"Yea, but what are the chances of a diamond cutter finding the largest diamond in the world? Slim to none is my guess."

"People win millions in the Lottery. Maybe the guy upstairs was looking out for him. Wanted to give him a little joy before his last day. From what Striker told me, Hillerman was a good man and always happy until the loss of his wife five years ago. Y'know, I have this inbred belief if ya work hard and lead a good life, you'll be rewarded. Good things you do, are returned, sometimes ten fold."

"Randall, your optimism disgusts me. We get what we deserve. I deserved my ten years in prison, but I paid my dues, and now I've been straight for the past two. Nothin's returned to me until now, and once again, it's all bad. People will think we did it, which we didn't. Here, it's back-"

"Tonight in the evening news, Paul Striker of Bala Bala Diamonds on 47th St. was shot on the sidewalk on Central Park West, in what appears to be a botched robbery. Mr. Striker was hospitalized with a single gunshot wound to the back. Two men fled the scene on motorcycle, one believed to be a well-known felon. We found a witness to the attempted homicide, now to Bethany Conitano:

"Good evening viewers, this is Bethany Conitano on the scene in Central Park. Facts are still merging in the shooting of a well known jeweler on the Park. Some believe it to be a random, or a well-planned botch up. What we have at this point is that Paul Striker, a well-known dealer in the diamond district, was walking North along the edge of the park. When the initial shot was heard, it echoed through the area. Tim Brussel, an eyewitness watched. 'Tim, can you tell me what happened?'

"I was about 200 feet away when I saw this man behind Mr. Striker. He talked to him then his body snapped forward. The man fell over in a puddle of blood. The guy pried something from the man's hands and a motorcycle shot out of the park to pick him up. That's when I yelled thief. Before I knew it, the men were gone."

"Sounds terrifying."

"It was Bethany. I hope he'll be alright."

"This is Bethany Conitano, back to you in the studio, Ann."

"Thank you Bethany. Mr. Striker's attempted murder is still in the early stages of investigation. We have an artist's sketch of our suspects drawn from several eyewitness accounts. If you see these two men-

"Christ, that's us!" yelled Randall.

"Sssssshhhhh," yelled Harry-

Please contact the authorities at 1-800-SE-CRIME. Mr.

Striker is currently in a coma and listed in critical condition at Mt. Sinai Hospital. And on to other news-"

Harry stood up calmly, walked to the TV, and turned it off.

"I can't believe it! We're suspects for the shooting of Paul Striker, what the hell are we gonna do?" Randall yelled in a panic.

"Take it easy, buddy. We go underground for a while and do our own investigation. You won't be able to go home for a while. The cops'll be all over your house like flies on shit. They'll find my place probably sooner than yours. I'm glad we came here," said Harry.

"You mean this isn't your place," asked Randall.

"No, it's a gang member's place, I'm watching over. He went to a biker's convention in DC and I told him I'd watch it for him. Good thing it happened when it did, otherwise we'd have no place to go."

"See, things happen for a reason," said Randall.

Harry smirked, "Wise ass. I have lots of friends that can hide us for a while. I'll get some information on Atari Gems through contacts. If he made a hit on you and he hit Paul Striker today, chances are they have some risky ventures."

Randall took a deep breath and calmly stated, "What if Milly saw the newscast? She'll be gone just like Jennifer Lovitska. She won't want to see a felon."

"For God sakes don't panic." Harry said. "You sell yourself short, Randall. You're a good-looking guy down on his luck. Call her and explain, she might understand."

"I did cancel our date because I told her my friend was in trouble. Can I blame you to get my girl back?"

"I don't mind if ya make me the bad guy, but avoid where we are. If the press find her, I'm sure to hang, and I was simply helping you out! Call her pansy."

Randall walked to the phone, picked up the receiver and dialed until he reached the last number; he stopped. *What am I going to say? How can I tell her? She's bound to know. I can't.* He hung up the receiver and looked at "the Heckler".

"Just do it. If you don't do it now, you'll have no excuse later."

He's right. I can't explain it later after everything's out. Randall picked up the receiver with confidence, and quickly dialed the number, hesitating before he hit the last. Finally, he pressed heavy on the 9 key and heard the dial tone. He paced the floor. It rang 3 times, "Hello?" she asked. "Hello?"

Randall's heart quivered in his chest and the words fell heavy on the end of his tongue. "Milly?"

"Randall, is that you?"

"Yes."

"My God, I was worried about you. What happened? I saw a sketch of you on the evening news. Tell me it wasn't you," she pleaded, "Please tell me it wasn't you."

"The sketch was, but I didn't do it. It's a long story, but you gotta believe it wasn't me.-

"Randall, how could you? I don't understand-"

"Stop. Listen," Randall said in a calming tone. There was silence on the other end.

"Go on," she said.

"I bought a cheap safe six days ago from an estate sale, a guy named Henry Hillerman. The combination was lost. When I got it home, I broke into it. I found a lot of paperwork and also a crystal, at least I thought it was a crystal. This afternoon, I visited the diamond district for an appraisal and the owner of Atari Gems offered me $3000 for it-"

"And you didn't take it?" she asked.

"No, he originally offered me $1000 and I sensed something fishy, so I decided to try someone else. He had two people follow me to Bala Bala Diamonds-

"Where you met the man shot, Paul Striker."

"Correct. Striker somehow knew the guys and after I showed him the stone he told me I was in great danger. I met with him in Columbus Circle tonight. Turns out he knew Henry Hillerman. During our walk I found out Hillerman was a diamond cutter."

"A diamond cutter!"

"Yea, that's what I said. He asked me to show him the stone again, and after he poured it in his hand, someone shot him. Fortunately for me, my friend Harry, who was close by, saw the shooter pull the gun and rode across Central Park West to save me. His Harley sounds like a jet engine, so I think many people connected the shot to us."

"Sounds like a novel," she shrieked, "go on."

"So Striker falls into my hands, the blood from his back drenched me. Harry knocked the shooter to the ground and I pulled my stone from his grip. I saw the thugs who followed me earlier in the day from a distance. Fortunately, Harry dodged the bullets, shot from silencers and picked me up four blocks down. The media, of course distorted the facts and now Harry and I are outlaws."

"Randall."

"Yea?" he answered.

Milly spoke softly and sincerely, "I believe you."

"Thank God! Milly, I was so afraid-

"-afraid of what?"

"Well, uh… afraid, that's all. I want to see you again."

"I want to see you too, but I think it's impossible for now. Can I do anything to help?" she asked.

"Not for now. There is one other thing."

"What's that?"

"You can wait for me."

"I will," she said. "However long it takes."

"Both Harry and I have to go underground for a while until we can prove our innocence. Harry was a convicted felon, but he's been straight for years now. So if they connect him to the crime, the media's bound to sensationalize him. Don't believe all you hear," he said. "I'll be in touch as soon as I can."

"I can't wait to see you again, Randall, really."

"When the dust settles, I'll make sure I treat you to the finest dinner and a movie you've ever had-

"And I'll treat you to something else," she said in a sultry tone.

"Can't wait."

"Me neither," she said.

Randall blew a kiss into the phone, "I'll be in touch. Goodbye."

"Bye," she said.

Harry looked at Randall and cracked a laugh.

"What?" asked Randall.

The Heckler stood up, puckered his lips, and imitated the kiss Randall blew into the receiver, again and again.

"Knock it off, Harry!"

"You're so sweet, Randall. If we get thrown in prison, would you be my girlfriend?"

"Shut the fuck up," Randall grumbled. "What are we gonna do?"

"First, let me call Eddie Z to see if he can find something on Atari Gem. Second, we're marked men, so we should get disguises. Unfortunately, I'll have to stop riding my bike. By now, I'm sure Johnny knows about our dilemma. Maybe he can be our grunt- buy us some makeup and different clothes. The stone's too dangerous to carry, so we'll have to hide it in a safe place." Harry looked around the room. "I've got an idea," he said, "If I can remove the molding from one of the wall panels along the floor. We'll carve a small hole out and put the stone there for safekeeping. I don't think anyone will pull the molding off. What da ya think?"

"Sounds like a great idea," said Randall

Harry went to the closet where he knew the tools were. He came back to the living room with a hammer and a chisel and pried back the molding next to an air vent. He pulled off a section of molding then chiseled out the exposed wall in a circular motion, a half-inch at a time, until he formed a large circle. He went three inches into the wall. "Randall, give me the stone for a minute." Randall handed him the pouch and Harry tried it for size, "once I get more depth, it'll be complete." He handed it back to Randall and continued to carve the hole to the right dimensions.

"One more time," he said. Randall handed him the stone again and he placed it in. "How does it look to you?"

"Perfect, now we'll reseal the molding and voila, instant safe." said Randall.

"Who's going to seal the molding?"

"Ok, you are," Randall said.

"Give credit where credit's due."

"Yes, sir, Mr. Heckler, sir."

"Randall, hold the molding while I put the nails back. If my friend finds I tore a hole in his wall, he'll kill me. I want to make it as perfect as it was when it came off." Harry hammered the nails back in, stood back, looked at its overall appearance, "good as new."

"I'd never guess to look there. Harry, you're a genius."

"Experience," he said, then winked. "Now, I'll call Eddie Z to see if we can find out what your friend does on the side. I call Eddie, Know-it-all, because of his uncanny ability to find out information."

"He's good?"

"The best- contacts everywhere." Harry picked up the phone and dialed. On the third ring it was picked up.

"Eddie, know-it-all here, what the hell ya up too, Harry?"

Harry nodded his head towards Randall. "Eddie, I'm in a jam. You know we're tight. I watch your back, and you watch mine- you know that."

"Course, Harry. Whatda ya need?"

"I need a favor. There's a place on 47th called Atari Gems. I think the owner, Sid Barchetti tried to put a cap in my friend. He must have a side business, maybe an illegal fence for gems. I'm not really sure, but I think he's no good. Could ya look into it for me and let me know?" I wanna make sure I can keep my pal clear of the guy.

"I don't talk ta ya for months then ya call only when ya need something. You're a good guy Harry and ya do watch my back. I'll check it out."

"Excellent."

"Was that you on TV?"

"Sketch did look like me, but I didn't do it. You know how it is; I have a habit of being in the wrong place at the wrong time. That's why I'm tryin to get down to the bottom of it."

"I never believe the news anyways."

"Thanks, pal. Contact me at 212-646-2331. Can you get back to me in a couple of hours?" asked Harry.

"Yea, shouldn't be a problem."

"I'll talk ta ya."

Harry hung up the receiver and looked at Randall. "He'll call back in a few hours. Until then we just relax. Can I get ya a burger or somethin?"

"Na, I'm gonna watch a little Jay Leno. I could use a laugh about now."

The two men sat down, watched the Tonight Show, and patiently waited for the phone call.

Chapter 11
The Plan

After Paul Striker was shot, without thinking, Gino threw Bill Barchetti over his shoulder and carried him to the subway. He sat him on a bench as others watched.

"Too much to drink," he said as he pointed to his friend.

When the subway rolled in, Bill Barchetti regained consciousness. They boarded the train and returned to Sid Barchetti's home, on the Upper East Side. They entered his penthouse on the 26th Floor, which overlooked the park.

"Did you get the stone?"

"No, Sid. We tracked Striker to Columbus Circle where he met that guy Randall. They proceeded up Central Park West together and when I saw Striker take the pouch, I pulled my gun and some biker out of nowhere clothes lined me from a motorcycle. I sent off a shot which accidentally hit Striker. Randall retrieved his stone then rode off with the biker," said Bill.

Sid approached his brother and slapped him across the face, "You fool! That's too public a place to shoot anyone!"

"I wasn't gonna kill him there!"

"You hit the jeweler for God sakes! Couldn't you have

taken him behind an alley or deep into the woods of Central Park, before you pulled your gun? Noooooo, you have to make a scene- just like you."

"I'm telling you, it was an accident!" Bill screamed.

"Turn on the TV; it's bound to make the evening news."

Gino went to the big screen and turned it on.

"Listen Sid, calm your nerves, we got it covered," said Bill reassuringly. "We framed the kid and biker for the murder. The police will track em down and since they don't know about the stone, we have a good chance to pick it back up. Once the cops lead us to them, we can torture them for its whereabouts- to death if need be."

"Christ. You know the cops'll find the bruise on Striker's ribs from my brass knuckles."

"Aw man, you didn't."

"He needed a warning. Make sure the cops nail these guys. My work has to be business as usual. Surely the police will investigate Striker's death. You're sure there were no witnesses?" Sid looked with concern, "You're sure Paul Striker's dead?"

"We're sure there were no witnesses, but I can't guarantee he's dead. I shot him through the back. If he's not dead, he's damn close," replied Bill.

"Ssshhh, let's listen." He turned up the volume on the television.

"In the latest on the Central Park shooting Paul Striker, the 47th. Street jewelry dealer, who was gunned down, remains in critical condition tonight. We remain skeptical on the reasons of the shooting, and police still search for the suspects who were seen fleeing the crime. According to eye witnesses, we've been able to do composites of the men." The screen prompted two sketches.

"That's them!" the young brother replied.

"Good job, Bill," Sid said. They listened intently.

"According to Police, Paul Striker remains in a coma at Mount Sinai Medical Center."

Sid Barchetti turned off the TV. "Paul Striker's our one major loose end. He could threaten our whole plan to get the diamond, and most likely finger you in the shooting. We have no choice but to kill him. I'll visit him in the hospital and survey the situation. Bill, make sure you talk to our friends in NYPD about keeping us updated. Have Officers Lear and Marrow drop by the shop, and we'll give them some incentive to lead us to our friends. Any information which will keep us one step ahead of the police," said Sid Barchetti. He walked behind a large marble top bar, grabbed a crystal glass, removed a few ice cubes from an ice bucket and clanked them in the glass. He filled it half way with Macallan 25-Year-Old Scotch, and then sipped it. "Ahhh, the comforts of home. Bill, do you realize the value of that gem?"

"I didn't think you'd go to the extremes for just any stone."

"The money and the power that come with a diamond of that size would be incredible." He looked at the men, "I'll make sure you're all amply rewarded."

"So whatda we do in the time being?" asked Gino.

"Follow up the motorcycle lead, you said it was a booming noise, right Bill?"

"Deafening… it was a Harley."

"So I'm sure he won't ride it again soon. He may belong to one of the local bike gangs."

"Yea, I'll look into that first," Bill replied.

"The diamond had distinctive cuts and was probably done by Henry Hillerman. I heard he died recently and his belongings were auctioned off to pay for his funeral. We can assume Randall somehow picked the stone up at his auction. Gino, see who held Hillerman's auction and see if you can get a buyers list for his merchandise. This could lead us to our next clue in this puzzle," said Sid.

The front door swung open and Tim walked into Barchetti's suite. "Did ya see the news? How'd I do?"

"Superb, Tim."

"It was beautiful. I stayed really calm."

"Did the news get your name and address or did you speak to the police?" Sid asked.

"No, I didn't give any information to either. I found the reporter, told her what I saw and she aired it immediately. After she aired it, we were off in the night before the police could speak with me," said Tim. "I didn't want to incriminate myself."

"Most likely the cops are looking for you. I don't want your face around here for the next few weeks. You need to go underground." Sid went to his bedroom and emerged a few minutes later with a bundle of cash. "Take this, it's your vacation money. Go somewhere no one will find you, somewhere quiet and far from the city. I'll leave it up to you, but take a train or car. I'm too worried about you flying. Four to six weeks should be enough time for this to be brushed under the carpet. When you come back, change your look. Grow a beard and moustache on your smooth face. It'll make you less conspicuous."

"Why don't I get the same treatment as him?" asked Gino.

"You're not a movie star and I need you."

Gino's face went sour. Tim smiled. "Maybe I'll go to Kansas City, I don't think anyone will search there," said Tim.

"You may be right about that," Sid said.

"Now, everyone knows their job. The clock's ticking and we have a lot of money at stake. Remember, business as usual."

The men nodded in agreement, and left Barchetti's place.

Chapter 12
Disappearance

Two hours passed when the phone finally rang; it was as loud as a fire siren, waking both Randall and Harry. Harry dived for the phone, "Yeah?" he answered.

"Heckler, it's me."

"What da ya got, Eddie?"

"Here's the deal, Atari's isn't a fence like you thought, but they run a protection racket that includes Bala Bala Diamonds. It's evidently a big operation and the owner, Sid Barchetti heads the collections. We have a small gambling operation hidden behind a jeweler close-by and one of my guys who play the numbers, saw Barchetti exit Bala Bala today. Turns out, they were late with a payment and I presume Barchetti went to catch up. I have no idea what transpired between the two. It's not unusual for Barchetti to be involved in murder, but he keeps his hands clean and lets his men take care of the dirty business. His brother Bill Barchetti, is an on-hands collector, deals out sentences and Sid's left-hand man. Sid also has a few cops on the take. So if you pissed the guy off, watch your nose. He's got powerful friends and connections everywhere. He fronts as the perfect jeweler. "

"Does he have any weaknesses?" asked Harry.

"He's obsessive compulsive, so if you got somethin he wants or he wants you, he won't give up! Find something he wants more! Anything else ya need?"

"No, not for now, Eddie. I appreciate your help. I'll talk to ya."

"Take care, Harry."

Harry hung up the phone, "did ya hear that?"

"All I heard was mumbles. Give me the lowdown," asked Randall.

"Sid Barchetti, the owner of Atari's runs a protection racket on the side. Bala Bala is one of his customers and he paid Striker a visit today. We don't know what happened there, but it looked like Mr. Striker was late a payment. Eddie told me, he lets others do his dirty work, so for me, it seems unusual he'd pay him a visit the very day you showed up."

"I agree."

"Also Sid Barchetti's is obsessive compulsive, which is a bad thing."

"How da ya mean?"

"The guy's gonna be hunting us like we're turkey at Thanksgiving. He also has a few cops on the take, so if the police close in, the chances are good that Barchetti's close by. He has connections everywhere, so we can trust no one," Harry said.

"Well, we've got a few people we can trust, Johnny for one and my gut tells me Milly's on the level," Randall said. "I can only think of one thing out of our situation."

"What's that?" asked Harry.

"Striker's survival. Maybe Milly can watch over the guy to secure our future. I don't think the police will have him under protection and even if they did, Barchetti could easily knock the guy off, and make it look like an accident."

"You really trust this woman?"

Randall paused, "looks like I trust her with my life. Strange isn't it? I only met her days ago, yet I feel I've known her for years. You told me Eddie Z can find out any information on anyone, right?" asked Randall.

"Pretty much."

"Could you give me his number encase I need it? God forbid, we get separated. I could find you through him."

"You know Randall, you're my best friend," Harry said. "I'll give you his number only under one circumstance."

"What's that?" he asked.

"That you never, ever, give it to anyone. When this situation's over, you destroy it. He's too valuable a source to me. I'll let him know you'll call only under dire circumstances and that it's okay to tell you my location. Promise me?"

"I promise," Randall said.

"I'll write the number with no name. You know who it is."

"So we know he's obsessive-compulsive, which would explain the shooting in the park. He wouldn't have killed a person over a valuable piece of rock crystal. Harry, my gut's tellin me this is a diamond, and he's obsessed with it."

"Keep dreamin, Romeo. If that was a diamond, you could buy anything you wanted," Harry ripped.

"What would you buy if ya had a million dollars, Harry?"

"I don't need much. I'd have a bad ass Harley with every option available. Customized to the hilt. A little home in the suburbs, a large screen TV with surround sound and a stereo that could blow the house down if necessary. How 'bout you?" he asked.

"I'd get myself a nice home in the suburbs too, not far from the city. A black Viper, my dream car, customized with a skull and crossbones. Maybe I'd hire a chef to cook for me all day long. Oh yeah, and a bar with my personal bartender to host wonderful out of control parties... You'd come, wouldn't you?"

"To your parties? Nah, probably be boring as hell," Harry said with an edge of sarcasm.

Randall didn't take notice. "It's good to have dreams, Harry. They help us get through, don't they?"

"Yea, you know when I was in prison all I dreamt about was eatin a freshly cooked apple pie. As a kid, I could smell the scent drift through the woods and call me from miles away. I dreamt about it all the time. First thing I did when I got out was search high and low for one comparable to what I remembered, but never found it."

"Shame."

"Not really, I must have eaten 20 pies the first week. I'd eat them morning, noon, and night, till I was practically sick. I still hope to find that perfect apple pie one day. Silly dream, I guess."

"Not at all. Things like that come to you when you're least expecting it. I think that's how most things in this world come. Hell, look at our situation. If you asked me two weeks ago what I'd be doing in two weeks, I certainly wouldn't have said- running from a murderer, cops, and keepin a million dollar diamond safe!"

"Give it a rest with the million dollar diamond, Randall. You'll only get your hopes up, to be defeated and crushed by the reality of life."

"Somebody wants that little baby and they're willing to kill for it. It's gotta be worth something!" replied Randall, "but you're right. Let's get back to our present situation."

"Let's call quick Johnny to get us clothes and disguises,"

Harry said. He picked up the phone and dialed Johnny's number.

Johnny picked up, "Hello?"

"Johnny, Harry."

"Where the hell have you guys been? I've been worried sick; your pictures are all over the news."

"It's a long story. Randall and I are together at my friends' place, but we need your help. We need disguises. Nothing eye catching, something normal everyday people wear. We also need actor's makeup along with either mustaches or beards."

"Where the hell am I gonna get that?" asked Johnny.

"It's New York, I'm sure you'll find someplace. There's plenty of people lookin for us, both cops and crooks, so watch your back and make sure you're not followed. We're stuck here."

"Who's gonna follow me?"

"I don't know," said Harry, "just be careful."

"What's my nickname?" Johnny spouted, "Come on Harry, let me hear you say it."

Harry shook his head while Randall looked on, "Quick, Johnny."

"What?"

"Quick Johnny. It's quick Johnny."

"Remember that." he said.

"Just get goin. Meet us at 13 Varick St. Apartment 606. The crossroad is Seventh Avenue- close to the Holland tunnel."

"Got it, I'll be there as soon as I can," said Johnny.

Harry hung up the receiver. "That boy has problems. Remind me to slap him around a little when I see him. He'll be over as soon as he can."

"Good," said Randall, "in the meantime, I'm goin back to sleep."

"Pleasant dreams, kid," replied Harry. "Let's hope Johnny can find somethin good this time of night."

After a half-hour, Randall fell into a light sleep. His body shifted to its side but fit the couch snugly. After a few hours, Harry lifted himself from the single leather rocking chair to check his friend. Randall's eyes vibrated behind his eyelids.

He'll be lucky enough to live through this ordeal if that's a diamond. I've known people to kill for a shitload less. Poor guy, wrong place- wrong time, but don't worry kid, I'll look out for ya. Thought Harry. Harry leaned over.

Randall's ears pricked up when he heard the creak of a loose floorboard. His eyes opened from a deep sleep to find Harry's face inches from his own.

"Ahhhhh, shit!" yelled Randall. His body jumped up in a moment of shock, "Jesus Christ, Harry! What the hell ya tryin to do? Kill me! Shit!"

"Sorry, pal."

"Did your cell mate have the same reaction when he saw your scary face?"

"He never saw my face. Just goes to show how special ya are, friend."

"You call that special?"

"Yaaaaaaaaaa," said Harry.

"Don't mess with me," said Randall. "I can't wake from this fantasy and I don't give a damn what you say, it's a goddamn diamond!" shouted Randall.

"Can I beat your fucking head in now?" Harry asked.

"My head on a good day is only worth the price of a cantaloupe. It's not worth a beating."

"I think you're overextending your value, man."

"Maybe you're right," said Randall with a giggle.

"You've slept the last two hours, so Johnny should be here

shortly. I only hope he's found something that'll fit us."

"He knows our approximate sizes, let's keep our fingers crossed."

Rap…Rap…Rap… went the door.

Randall sprung from his chair, and then retreated in silence. Harry raised his hand to stop Randall's motion. He stood attentively and listened.

"Harry, it's me. Open up, hurry," whispered Johnny.

Harry leapt for the door, pulled it open quickly, and grabbed Johnny by the shoulder. He pulled him in, along with a large suitcase. "Geeze, Harry, could ya be a little more gentle? You scuffed my shoes," said Johnny.

"You're lucky I'm not scuffin your face. How'd ya do?" asked Harry.

"Now keep in mind, it's the middle of the night and I had limited resources. I don't think people will recognize you," Johnny said. He opened the suitcase and pulled out a dress, wig, lipstick, eye shadow, rouge, and some fake costume jewelry.

"So this is good for Randall. Where's mine?" asked Harry.

Johnny pointed down at the suitcase, "The large one's yours, honey," said Johnny. He handed Harry a deep floral blue dress. Johnny bit his tongue to contain his laughter.

Harry got up and grabbed Johnny by the throat. "Do you think this is some sort of joke, you fuck! If we're recognized, you can kiss our asses goodbye. You'll be in shit's creek cause I'll have every mother fucker from every prison in the US after you." He jacked Johnny up against the wall. Johnny struggled to breathe.

"Harry, Harry, take it easy," said Randall in an even-tempered voice. "This might not be so bad. It'd be smart to change our sex. Who's gonna look for a couple of women? Trust me, I'm no closet drag queen, but we can't afford to be spotted.

There are enough queens in the village that we'd blend in perfectly. Let him down."

Johnny quickly retorted, "That's what I thought. Harry, I know the last thing you wanta do is wear a dress, but they'll recognize your tattoos."

"I'm not gonna do it. Randall, I wantcha to use it. I'll make some phone calls to my connections and they'll watch our backs, I'll take my chances," Harry said.

"You know as well as I, all ya need is a former rival to see ya. I mean, there's no doubt some of your enemies have seen the news. You don't think they'll be spillin their guts to try and get ya put back in the pen?" said Randall.

"I'll be fine," said Harry.

"No, man, you've worked too fuckin hard to stay clean and just cause some shit goes down…" Randall walked over to him, "Do I gotta get in your face?"

"You don't want ta go there. Kimosabe."

Randall stepped back, "Ya know what I'm talkin' about Harry." He looked at him sincerely, "I'm beggin' ya- please."

Harry looked at him with all seriousness, "Try out the new stuff for size, Randall. Let me see how it looks."

Randall took the suitcase into the bathroom and shut the door. He looked at the razor stubble on his cheeks, and then opened the bathroom cabinet. He found a razor and shaving cream. *I'd better take this five o'clock shadow off. Nice, clean, neat and feminine.* He filled the sink with steaming hot water, shaved his face, shut the lid of the toilet, and opened the suitcase. *Christ.* His hands reached in and grabbed a long black dress and a pair of stockings. *What the hell do I do with these?* He laid them across the sink and frowned. "Foundation, rouge, lipstick? Can this day get any worse?" He unscrewed the cap of the foundation, and scooped a palm full of the material – "Uh." He smacked the small pile on and pasted it over. It was heavy and thick. He moved the dress and stockings to the toilet and rinsed his hand under the water. He grabbed the lipstick and cringed when it touched his lips. He slid it across and watched the contorted expressions in the mirror. He rubbed his lips together. "I think this is how they do it." He slipped his lanky body into the frock. *Oh shit, no, no, no…. I can't, I can't.* He stood back and looked at his hairy legs in the mirror. *Randall…you gotta do it otherwise, prison.* He picked up the razor and stretched down to the bottom of his ankle. His head turned from side to side and began to cut a lifetime's growth of his precious leg hair. He rinsed the razor under the bath tap frequently as truckloads of hair fell from his skin. *I can't believe I'm doin this!* He did this until both legs were as bare as a baby's bottom.

He pulled the blouse over his head and stuffed the breasts with toilet paper. He boosted them up for lift until both were in place. The skirt fit Randall like a glove. He yanked the stockings up his legs and tried to fit them comfortably in his crotch. *How do women do this?* He lifted the curly brunette wig from the suitcase, placed it on his head, and tossed the long hair to the side as he bent his head back. He stood with his legs apart, one hand on hip, looked at himself in the mirror, puckered his lips and blew a kiss. "Wow, you're one ugly broad!" he said to himself.

"You think he's playin with himself in there, Johnny?" asked Harry.

"I don't know. It's been 20 minutes. Maybe he's getting off in those clothes. I hope he doesn't turn into a cross dresser. Last thing we need is THAT kinda of mess."

"Aw man, bag that talk," Harry said, "this sucks."

"It's just temporary. These things resolve themselves."

"No, we gotta resolve this one."

"So whadda ya gonna do, Harry?"

"I'm gonna take a trip uptown to check out Atari Gems. It's not safe for Randall, so I'll go alone. You should go to his place and get any necessities he'll need for a few weeks. You've gotta make sure you're not tailed, cause this place has to remain our sanctuary. If the cops found anything within the last 12 hours, they could beat you back to Randall's place. Chances are it's still vacant, but I wantcha to case the joint. Take Randall and work together. You should go in only after you signal him. I don't want you in that place for more than 15 minutes: in and out. Wear gloves because when you leave, I don't want any hints you were there. It's only a matter of time before they find his place. Barchetti may already have a handle on it considering his connections."

"Who is this guy, Barchetti?"

"It's a long story, but the guy's out to kill Randall and me. He wants Randall's stone."

"What stone? Where'd he get the stone? How'd he-

Enough already. You only need to know we're in the crapper," said Harry.

"Alright, where da ya want to meet?"

"Well, I figure I'll be about five hours. Let's say I meet you mid-day, 3pm at the marketplace. I figure that should be relatively safe. Pray Paul Striker recovers cause he's our only way out."

Randall opened the door to the bathroom and both men stood dumbfounded.

"Hey kid, you make a pretty good woman," Harry said. "Just don't get caught in that garb, or you'll be some guy's love slave in the joint."

Johnny got up from his seat, and walked over to Randall. He leaned his head back to take in the whole picture. He slowly walked around him and studied his features. Small razor cuts adorned Randall's legs. "You've made a mess of your legs. Until now, I've never noticed how shapely they are."

"You ever shaved your legs?" asked Randall. "Christ, I don't know how women do it!"

Harry interjected, "Just be thankful they do!"

They all burst out laughing.

"You sure you've never done this before Randall?" Johnny inquired. "I think I saw someone like you a couple of weeks ago on Avenue C!"

"Not me. Besides, I'm a born again virgin."

"You won't be for long, looking like that," Harry chimed in.

Randall cleared his throat, "come on now- enough of this- the first guy that hits on me and BAM!"

"Don't make me get up," replied Harry with a grin. "All kidding aside, let's get down to business. I told Johnny I'm checking out Atari Gems this morning, while you guys visit your place. Get enough clothing for about three weeks and bring it back here. Make sure you're careful, while Johnny scouts out your apartment!"

"Harry, you should really wear a disguise. You're a felon and our faces were all over the news. If you don't, you're bound to get seen and then you're really up the creek," Randall said.

"I'll get something, don't worry. I'll wear a long sleeved shirt, and before you can say 'Boo', I'll be back," he answered.

"You better. Take off and we'll meet back here around 3:00 pm," Randall replied.

"Peace," said Harry as he looked as his watch. He took a deep breath, opened the door and left.

Chapter 13
The Network

Bill Barchetti thumbed his Rolodex and came to a single name, Nelson, scribbled on a white card, a phone number beside it. *Nelson, it's been awhile since we've spoken. I hope your girlfriend is better, since the hit and run. She was like a cat, but if you're not careful we might have to use up another one of her lives.* Barchetti picked up the receiver and dialed the number. He waited.

"NYPD, Nelson Lear."

"Nelson, Bill Barchetti here, how are you?"

"What da ya want, Barchetti?"

"I need a favor of you and Sal Morrow."

"You're lucky you're not in prison after tryin to kill my girlfriend," Lear whispered.

I'm sure N-Y-P-D would be happy to see our 'donations' to you and Sal. Ever think of what prisoners do to 'ex-cops'? Besides, we take care of ya, we always make it worth your while," said Barchetti.

"So what's this favor?"

"I wantcha ya to let me know when the PD closes in on the suspects from the Central Park shooting. I wanta know what evidence was at the scene and any other info pertinent to the case, especially the type of Harley they escaped on. We want these guys ourselves."

"And what's it gonna cost?"

"My silence. As good amends, we'll give ya a beautiful diamond tennis bracelet for your girlfriend. Sal'll get the same thing. I need ya to tell him when it's convenient."

"Do I have a choice?"

"Not really," said Barchetti.

"I'll let Morrow know. We'll be in touch."

Barchetti hung up the phone and again picked up the receiver then dialed 411. "Could I have a listing of the Harley Davidson dealers in Manhattan, please?"

"One moment." A few seconds went by and the operator returned. "There are three."

"Fantastic. Could you give me the addresses?"

"Certainly," she replied.

Barchetti scribbled down three dealers the operator quickly rattled off. *All located in Manhattan, fantastic!*

Gino walked down 47th until he found a small doorway with the number 1020 above it. To the side he found a directory with several companies listed. He followed his finger down the listing until he found a company named "Wish upon a Falling Star." He stepped through the doorway, took the elevator up and exited on the tenth floor. He came to a small window where he could see a man and woman talking behind the receptionist desk.

"Can I help you?" asked the woman.

"I'm here to have Henry Hillerman cut a diamond for me," said Gino.

The man looked across the receptionist desk at Gino, "I'm afraid Mr. Hillerman passed away, August 17th."

"Oh, how awful. I heard he was the best diamond cutter on 47th Street. I'm so sorry," said Gino, "Can I presume you're the owner?"

"Yes, my name's Ubi Cancade. He was not only my best worker, but my best friend." He pulled out a handkerchief to wipe his nose. "You'll have to excuse me; I still get choked up talking about it. We only buried him a few weeks ago."

"His family must be grief stricken," said Gino.

"He had no kin, we were his closest family. The worst part is I had to sell all his valuables to pay for the funeral. Things haven't been so good around here."

"I see. At least the auction house must have been accommodating."

"They're a bunch of low key crooks. Most of them charge outrageous fees which off balances the money you raise. I was lucky to find one which wasn't as cold as the others and accommodated me. They got us out of our awful predicament."

"Who was that?"

"Geller & Associates. If you have to auction anything off to raise funds in a pinch, see them. I'll recommend them to everyone I know. I spoke with a woman, named Helen, who was a tremendous help."

Helen of Geller & Associates, huh- noted. He nodded his head, "Sad thing, I'm sure there's no replacing him, right?" said Gino.

"Very few cutters could meet Henry's expertise. Right now, we're looking for one, so you're outta luck today. If you want to check back in a few weeks, we should have a full time cutter by then," said Ubi.

"I need it in a hurry, so I'll find someone else. I appreciate your time," Gino said politely.

"Thanks. Take care." he said.

Gino exited the door. *Geller & Associates. Let me find out when the auction was and who Helen is. Maybe they'll give me a roster of merchandise if I pose as a relative. I'll tell her I'm lookin for something great uncle Henry wanted to give me. If I can get Randall's whole name, I can resort to the phone book and get this scoundrel.*

Gino went back to Atari's and thumbed through the phone book until he reached Geller & Associates. *123 East 57th St, phone 212-967-4052. I gotta go there in person.* Gino scribbled the number down on a piece of scratch paper, closed the phone book, and ran out the door. He hailed a cab, and rode it to 57th Street, where he paid the cabby and walked into 123 East 57th. He found Geller & Associates on the 10th Floor at the index. He took the elevator there and found them the last door on the right side of the hallway. He stopped outside, ruffled his jacket, and pulled out his shirt. He walked through the entrance and greeted a beautiful blonde secretary. *This should be easy.*

"Miss, I hope you can help me. My great uncle Henry Hillerman died a few weeks back. His business partner, Ubi Cancade, sold his valuables to pay for his funeral before I was notified. I know the auction's been held and I presume many of the items have been sold. There was a lamp and some other family heirlooms I couldn't locate. I hoped the people, out of their kind hearts, would sell them back to me for what they paid. Could you help me?"

"You poor thing. Where did you come from?" asked the secretary.

"From West Pennsylvania. Anything you could do would help." Gino forced some tears from his eyes, "Do you have some tissues?"

"Certainly, hon," said the secretary. She handed him a tissue from a box on her desk. She watched him wipe his eyes. With sympathy she continued, "Now, now, everything's gonna be alright.

Normally we're not allowed to give the public any information on the buyers of merchandise, but since you're a relative…" She looked around, then at her watch. "My boss leaves for lunch in 5 minutes. I'll get you a copy of the buyers list with the merchandise sold. It won't have personal information on the buyers, but it does list phone numbers. I hope that'll help."

"That'll help a great deal. I really appreciate your kindness," he said.

"If you take a seat in the lobby, you'll see him when he goes. In the meantime, I'll print it out. He's about 6 foot with dark black hair. When you see him go, come see me and I'll have it."

"Thank you so much." Gino said. He walked to the lobby and sat down in one of four wooden chairs.

She pulled the information on Hillerman's auction from her computer files and sent it to the printer. Once it stopped, she pulled the seven pages from the printer and stacked them in a neat pile on her desk. Her manager opened the door to his office.

"I'm going to lunch, Helen. Hold my calls."

"Yes, sir."

The man went through the lobby to the elevators and disappeared. Gino came back inside. She smiled.

"Here you are." She handed him the papers. "I hope this helps, but remember, you never got'em from me."

"Your secret's safe. Have a good day," said Gino.

"You, too," she said.

Gino exited the auction house and walked to Central Park. He took a seat under a large oak tree and flipped through the items. *Corner desk/Safe-no combination, Randall Becks- buyer! That's got to be it!* Startled by his find, Gino jumped up and ran to the subway. He exited on 47th and jogged to Atari's.

"Gino, you look elated," Sid Barchetti said.

"His name is Randall Becks. I need your phone book." Gino brushed through the pages till he found it. "Randall Becks 162B Avenue A. Bingo!"

"Excellent job, Gino. Go to his place and search his apartment high and low. I doubt he'll be there, especially since the broadcast last night. Rip it up, until you find it," said Barchetti. "I'm going to visit our friend Paul Striker, in a few minutes. Meet me back at my place tonight."

"Righto. Send my regards," Gino said with sarcasm.

"Hello?"

"Hello, Milly? It's Randall. I hate to be abrupt, but I need a favor. Remember when you said, did I need anything?"

"Yes, of course. Are you ok?"

"I'm fine, but I need ya to stop by Mt. Sinai Medical Center and see how Paul Striker is. We're relying on his testimony when he's out of a coma. I'm praying he'll be alright."

"Me too. I'd be happy to check on him. Who am I if anyone asks?"

"He must have countless friends in his line of work, since he's a jeweler. If ya find they're only allowin family members, then let me know. Johnny and I are gonna take a quick trip to my place, so I can pick up some clothing. I shouldn't be gone long, my number's 212-664-5243. I can't wait to spend time with you."

"Me too. I'll speak with ya soon." she said, and hung up the phone. She grabbed her coat and left for the hospital.

Sid put his overcoat on, hailed a cab and took it uptown to the corner of 100th St. and Madison. He entered Mt. Sinai and spoke to a receptionist.

"Excuse me miss, could you tell me what room Paul Striker

is in? I'm a good friend of his."

"One moment, let me find out," she said. She tapped the keys on her computer, "Room 1214. You have to go down the hall, make a right, then a quick left. You'll see the elevators right there. Take one to the 12th floor and when you exit, speak to the receptionist on that floor for directions to his room."

"Thank you," said Barchetti.

Why the hell are hospitals always in the shape of a labyrinth? I feel I should lay some string down, so I can find my way back to the front. I hate this! Barchetti entered the elevator and pushed the 12th floor button. He exited it, went through two glass doors and found a nurse.

"Could you lead me to room 14 please?" he asked.

"Certainly," The nurse grabbed a room pass from behind the station and led him around the corner to Striker's room. "He's still in a coma, but I'm sure he can still hear," she said.

Barchetti entered the room. "Wow, all these wires, he looks like a machine. Do you think he'll make it?" he asked.

"He lost a lot of blood, but I think he'll pull through. We're not sure when he'll emerge from the coma. That's up to him," she said. "Obviously, he's been stabilized and no longer in ICU. Your friend's lucky he arrived when he did, another few minutes and he wouldn't have been so lucky."

Barchetti looked down at the bed. *If only the police weren't so quick, or the traffic backed up, I'd be free and clear. You're a lucky man, Mr. Striker.* "He looks so helpless."

"We believe his a coma will be at least a few days. We have orders to notify the police as soon as he comes out of it," said the nurse, "I'll leave you alone with your friend."

"Thank you, nurse," said Barchetti. He waited for her to exit, and then pulled a chair to the side of the bed. He leaned over Striker's limp body and whispered, "Paul, Paul, Paul. You do get yourself into trouble, don't you? I think you've just stepped into the worst trouble you've ever had. We could've saved this headache if only you'd told me the truth about your rendezvous with Randall Becks. I only want the stone," said Barchetti. "For God sakes, he had no clue what he had! It should have been easy, but he had to flake out last minute. Did you tell him what it was?" The man sat back in his chair and watched the heart beat monitor attached to Striker. It bounced faster. He bent down, "All I have to do is unhook the switches and wires that make you this living machine and you'd be dead. You're the only person in my way, so unfortunately I have to kill you. But don't worry, we'll bury you in peace with all honors." Barchetti kicked out the legs of his chair and placed it back in the corner from which it came. He looked at Striker's heart monitor rapidly beat. "But for now, I'm just giving you brain candy to chew. From all accounts, the afterlife's not bad."

A nurse came in unexpectedly. "Excuse me, Mr. Striker's monitor was a little erratic, I need to check the connections."

"That's ok, we're done anyway." He leaned over, "Trust me, I'll be back." Barchetti stepped away from bed and watched his monitor continue to bounce. *You heard everything, didn't you?*

Barchetti left the room and walked back to the nurse's station. He handed the pass back to the nurse, nodded and walked into the elevator. When he reached the lobby, he heard a woman at the reception desk.

"Could you tell me where to find Paul Striker?" she asked.

Sid Barchetti turned around to look at the woman. *She doesn't look familiar, I wonder if it's Striker's daughter?* "Excuse me, miss?"

She turned around, "can I help you?"

"I'm sorry to bother you. I overheard you're looking for Paul Striker. I just came from his room, but it's hard to find. Let me take you there," said Barchetti.

"Thank you," she said, "I can't believe what's happened."

"It's horrible. You wouldn't think an attempted murder could happen on Central Park West. It's such an open area. Are you his daughter?" asked Barchetti.

"No, I'm a friend. We work in the same business," she said. "I'm a jeweler."

"What a coincidence, so am I." said Barchetti. He watched her body shift uncomfortably. "Are you on 47th?"

"No, I work downtown. Are you familiar with downtown?" she asked, her voice cracked on the last word.

Barchetti stared at her. Her eyes moved from side to side to avoid his piercing stare. "No, I'm not familiar with many places downtown, in fact, I rarely get down there. I keep myself pretty busy up here. I'm a few stores down from Paul. What's the name of your place?" he asked.

"It's called," she stalled momentarily, "The Diamond Star of New York. Have you heard of us?"

"Hmmmmm, no, doesn't ring a bell. Are you JBT rated?" he asked.

"JBT what?" she said.

She doesn't know the Jewelers Board of Trade, that's suspicious. "What are you known for?"

"Well, we carry a bit of everything."

"Like what?"

"Do you have ta be so rude? I'm here ta visit my friend Paul, I didn't come here to talk shop and I don't need you to drill me on my business. Lay off, ok? I didn't come here for this." she strongly stated. Her eyes pierced him in fury.

"My apologies miss. I was just curious," said Barchetti.

They approached the nurse's station, grabbed a pass and turned the corner to Striker's room. They entered the doorway.

"I can't believe how terrible he looks," she said.

"He's in bad shape, but better then he was. The nurse said he's stable but doesn't know if he'll come out of a coma. He's lost a lot of blood."

"I'm surprised the police aren't guarding him, given the circumstances."

Police guarding him? Why would she consider police guarding him, in the case of a botched robbery? Maybe she's with the two guys from the park? They need him alive, the same way I need him dead. "I was as surprised as you. You'd think in the robbery of a jeweler, they'd be close by."

"You'd think," she paused momentarily, "do you think he'll wake from it?"

"Hard to tell."

He watched her lean over Striker and stroke his face. Compassion filled her eyes as she watched him lay motionless in bed. She bent in close to his ear and whispered, "Our happiness relies on you making it out of this coma. Please, I beg you. I love him," she said. She kissed his cheek, and stood up. Water filled the wells of her eyes.

"Hey, he'll be alright." *Once he reaches the grave.* "Can I treat you to a cup of coffee?"

"That sounds good. I didn't get your name," she said.

"Sid Barchetti."

"Mine's Milly Van Lowe."

Gino arrived at Randall's place and stood there in shock. He walked around the outside and looked at the boarded window, the plywood which seemed to secure the front door.

He scratched his head. Gino went to what appeared to be the entrance. His fingertips reached around and gripped the sides of the 4x8 and moved it slightly. He saw the wood move.

I'll be damned. Looked like the fuckin thing was nailed solid. Clever shit.

He slid the board to the right and slid his body in through the opening. The scented candles filled the air. He found a small stand near the handrail which had a few old newspapers and loose letters strewn upon it. He sorted through them. "Randall Becks #162B, ah hah!" He looked at the dusty staircase and ascended the stairs until he reached the third floor and found the apartment, a lone door at the end of the hallway. He slipped a set of keys from his pocket and some workable tools. He manipulated several skeleton keys in and out of several dead bolts with no luck. He jammed a small tool into the lock and worked the mechanism. After the course of 10 minutes, he heard a click to the last device and pushed the door gently with his shoulder. The door opened to reveal a railroad apartment. *What a sty. I can't believe someone actually lives here. Shouldn't take long to rip this place up.*

Gino found a set of dress clothes laid neatly on the sofa. *Probably hasn't been home since yesterday. Why would someone be getting dressed to go out if the whole city is looking for him? I suppose I should start with the bathroom, the back of the toilet is a typical hiding place.* Gino walked into the room and lifted the back of the toilet. *Nothing! If I'm going to get anywhere, I'll have to throw his shit around, the punk asshole!*

Chapter 14
Red Handed

H arry put on his black sunglasses, grabbed a rubber band, tied his long black hair back and left the apartment. He searched the streets for a curbside vendor and found one on an neighboring street that sold large woolen plaid shirts. He paid the man $15.00 for an extra extra large plaid shirt. He immediately put it on to cover the large tattoos that cascaded down his arms. He started to walk the street and found himself listening to the thumps of his large biker boots. *No use in wearing these boots on the run. They'll get me caught if anything.* His eyes caught an illegal shoe vendor, so he purchased a new pair of hot Nike sneakers, slipped them on his feet and carried on. He put his boots in the plastic bag and found an empty alleyway. *You've been good to me old friends, hopefully, you'll save someone else's dogs.* He kissed the bag and put them next to a Dumpster.

Now, down to business. He walked with confidence down Broadway, avoiding the yellow line of cabs that moved past. It was noon when he finally arrived in front of Atari Gems. He gazed in the window. *There's the motherfucker who shot Striker! I should kill him, now.* He stood up straight and turned his back to the window. *Easy Harry, easy, take a deep breath. You need to stay relaxed. He probably sees hundreds of people a day; no way he could have made me out that night. Things happened too quickly.* Harry waited for the store to empty out before he entered. He left his sun glasses on.

When Harry entered, Bill Barchetti approached his two salespeople, "Watch this man carefully," he whispered. He moved swiftly to the manager's office, sat below the window, picked up the phone, and hit speed dial 10. The phone rang three times before it was answered.

"Marrow here."

"Marrow, Bill Barchetti here."

"Yeah, Barchetti?" he replied. "If you're calling about any leads to the case, we have none now."

"I have the first," Barchetti said. "The biker's here."

"He can't be that stupid, Barchetti."

"Sal, I'm not one hundred percent sure, but I guarantee this guy's trouble. I'd advise you to get over here. Something's going down, and it's going to be soon. Hurry!" Barchetti urged.

"All right," he conceded, "I'll be there in about five." Marrow hung up the receiver and looked at his colleague. "Nelson, do you believe this guy, Barchetti?" A disgusted look crossed his face. "What an arrogant prick! If only I stayed clear of that piece of garbage. He thinks the wanted biker is in his store."

"Really?" Nelson said.

"Yea. Can he be that stupid?"

"I wouldn't think so, but I suppose we should check it out." He added, "You know he's got both our balls in a vice. It's better to just listen ta what he says, and check it out. If we can nail these guys, maybe we'll get a nice trip to the islands. Some pina coladas on a beautiful sandy beach is what we need."

Marrow snapped at him, "Yeah, but if we're gonna catch'em, we better hightail it to Atari's. Avoid the lights and sirens; we don't want to alert the guy."

"Let's go," replied Nelson, as they left together.

Bill Barchetti opened a small safe at the bottom of Sid's desk. He worked the combination until the door clicked. On top of a stack of money, he found a .45 caliber pistol, which he tucked behind his back. *Now, I feel better.* Barchetti stood up and looked out the small window that separates the office. He saw the man lean down and look inside the glass cases, opposite the office. The man glanced up and nodded his head. Barchetti opened the door and moved toward him.

"Can I help you, sir?"

Harry's head swayed back and forth. "Could I speak to Sid Barchetti? I have a stone I'd like to get appraised."

No! He couldn't be that stupid. "Sid's not here right now and I'm not sure when he'll be back. Perhaps, I could help you. My name's Bill Barchetti, I'm Sid's brother."

That explains some things. "Well…Bill. I wanted a gem appraised that could be worth a lot of money. It's tucked in my pocket." He reached into his pocket, "Let me show you."

Barchetti leaned his left hand on the counter and reached around with his right. The back of his hand smacked the gun's handle and his fingers fondled the grip of the gun. He watched the man pull a small paper bag from his pocket and place it on the counter.

"There," Harry said. "I wantcha to look in there. I can promise it's worth your while."

Bill stood there. *I don't know, seems fishy to me.* Bill stared at Harry's eyes in a mesmerizing glare. *He doesn't look very bright.* He shifted his look to the bag. *Maybe he stole it from his friend. If he had any inkling to its value, he'd undoubtedly pawn it himself. Yeah, he's not so stupid; I bet that's what he's doing.*

Bill removed his right hand from the gun and stood upright. He grabbed the bag and positioned a small velvet pad beneath it. He uncurled the end of the bag.

Harry eyes searched the store, until he focused on a reflection of Barchetti's back in the small office window. *Shit, he's armed. Keep cool.*

Barchetti spilled a piece of coal from the bag. "What the hell's this?" He demanded.

With an innocent smirk, Harry replied, "You're a jeweler, aren't you? You tell me."

"It's a goddamn piece of coal! What's the meaning of this!"

"Diamonds come from coal don't they?"

Barchetti looked at him. "Carborundum," he enunciated clearly. "Diamonds come from carborundum."

"I suppose rock crystal can't be turned into diamonds can it?" Harry looked at Barchetti's shifting expressions, and then flashed a crooked smile.

Barchetti's right hand quickly flew around his back, as Harry hurled himself over the counter. He crushed Barchetti's body into the wall with his shoulder, pinning his arm. Harry pulled the man's limb higher than the gun and Barchetti screamed as a bolt of pain surged through it. Harry's free hand flew around and caught the handle of the gun. He pulled it from Barchetti's belt line and, in an instant, he turned it back on him, "you move and I'll shoot a hole in ya the size of a grapefruit," Harry threatened.

Shocked at the speed of the altercation, the salespeople froze. Harry yelled, "one of you, put the 'Closed' sign up. If you cooperate, no one'll get hurt."

"Do as he says. Adele flip the sign," shouted Barchetti. She ran across the shop and turned it over.

He waved the gun. "Now, I want ya'll in the office and

down on the floor!" Harry checked his watch. *All I need is five minutes.* "Move!" he yelled. "If I so much as see one of ya flinch, you're dead," he threatened.

They walked single file into the office and knelt on the floor. Harry kept Barchetti pinned against the door. "I know ya tried to kill me and I don't take kindly to dodgin' bullets." He pulled the trigger back and brushed Barchetti's ear with the nozzle of the gun. "I know you're in the racket, and I know all about your business, but what da ya want of my friend? Why do ya want us dead?"

Barchetti remained silent. Harry threw him on his knees. "Tell me, you fuck!" He kicked his chest. Harry saw Barchetti's feet angled to the ground, so he lifted his own foot, and with a sudden charge of energy, slammed his foot into Barchetti's heel. Barchetti screamed in agony.

"You crazy fuck!" he shouted through gritted teeth, "you broke my fucking ankle!" Barchetti pulled himself into a fetal position using his hands. His fist pounded the wall.

Harry took the butt of the gun, and smacked Bill's head. "I don't think you get the seriousness of this, dickhead," he said calmly. "Now, I'm gonna ask again… really nice. If you don't answer me, I'm gonna break each finger until ya tell me. You don't want that do you?"

"No, no, no," Barchetti pleaded.

"OK, now we understand each other. Why do ya want my friend?"

"My brother wants his stone. He's a big collector of rare quartz." Barchetti replied.

Harry took one of Barchetti's fingers and with a flash bent it backwards. Barchetti winced in pain. He continued to move the digit further and further when suddenly he used all his strength. A loud crack filled the quiet shop. Barchetti screamed.

"Fuck!" he exclaimed. "Please, please."

"I guess ya think I'm an idiot, cause I'm a biker," Harry told him. "I have news for you, my patience is runnin' out. I have no time to fuck around. Quartz ain't worth shit! It's a diamond isn't it?" he paused, "isn't it!" He grabbed the index finger of Barchetti's other hand and moved it slowly backwards.

"All right, all right!" he yelled. "It's a diamond! The fucking thing's a diamond!"

Harry looked at Barchetti and bent it farther back. "You sure now?"

"Yeah, yeah, I'm positive!" Barchetti replied in a cold sweat.

"Okay." Harry let go of his finger. "I know your brother has a protection racket, and I know where your family lives. I got friends who could shoot ya from the top of the Empire State Building, if necessary. I'll forget this whole incident and keep my mouth shut if you do the same. It'll be our secret," said Harry. "My only provision is you've gotta leave my friend clear of this mess. Ya don't and I'll hunt ya down like an 18-point deer at hunting season. If ya have to pay your people to keep their mouths shut, do it. Understand?"

"Yeah," Barchetti replied. "I understand."

"Good. Now, keep your mouth shut for the next ten minutes, then talk to your people." Harry opened the door to the office and heard the saleswomen whimper on the floor. "Keep your goddamn faces to the ground until I say, or I'll break your legs like I broke your boss's foot. I'm watching you." Harry slammed the door. "I want silence for the next 15 minutes!" He looked at Bill Barchetti, "Lay here and think about what I said. Turn your face to the wall."

Barchetti turned his body in and Harry leapt towards the front door. He pocketed the gun, quietly opened the door, stepped out and shut it again just as quietly. He began to run.

"Freeze asshole! Hands in the air!" a voice shouted from behind.

Harry spread both hands away from his body. He moved the fingers on his right hand.

"Don't think about it, Billy the Kid, we don't take kindly to trigger fingers."

Nelson Lear came up to him and patted him down. Lear pulled the .45 from his pocket. "Hey Sal, look what I found. You're busted, friend. Let's go see your friends in Atari Gems."

Sal Marrow held his gun on the suspect, as Lear opened the door to Atari Gems.

"I need to speak to Bill Barchetti? It's me, Nelson Lear."

Barhetti lay behind the counter, his face against the wall. "You fuckin idiots, I told you cops he was here! He walked out the door a minute ago!"

He stuck his head over the counter, "Stop your cryin," said Lear. He pulled Harry's head over it also, "Is this the guy?"

Barchetti struggled onto his good foot then grabbed the counter and pulled himself up. His flaring temper flowed like white water rapids. "That's the fuck. He broke my finger and ankle, threatened to break others if I didn't give him information."

"What kind of information?" asked Lear.

He cooled his temper immediately. "It's not important." Barchetti hopped closer to Officer Lear. He whispered, "I want this guy dead. He knows too much. If you and Marrow take him to Jersey and 'make him disappear,' it'll mean a quarter of a mil for each of you. We'll deposit it in a Swiss bank account, so no one'll know. You could both leave this rotten city. Problem is I need it done now. What da ya say?"

"Let me talk to Marrow," he replied. "I think he'll agree." He stepped over to his partner. Lear's hand covered the front side of Marrow's ear. Marrow nodded as Lear whispered away.

Barchetti watched their hands move until they nodded in agreement. Lear walked back to Barchetti.

"We're in, but how do we know you're not BS'ing us?"

"Come here," he said. Barchetti looked cautiously towards the office. He saw no salespeople. He limped to the diamond case, and grabbed two diamond tennis bracelets. "These are $25,000 each, take em," he told the officers. "Put'em in your pockets, but don't let the biker see'em. He 'stole' em."

Harry's mind reeled as he watched Barchetti over the diamond case. He saw Officer Lear quickly pocketing something. *I don't like where this is going. Two cops, probably on the take, and a jeweler who wants to see my balls flying from a flagpole. Randall and Johnny better do better than me.* He looked at the ceiling of the place. *Guys don't let me die in vain.*

Chapter 15
Home Sweet Home

August 17th 8pm Gio's Italian Restaurant:

"Signore Hillerman, Como stai?"

"Excellent. I feel wonderful, my usual table?"

"But of course," said the maitre-d'. He picked up a menu, led Henry through the busy restaurant and took him to a small table in the right hand corner beside a small stream, which trickled through an open garden.

"Thank you for saving my spot."

"But of course. You've only arrived the same time every Friday night for the past 10 years, this is Hillerman's retreat."

"That's sweet. Thank you. You know this place means more to me than anything in the world. He thought momentarily and added, "almost".

"Have a scrumptious supper, signore Hillerman."

Henry took the corners of the neatly folded cloth napkin and swung it back and forth until the folds fell loose. He covered his lap completely then opened an article on London in Conde` Nast. *I have to get out of New York! When I finish that diamond the first thing I'm going to do is take a world cruise to London, then Amsterdam and around Scandinavia. I'll visit Athens and watch nude women on the hot beaches of Greece, to Tuscany for some bruschetta and Chianti, and I can't miss Cairo and the pyramids. I can't imagine what it'll be like to have inexhaustible time and money. If only I was thirty again.*

The waitress arrived at his table, "What shall we get you this evening, Mr. Hillerman?"

"First, I'd like a dry martini. Is Enrico working the bar tonight?"

"Yes, he is."

"You know he make's the best dry martini I've ever tasted, don't you?"

"You're not the first to tell us that. I don't know where we'd be without him. He's a great bartender. Let me tell you what our daily specials are. First, we have Pasta Carbonera, an incredible dish of linguine, chopped bacon and a hint of parsley. Second, we have fresh tomato and mozzarella salad with black olives and our special house vinaigrette. Third, we have Osso Bucco, a beautiful dish that combines only the finest veal and Italian spices available in the US. It's bound to make your palate beg for more and is highly recommended by our chefs."

"It sounds wonderful, Penny. I should be ready with my decision when you return with the martini. Thank you."

The waitress left Henry's table and immediately greeted the bartender. She placed the order at the edge of the bar. When the bartender picked it up, he glanced across the restaurant, saw Henry, and waved. Henry waved back then buried himself in the Conde` Nast.

The waitress returned minutes later with his dry martini, "Enrico sends his regards. Are you ready to order?"

"Yes, I am. I'm going to order the Primavera Stroganoff."

"It's been sometime since you ordered the Primavera Stroganoff. Is it a special occasion?"

"No. The doctor says I can only eat my favorite dish once a month because of a blocked artery or something. Nothing really. Sometimes I listen, depends on how I feel. So I'm ready for the special. My rent's paid and the other bills are up-to-date, so while I'm celebrating, I'll visit the Marble Corridor for a few drinks afterwards. They're my only family outside of work," Henry said with a laugh.

"It's always good to make appearances," said the waitress.

"Besides, sometimes you need someone to bounce things off. I know the bartender Maury like I know Enrico- he's another good one."

"Sounds like a good way to top off an evening. I know they love you over there," said the waitress.

"It's good to be loved."

"Enjoy your drink, Mr. Hillerman and I'll be back shortly with your meal."

"Thanks, Penny."

Henry spent a half-hour with his dry martini, reading and dreaming, before the waitress served his meal. The magazine had captured his attention to the point that he couldn't put it down, so he laid it in front of him as he ate. When he finished his meal, he requested the check, refolded his napkin, and placed it back on the table. The bill came to $47.50 and he left $60.00 in the black bill folder. He stood up then gently grabbed Penny by the arm as she passed.

"Thanks for the wonderful service, Penny. I can always count on you. There's a little something in the folder for you. Make sure you pick it up before someone else does."

"Thank you Mr. Hillerman. We'll see you next week."

Gino ransacked Randall's bathroom in his relentless search for the diamond. He threw the contents from the cabinets all over the floor, bent down and stuck his head beneath the sink. He probed the darkness with his fingers and found his hand quickly covered in thick black mildew. *God, I better not get a disease from this filth.* He reached for a single creased towel that hung over the curtain rod, wiped his hand and threw it in the shower. His eyes scanned the corner of the shower's tile wall. *Looked behind the shampoo bottles and soap.* In a frustrated fury, he stormed out into the living room. *The print out said he bought an end table safe. The guys too poor to have it re-drilled, so I think I'd find it there.* He spotted the end table tucked away in the corner of the living room, so he ran over, and opened the cabinet door. Inside he found another steel door with a combination and a hand crank. He twisted the chrome handle and heard a loud clank, which opened the heavy door. He looked through the safe.

"Henry Hillerman, Henry Hillerman," he said. He tossed the man's personal papers over his shoulder. He reached into his pocket and pulled out a small flashlight attached to his key ring. He aimed it inside the safe, and then tilted back the shelves to make sure there was nothing caught between. *What the hell's all this useless crap! God damn expired license, used checks, what a waste of time!* Gino threw a small table towards the window in a fury. Its leg broke as it bounced from the floor. He tossed the couch on its side and noticed a small sack that fell forward. It swung from its perch like a glow stick in the night. *Finally, St. Anthony you've done it.*

He reached for the bottom of the couch. His calloused hand grabbed his hidden prize and ripped it from the staples that secured it to the wood. He opened the zipper. "Jesus!" said Gino. He grabbed the middle of the bills and flicked through the pile of twenties. "There's gotta be $5000.00 here!" He stuffed the pile of money into his pocket. *Some people are meant to live poor and you, my friend are one of them.*

"Johnny, it's only another block. Come on! These high heels are killing me!" said Randall.

"I'm sorry pal, I just can't stop laughing. You gotta walk like a woman, if you're gonna be a woman. You're the most awkward lookin lady I've ever seen! I've seen truckers walk better, but on the good side, ya gotta a cute behind."

Randall cussed quietly. "Watch your step, or we'll see just how quick ya are."

"You should pat me on the back instead of swearing under your breath. It's the perfect disguise."

"Really and sincerely, Johnny, I thank you. I'd probably still be locked up in Harry's friends place without your help."

"It's all right, Randall," he put his hand on his shoulder. "You know I'll always be there for ya, pal."

"My apartment's a little farther," he said. "I can't wait to contact Milly and find out Striker's progress. I want to see her."

"Are ya fallin for her Randall? You know it's only been a couple of days, maybe you shouldn't get your hopes up this early."

"I stepped in front of a freight train when I met her. I can't explain it, just got this feelin." He took a breath, "There's something I need your help with."

"What's that?"

"I need ya to help find Jessica Lovitska, a woman Harry knew long before his stint in prison. I want to reunite the two."

"It's an old girlfriend?"

"Yea. It's a long story which I promised Harry I'd never divulge. Don't mention her name to anyone."

"Mum's the word," Johnny said.

"I can count on you, right?"

"Yea," he moaned. "You can count on me. What time is it?"

"Noon. My building's the brownstone with the girders around it."

Johnny stared at the building, "looks like a squatter's residence."

"It's a shitty hole in the wall and ya can't get cheaper. It's a roof over my head and most of the time the water's warm."

"Wow, has Milly seen it?"

"You kiddin? I doubt I'll bring her by anytime soon, I'm too embarrassed to bring her here. She'd never wanta see me again! I think sometimes, she's just too classy for me," said Randall. "I wanta break in life, John. Just a little break."

"Don't bang yourself up about it. Maybe she'll accept you for yourself, what more could ya ask?"

"I can't take the risk. Hang on, let me get my keys." He pulled out the enormous key ring buried beneath his dress and sorted through.

"Let me go first, chief." Johnny replied. "Remember, I'll signal you from your window?"

"Here's the key, #162B on the third floor."

"If you don't see me in the next two minutes, don't enter," Johnny whispered. "I'll wave my hand back and forth if there's a problem. If there is, don't come after me."

"Right, later," said Randall. He crossed the street, and sat down on a bench at the edge of the curb. He watched the open curtains at his vacant apartment. Johnny slipped in through the plywood and jogged up the stairway. He spotted the shut door of Apartment #162B, crept up to the door, and stopped momentarily to listen. *Nothing.*

Gino's face was just outside the cabinet below the kitchen sink. He squinted to see the dark corners, bent over, and ran his fingers along the drainpipe only inches below a gun taped to the cabinet ceiling. He withdrew his hand quickly, when he hit a glob of sticky goo that surrounded a pipe seam. *Goddamn this place! Fucking shit!* He stood up, washed his hands in the kitchen sink, and then opened the refrigerator. In front of him was the half of a pastrami sandwich loaded on to a couple of pieces of rye bread. *Finally, something worth sinking my teeth into.* Gino went to the kitchen table and sat on an upright wood crate. His jaw opened wide to bite the pastrami. *No wonder the Goddamn guy's so thin. Hardly anything.*

He heard the jingle of keys and a slight turn of the door-knob, so he jumped up, and pressed his body flat against the wall. His head peeked from around the corner. The door slow-ly opened. He tucked his head back carefully.

"God damn fucking hinges! I bet Randall hasn't oiled'em since he moved to this sty," Johnny said to himself. Johnny's glare glazed over when he saw the couch on its side. Lamps were broken on the floor, rugs and clothes were tossed every-where. *Someone's found this place. It's like the remnant of a tornado ripping through Kansas.* He stood in the frame of the doorway shell-shocked. He surveyed the landscapes destruction then carefully listened. He took two steps into the apartment, his fingers wiggled, ready to run at a moment's notice. *Come on, baby.*

Gino's body was flush with the wall. He watched Johnny's foot come into view. The foot stopped then seconds later, it disappeared as he stepped to the right of the doorway. He tip-toed towards the bathroom like a Siamese cat.

Gino listened for any clue to the intruder's location. He

heard the squeak of a loose floorboard and recognized the same sound when he searched the place. *He's entering the bathroom.* Gino pulled a pistol from his shoulder holster and bobbed his head through the living room. He saw Johnny's back as he crept down the hall. From a distance, Gino shadowed Johnny like a church mouse. *Maybe, he knows where the stone is.*

Johnny popped his head in the bathroom. *Randall's gonna be bent when he sees this. What a mess.* He stood upright and walked in. *Something's not right here.*

Gino quickly crept across the floor and closed his distance to five feet. Avoiding the loose floorboard, he swept his right foot around and closed Johnny in. "Don't move. If you make even the slightest budge, my itchy finger will do the talking."

Shit. Johnny raised his hands. "I got nothin. Take whatever you want. I don't live here."

"So, who the hell are you, and why you lurkin around?" asked Gino.

"I live down the hall. Randall leaves me the keys to feed his cat. Have you seen him? Here kitty, kitty, kitty."

"Knock off the crap," said Gino, "I know you're friends with him. Where is he?"

"I don't know. I haven't seen him for days. The cat's been meowin' like crazy and I thought I'd come by to make sure he's fed. Poor cat," said Johnny. "Sometimes, he hides behind the curtains. Can I check?"

"No way. Don't think I'm gonna be stupid enough to let you by the window, so you can alert someone. Now, I want ya to get outta the bathroom and step to the side."

"You're the man," said Johnny.

Gino let Johnny pass and followed two-foot lengths behind. Johnny made his way to the window until he came to within a couple of feet of the windowpane. "Dammit, did you see that horsefly? It's enormous. These things get so big they've been known to prey on small children," He waved his hand back and forth pretending to shoo the fly away.

Is that Johnny's hand? Randall repositioned himself, backing up against the building. He held a hat, firmly on his head. *Not good, he's waving his hand back and forth.*

"What da ya think your doin, guy? There's no damn fly around this place," said Gino. "Are you trippin? Move aside and no false moves while I shut these curtains," said Gino. He kept the gun aimed on Johnny. Gino stepped close to the window to reach up for the curtain rod. He looked on the people below.

Randall pulled the large hat over his face before Gino focused on him. *Shit, Johnny shit.* He stood still as Gino's face looked down momentarily on his white and yellow frilled hat. *The goon from Columbus Circle!*

"I bet the woman under that hat must be cute as hell," Gino said.

"I doubt it," Johnny said under his breath with a smirk. He made an odd nasal noise in his attempt to subdue the cackle that boiled inside. Gino looked at him. He faked a cough. "Ahem! My allergies acting up."

Gino closed the curtains.

After a few moments, Randall glanced at the window. *I gotta go in.* He crossed the street and waited impatiently at the walkway. He finally bolstered enough confidence to open the barrier. He stood at the base of the stairs.

I've got to get help from Mrs. Alexander; she's got my spare keys. He walked to a doorway on the ground level of the building and rapped gently on the door, then a little harder.

"Who is it?" a voice warily asked.

Randall looked at his watch. *She usually gets her meals delivered about now.* "Meals on Wheels," he said in a falsetto voice.

"Very good," she responded. Mrs. Alexander went to the door and slowly unbolted the three deadbolts. She opened the door.

"What can I do for you, dear?"

"Mrs. Alexander, it's me, Randall. Please... you've got to help me!" he whispered.

"Randall, I only know one Randall, but he's not a woman." Her face changed suddenly. It drew back in recognition, and her mouth opened wide. He inserted his foot in the door and covered her mouth before it came.

"I know you've seen the news, but it's not true," he vowed. "One of the men who did it is in my place upstairs ready to gun me down. You've gotta believe me, I'm innocent." He held her hand tightly. "Please, I'm not gonna hurt you. I only need a favor," he pleaded.

With her mouth covered, Mrs. Alexander gently nodded.

Randall removed his hand gently. "A friend of mine went to check the apartment for intruders before me. The drapes closed as I watched from the street. Could you alert someone if I don't come out in a half-hour? It'd be an enormous help. My friend had my keys, so I'll need your set." He stopped for an instant. "Can you still act?"

"You know I was the best in the theater district decades ago."

"I've got an idea!" His eyes glimmered. "We can go there together, I'll knock on the door chaotically and pretend to be your sister looking for help after you've had a heart attack. We're gonna ask, no, beg Randall for help. Since he's not there, we'll beg his friend!"

The old woman looked at him, "Sounds exciting, but dangerous, Randall."

"It could be Mrs. Alexander, I won't deny that, but you'll save my soul. Don't you want to relive your glory? You remember all those dramatic roles you played when you were young? I know you were a famous. You could relive those times here. Only thing is your performance could make or break me, so I'd expect nothing less than your best."

"You know, you're quite the talker- you should be a Director," she said with a smile.

"My whole life's been played by ear, but now I'm outta time, Mrs. Alexander. We've gotta move," he said soberly. "Now, if you see me move quickly, and some kind of confrontation breaks out, I want you on the floor."

"Don't worry, I'll play your part, then you'll see why I was famous," she assured him. It'll be an Oscar performance."

"If I get outta this mess, you'll get more than an Oscar."

"It'll be my last and greatest performance!" she said enthusiastically.

"Now, keep it down while we sneak upstairs."

The two slowly crept up the stairs until they reached Randall's home. He put his ear on the door and listened carefully. *I can't hear a thing. Maybe they're in the bedroom.* "Mrs. A," he whispered, "you ready for your award winning performance?"

"You're such a cute boy," she whispered back. "Roll 'em."

Randall knocked loudly and erratically on his own door.

"Help! Help!" he yelled in a high-pitched voice. "Randall, I need your help! Sherry's having a heart attack! Please, you've gotta help me! I know you're there. It's an emergency!"

Alexander hunched over, clutching her chest. She coughed and fell to one knee. "Ohhhhh...please," she exhaled.

The thunderous knock came as a surprise, both men

jumped.

"Who the hell is that?" asked Gino.

"It's the other neighbor, Sherry Alexander," he replied. "She's a decrepit old woman, in poor health. It's gotta be something important," he paused, "she never bothers anyone. We've gotta check it out, or she'll knock until the door comes down."

"No," Gino said adamantly. "We wait quietly. As far as she knows, we're not home."

"I'm tellin you," Johnny continued, "it sounds like an emergency!"

The knock came again, louder than the earlier one. "God, please, Randall" the voice cried. "I know you're home. The paper's missing from the front door. It's been there for days. Sherry's gonna die if you don't help her!"

Randall, you son of a bitch, you don't get the paper! Thought Johnny. "If you don't let those women in, they'll have everyone in this whole building here to see what's happening," Johnny spouted arrogantly. "Jesus Christ, you don't want that do ya?"

"Get 'em in here quick, and no funny stuff!" Gino shouted.

Johnny pulled the door open violently. He saw Mrs. Alexander hunched over, as Randall winked at him.

"Where's Randall? Please, you've gotta help me!" Randall spouted in his disguise. He crouched over holding Mrs. Alexander's right arm.

"It's all right, we'll getcha help. Come in, come in," Johnny told them. He secretly moved his hand to his front and made a finger gun. He wiggled his thumb as if he was shooting it.

Guy's got a gun, shit. Randall bent his head at the chin, so the hat hid his face. He turned around, slightly nodded and backed into the apartment. Johnny stood back, as he dragged

Mrs. Alexander in.

Gino backed himself into the kitchen, pushed the gun into his pocket and watched the three people make their way to the couch. Johnny flipped the couch to its original position.

"My lord," exclaimed Randall. "Can you call 9-1-1 young man?" *All I need to do is get beneath the kitchen sink.*

"No, he can't," Gino answered from the kitchen. He faced the living room scene.

"Who's this?" Randall asked Johnny. He turned his face to Johnny avoiding Gino's eyes.

"Probably a burglar, but I'm not sure," Johnny replied.

Randall faced Gino, "please, we need medical help. Can't you see my sister's dying?"

"Do I know you?" Gino asked.

"Maybe you know one of my relatives. I'm from a big family," he said sweetly, "can I get her a cloth at least?"

Gino stared and surveyed Randall's body. His eyes were doused in blue mascara; blush filled his cheeks. His hair was pulled back beneath a brunette wig and the long eyelashes barely fit. Randall watched Gino's eyes stop at the pretend breasts Randall made. They stood erect, enough to fill a C-cup bra.

"Do you mind?" Randall said indignantly.

"Go," replied Gino, "get your cloth."

"So whadda we gonna do here, guy?" Johnny asked Gino. "The poor woman's dying. Come here, just look at her!" He pointed at Mrs. Alexander.

Gino looked at Randall and returned to the two on the couch.

In the kitchen, Randall turned on the faucet and ran it on high. He watched Gino walk to the couch, as he quietly opened the cabinet doors below the sink. He dipped his head and peered inside. He saw his gun taped to the cabinet's roof. He stood up, looked in the direction of the visitor, and nodded quickly to Johnny, mouthing the word "talk".

"What are you gonna do with us? I mean, if you're not careful…." Johnny collapsed to his knees and begged, "Please, I don't want to die!" The level of his voice rose, "I'm too young to die! I think I'm having a nervous breakdown."

Alexander gripped her heart tighter. She leaned forward, and fell onto the ground. Her face landed on a pile of shirts.

"Ohhh God!" she exclaimed. "Call 9-1-1!" she screamed. Her body curled up.

Amidst the screams from his friends, Randall ripped the gun from the tape.

"Easy lady," said Gino. He leaned over and placed his hand on her neck to check her pulse, his back towards the kitchen.

Randall stepped out of the heels to his bare feet and moved like a flash of light across the room. He brought the gun down on Gino, "don't move, unless of course you wanta lose your brains over the floor. I got my gun on your jugular, so if you so much as breathe too hard, my place'll be splashed with your blood. Drop the gun."

Gino froze. He listened to the tone of Randall's voice, reluctant to look back. His eyes shifted to look at Johnny's face as it turned from overwhelming anxiety, to absolute anger. He dropped the gun.

"Johnny, get it," Randall ordered. Johnny went to Gino, picked up the gun, gripped the handle tightly and pistol-whipped Gino's face.

Mrs. Alexander got up. "How'd I do?" she asked.

"An Oscar well deserved," replied Randall with a wink. He returned his stare to Gino. "What the hell are ya doin here?"

Gino looked at the floor in silence.

"Come on! Speak up or my friend here will play football with your face," Randall demanded angrily. "Were you expectin to find a stone, perhaps? Why do ya want it so badly? Answer me that!"

Gino didn't move, He stared at the patchy linoleum floor.

Johnny edged closer to his face. "I don't think you understand, friend. If you don't talk, we'll kill you and call it self-defense. Remember? You took me captive after I walked in on your robbery. Besides, the cops'll find this place sooner or later, and wouldn't it be a surprise if they found you here tied up? We'd be sure to leave a note for em'. You must have some kind of rap sheet, and in case you didn't know, the other person you set up, is also an ex-con. I'm sure he has plenty of friends to keep ya company in the pen. If you give us some answers, I'll put in a good word for ya. Now, I'll give you two minutes to think about it," he looked at his watch, "Time."

Johnny watched the second hand tick away. He held his finger to his mouth in a gesture to silence, his friends. They all stood peering at Gino in dead silence. Gino's body shifted. He looked at the ground, then up again at Johnny. Johnny's eyes were glued to his watch. He looked at Randall and Mrs. Alexander; they returned their stares. Gino's mind turned and his eyes shifted around the ground in hopes he would find some type of weapon. His sight returned to the barren floor in front of him.

"One minute," reported Johnny. Johnny, made a finger gun, and pulled back the imaginary trigger as Randall watched. Randall put his left hand on the mallet of his gun and cocked it back, raising his eyebrows in question.

Johnny nodded, confirming Randall's thoughts. He waved his hand in a stop motion and mouthed the words, "When I say."

Randall nodded back and stood awaiting Johnny's signal.

The silence remained.

Gino's body twitched then moved sporadically.

Randall pushed the barrel harder into Gino's head.

"You wouldn't pull that trigger," Gino said.

"I'm already framed for an attempted murder which I didn't do. If I kill you, I'll only end up where I was gonna end anyway. Try me."

"Now you better speak you fuckin asshole," Johnny spat, "You got 30 seconds."

Gino's body trembled as he felt the gun push into his skull. Again, the silence fell for another 15 seconds.

"Now! Who da ya work for and why are ya here!"

"OK, OK," Gino relented, "I work for Atari Gems." Gino pointed directly at Randall. "I was here tryin to find a clue to who he is."

"Johnny," Randall explained, "this guy followed me outta the gem shop yesterday." Randall redirected his gaze. "Who's your boss and why's he want me?"

"Sid Barchetti's my boss and when he wants somethin, he gets it."

"So, he wants my stone?" Randall asked angrily.

He shrugged. "Guess so."

"What did he say about it?"

"He said nothing. He didn't volunteer, I didn't ask. All I can tell you is he wants it, and that's why I'm here. I was sent to track you down," Gino replied. "Looks like I beat the cops." Abruptly, the song "Tubular Bells" sounded from his cellular phone attached to his belt.

Johnny stood back as he imagined Gino reversing the situation. He looked up at Randall in question.

"I want you to get that, and be really cool about it. John, hold the gun on him, cause I'm gonna listen in. It could be this guy Barchetti, tryin to see what he's found. If you make any false move, anything to let the other guy know you're in trouble, my friend here will torture you until your death. Understand?"

"Yea," said Gino. He picked up the receiver, "yea, Gino." Randall's head closed in.

"Gino, Barchetti. What the hell's going on?"

"I'm searchin the kid's place for the stone."

"I had some fabulous luck. I was visiting our friend Paul Striker in the hospital when I overheard a young lady named Milly Van Lowe-

Randall backed up in horror. He shook himself out of astonishment regained his sharpened senses and closed back in.

-she claims to own a store downtown, but she got really feisty when I asked her questions. I have a hunch she's with this guy, Randall. I think she was checking on Striker for their sake."

Randall grabbed a piece of paper and pen from the table and quickly wrote, "where are you?" He tapped his index finger hard on the pad facing Gino.

"Where are you?" asked Gino.

"I'm at a coffee shop with the girl called 'For the Sake of Coffee'. It's on 96th. and Madison. I'm sure I can occupy her for the next half-hour. Can you get here quickly? I need you to tail her."

Gino looked at the men. Randall nodded in unison with Johnny. "A half hour it is. I'll wait on the opposite side of the street for you to bring her out."

"Good. I'll see you then," said Barchetti. He hung up the phone.

Gino hung up the receiver and inhaled deeply, "do either of you have a cigarette?"

Randall pulled a pack of Marlboro's from his top pocket. He tapped the end of the pack and handed one to Gino. "We're gonna hop a cab. John, you hang on to that gun and I'll hold his. Hide it inside your pocket. Mrs. A., I'll reward you when I'm in the clear. You've been a tremendous help."

"My pleasure, boys. I'll keep my fingers crossed for you both. Good luck," she said.

"Good luck, Alex," said Johnny.

Randall grabbed Gino in his right arm, the gun in his left, and buried it in his pocketbook. They exited the building and hailed a cab. Randall slid across the seat first, then Gino and Johnny sealed him in.

"96th and Madison," said Johnny.

The cab took off.

Chapter 16
For the Sake of Coffee

August 17ᵗʰ, 1992 6pm Henry Hillerman's Apartment:

H enry opened his door and went straight to the bathroom. He unbuttoned his sweaty shirt and looked at his protruding ribs. He studied his sparse grey hair in the mirror. *Who is that strange old man?* He stepped closer and rubbed his palm against the grain of his sunken cheeks. He pulled his face down and tightened the loose skin beneath his aged eyes. The permanent bags disappeared until he released his hand. *Damn! If only I had a full head of hair again, some muscle, and firm skin. I'm so damn ugly.* One cough after another came until he sat down on the lid of the toilet seat. *I had better not come down with a cold. The last thing I need is to lose any time cutting. Only two months, Henry, then you can relax.* He took a deep breath. *I feel so weak.*

Henry put his hands on his knees and pushed himself up. He took his silk robe from behind the bathroom door and draped it over his shoulders. His crooked old fingers reached inside the pocket of his pants and pulled the clean velvet pouch out. He buried it in his hand and walked into the kitchen, opened the refrigerator door, and looked inside. The bottle of VO and milk filled the barren landscape like an oasis on a desert-filled plain. He grabbed the VO and a crystal glass from the cabinet. Two ice cubes clanked into the glass, which he filled halfway with the aged scotch. He licked his lips before he sampled the drink, and exited the kitchen, moving to the living room couch. The small indentation on the cushion fit him like a glove. He put his scotch down on the coffee table, and leaned over to open the cabinet door. Inside was a large steel door. He spun the locking dial right then left and right again until he pulled the door free. The safe opened. *In you go precious one.* He bent down and pushed his whole arm into the safe. He wedged the diamond pouch at the back and jarred the top shelf until the diamond sat securely. He returned the door to its place.

The CNN theme blared on the television. He watched the headlines scroll by and listened to the news updates. He sipped his whisky and 20 minutes later got up for a refill. When he finished his second drink, he dragged himself into a hot shower. His pores opened and he felt the days poison wash from his wrinkled body. The steam rejuvenated him enough to revitalize his hunger for human contact. When he stepped from the shower, he opened the medicine cabinet, grabbed Vitalis, and rubbed it through the thin hairs that glazed his scalp. Old Spice filled his palm and splashed over his neck. He massaged it into his cheeks and neck, and the remainders down his chest.

"Like a new shell!" he said. He walked into the bedroom, pulled open his chest of drawers, and grabbed a tan pair of khakis and a green knit shirt. He slipped them on and returned to the mirror. *That's better! I feel young again! Now, I can be seen in public!*

"Dinner, here I come!" he said as he exited his apartment.

Sid Barchetti stepped into the coffee shop and jogged up to the counter, "sorry, Milly. I had to make that phone call. I have a customer coming in later to pick up a diamond ring. It was finished, but the size needed adjustment. She takes a size 8 ¼."

"Not a problem, Mr. Barchetti."

"Call me, Sid."

"Ok, Sid. Have you ever been here before? I love the lounge music echoing from the back of the room."

"The name of the band is Sunrise, Sunset- I saw it on a chalkboard when we entered. Unusual, eh?"

"Yes, but beautiful. You know I was once in interior design. The back room has the same vibe I try to create; it's like a sketch in my notebook. See the plush maroon couch with the bamboo coffee table, the one with papers draped all over it? I had a similar set up in a room I named Africana. The abstract paintings are so varied; they must be from local artists. What an eccentric atmosphere. The music adds a hint of the sublime. I'll learn from this," said Milly.

"I like the fact they have a bar to the left of the room. How many coffee shops have bars built in?"

"It's the first I've seen. Looks like all the living room chairs and couches overlook the stage. The acoustics are fantastic!"

"It does sound clear," replied Sid. "If you ask me, I'd be drawn in by the smell. These croissants are making my mouth water. I may have to order a full course of these crumb cakes." He picked one up the size of a softball. "Jeez, feel the weight of this! It must weigh two pounds!"

Milly grabbed it. "Impressive, I've never eaten crumb cake this dense before, it'd make a whole meal. I'll get a miniature pecan pie; it's my favorite."

"Would you like a cappuccino?" Sid politely asked, "It's on me."

"That sounds fabulous," she replied. "I hope the coffee is as good as the atmosphere."

"Me too," he agreed. He went to the register, "two cappuccinos, a crumb cake, and this pecan pie."

"Will that be all?" the clerk asked him.

"For now."

"That'll be $14.00," she replied.

Sid pulled out a 20-dollar bill and handed it to the clerk. He received his change and went with Milly to the back room.

"That was awfully sweet of you, Sid."

He replied with a smile, "It's my pleasure." Sid sat himself on a plaid recliner.

She grabbed one of the newspapers scattered on a nearby table and flipped through it briefly. She placed it back on the table and turned to Sid, "these papers look well read. I wonder how many hands they've found their way into?"

"Probably hundreds," Sid replied, "it wouldn't surprise me if some of them were fished out of trash bins."

"Ewwww," she made a face. "Now that's a disgusting thought."

"The homeless constantly pull newspapers from garbage cans. It's disgusting," responded Sid. "Who knows what kind of disease you could get."

Milly rethought her reactive statement. "We really shouldn't criticize the homeless. If you ended up there, what would you do?"

"I wouldn't end up there," Sid said with resentment. "I'd resort to stealing first."

Milly was taken back by the statement, "but what about ethics? I mean, who would you steal from?"

"Anyone," he said with a shrug. "Who wants to live on the street?"

Milly thought about this for a minute before she answered his question. "I suppose there are some of us who'll adhere to principles that could take us into the bowels of a penniless life. I know there are people who get there because of their own selfish ideals, but I believe there are those who are in the wrong place at the wrong time and as a result, become homeless. I've heard of people who have gone from rich to poor and back again." She looked at his skeptical look.

"I'd like to hear you name one," he said with a sneer. "These people are miserable urchins. If they're homeless, they deserve to be, no matter what their circumstances are. If they worked hard for a living, there should be no reason they're homeless."

"I don't think you understand, Sid. First of all, if you were homeless with only a couple of rags on your back, how are you going to get a job?" She leaned forward in her seat and looked at him annoyed.

"By using your brains," Sid replied defiantly.

Milly snorted at this, "Who's going to let you use your brains if you look like a bum? Didn't you just tell me you would steal from anyone to keep you from getting there? You're a man of action…brains? I don't know."

Sid's face soured with anger. *The nerve of this little bitch.* Sid reached into his top pocket for his pack of cigarettes. He tapped the box and pulled a cigarette from it. He quickly lit it and took an enormous drag. He sat back, blew the smoke from the corner of his mouth, and regained his cool.

"And I suppose you would choose homeless life because of your principles?" he asked her calmly.

"Really, I don't know," she honestly replied. "I'd never want to make the choice of homelessness for my principles. I suppose we all make decisions, some right, some unethical. I can only hope that if I have to choose, I choose the right and ethical path. I'd rather die a free spirit than die bound by the chains of hell."

"You have no clue what you're talking about," he spewed at her. "There's no such thing as a martyr, lady. How'd we end up on this thing anyway?"

She frowned at him, "you started it with the newspaper thing."

He gritted his teeth and inhaled, "I see." He paused. "Let's talk about something else."

"I'd prefer that."

"So, what do you think of the coffee?"

"It's delicious, but the music is even better. Do you like this type of music, Sid?"

"It's wonderful. I like the early greats like Frank Sinatra, Ella Fitzgerald, Duke Ellington, along with this lounge music." He opened his eyes and looked at her. "How about you?"

"I like a little of everything from punk rock to smooth jazz like the ones you mentioned."

He was stunned, "punk? That's for idiots. It's pointless aggression."

"It's expression in aggression. You should really open your soul."

Sid's patience wore thin as he abruptly answered, "My soul enjoys soothing music like an opera. The expression's true."

"So, is the expression in aggressive music. I suppose it's in the way we react to stimuli around us. Those who bottle up anger tend to self implode, unless they find a useful source of release. The mosh pit is acceptable form of behavior where kids release those feelings. It's constructive, instead of destructive behavior. I don't suppose you've ever witnessed violence in a mosh pit," Milly said. "It's an oddity, but I was in one or two when I was younger. I felt uplifted after it." She had a faraway look in her eye.

"It's childish; foolish," he said. "No matter what argument you raise, I won't change my feelings regarding this."

"You're set in your ways and that's all right," she patronizingly replied. She sipped her coffee and bit her pecan pie.

"How long have you known Paul?" Sid inquired.

"A few years," she replied, "he's a very kind man." Milly calmly took another sip and quickly changed the conversation. She pointed at the band on stage, "have you seen these people play before? They're good."

"No, I haven't," he answered then redirected it back, "do you know Paul's wife?"

"Yes, I've met her once, quite some time ago," she said, "at a trade show."

If she really knew Paul as she claims to, she'd know he was never married. He's probably as queer as a three-dollar bill. "What trade show was that?" he arched an eyebrow at her.

"Here in the city. What's the name of that building? My mind's drawing a blank."

He leaned forward in his chair and looked with eyebrows drawn, "you're talking about the Marriott in Times Square?"

She shifted uncomfortably, "Yeah," she said. She avoided his glance, "sorry, my mind's not been right. Do you think he'll be OK?"

Wrong, Missy, it's the Javits center. He sat back. "Not sure really," he said. "I hope they get these guys soon. Imagine, gunning someone down in Central Park. They should hang."

"What if the guys didn't do it?" she asked.

"What do you mean? The motorcycle came and picked up his accomplice after the jeweler was gunned down. It's been all over the news."

She went on the defensive, "I'm sure they're guilty, I'm just playing devil's advocate here." *Could they be guilty?* Milly rubbed her temples with the middle finger of each hand. "I hope he wakes from his coma soon. I'd love to speak with him."

"I'm sure you'll have that chance soon." *Not if I get my way you won't, thought Sid.*

Milly thought, he looks so relaxed. Maybe I should tell him, he seems like an honest guy. He's a jeweler. He might believe me.

"Mr. Barchetti?" she quietly asked.

"Yes, hon?" he replied, as he looked back at her.

She shifted in her seat. "I have this friend, who's got some problems," she began. "He tells me I have to believe him and that he's an innocent bystander of an incident."

He leaned closer. *Come on baby, tell me what you know.* "What type of incident," he asked gently.

"This friend hasn't been a good friend for long, but you know they say you can see someone's soul through their eyes."

Sid leaned back to avoid her gaze, "of course."

"His soul's good, I feel it, but I haven't known him long enough to tell. He's asked me to watch out for him, even though the arrows point to him being guilty. Should I trust my heart?"

Sid thought for a minute, "I think we're misguided by our hearts. Let your brain answer, it'll bring you to the ultimate truth. If you haven't known him long, you should ask about his past. Certainly you can't judge him based on a few moments you've had together. It takes years to earn a strong level of trust. Maybe after a few years together you'll be able to learn that."

If we have a few years together, Milly thought. "There's something about him," she continued. "It's as if we've known each other for years, when in actuality we've only known each other for days. It's like we're mystically connected. Have you ever felt that with someone?"

"Can't say I have. I'm a man dedicated to my work. If you get attached to someone or something at first sight, it's just an obsession. I'm obsessive, but I'm not mystical. I've had many girlfriends throughout my life, but none I'd consider to be a soul mate."

"That's it. He feels like; my soul mate," she thoughtfully said.

Gold, this is pure gold. Wait 'til I get that guy. Mystically together; soul mate; they're practically married if she had her way. "You know, sometimes a person can judge a character by his name. My guess is his name begins with an 'R'. Robert maybe?"

Milly was nervous, "you got the letter but not the name," her heart sputtered, "try again."

"Ralph? No, scratch that, I can't see you with a Ralph, Ron maybe. Wait, what's your last name?"

Milly smiled, "Van Lowe. It's Milly Van Lowe."

"Sounds Dutch," he said. "Van Lowe. Hmmm. What would fit with Van Lowe? How about Randall?"

Her eyes opened like two large saucers. "That's incredible," she said breathlessly. "How did you….."

"…Let's call it mystical. Sometimes, I simply get a feeling."

"It's amazing," she replied. "You're an interesting man, Mr. Barchetti." She sat back and started to think.

He did the same.

"Can't this cab move faster?" demanded Randall.

"Its gridlock, kid," spat the driver. "I can't help it if you chose the wrong time to take a cab."

"We'd be better off in the subway," Randall grumbled. He threw his back against the seat.

"Randall, take it easy," Johnny urged. "We'll be there soon. Barchetti's not going anywhere cause he's waiting for this guy.

Milly will be fine, besides what could happen at a coffeehouse named 'For the Sake of Coffee'? A crack head overdoses on caffeine, right?" The statement brought a smile to his face as Johnny tried to ease Randall's tension.

"Crackhead," he said, "that word always makes me laugh. Thanks Johnny."

"What are friends for?" he chuckled. "Now, what are we gonna do about this guy? How we gonna work this?"

"I'm not sure yet." Randall's head turned to look out the window. "Hopefully, Barchetti will be outside the coffeehouse when we arrive. We can approach from a couple of blocks down. We'll exchange this guy for Milly."

Johnny looked out his window. "You know, he wants the stone. If he's willing to kill for it once, who's to say he won't take his own man's life?"

"Hey, wait a minute. No offense, but he'd never take my life," Gino chimed in. "We've been loyal to each other for decades."

"Even for a diamond worth millions?" whispered Randall.

"Millions?" Gino's eyes popped when he looked at Johnny. "He has me looking for a stone worth millions? He didn't utter a word why we're making these sacrifices."

"Hasn't he always kept you in the dark?" Johnny replied with a shot. "You're willing to go to jail for him, but he's not willing to tell you what the deal means for you. If you ask me, that's no friend."

Gino sat back. *Maybe they're right. Could Sid take me for a loyal idiot? I bet the fucker is. He better cut me in on part of this take, cause I'm not gonna be his puppet any longer.*

"We're approaching 94th. We can walk there from a safe distance," Johnny suggested. He looked to Randall for approval.

"Yeah," Randall agreed, "good plan." He leaned forward and addressed the driver. "Let us off here, cabby."

The cab pulled to the side of the street. Randall hastily paid the fare, and the three men climbed out.

"There it is," Johnny said quietly. 'What time is it?"

"It's a quarter to two," replied Randall. "It's taken us 40 minutes to get here," Randall asked Gino, "do ya think he'll be outside, guy?"

Gino looked angry. "Why should I tell you?"

"Cause my gun's aimed at your kidney," Randall threatened. "You ever seen a kidney explode from gunfire?"

Gino smirked as he answered, "actually, I have."

Johnny interrupted. "Come on, move," he ordered. He pushed Gino along.

They walked up the opposite side of the street towards 96th when they saw Barchetti emerge with Milly Van Lowe. She didn't look scared of him, on the contrary, they were engaged in a cheerful conversation.

Randall looked concerned. *Be careful, honey, be careful. You're a naked sheep in the wolf's den. Please let this work.* Randall looked at Johnny, "what do ya say, champ? Wanna make a little noise?"

"Oh, yea." Johnny's smile grew crooked then slowly lit his face from ear to ear.

"I've got an idea!" Randall said with a glow of inspiration. "Cross the street and move in on them. He doesn't know you. I'll keep this guy with me at gunpoint and attract Barchetti's attention. You run and grab Milly out of his reach. He'll make a grab for her, but I know you'll do it when the time is best. Do it quick and make sure she's safe. I trust your judgment."

"Come on, Randall, say it," Johnny grinned.

Randall sighed with a smile. "OK, they don't call ya quick Johnny for nothin."

Johnny winked, gave the OK sign and proceeded across the street.

Chapter 17
Awakening

P aul Striker's body lay motionless. *The ice, please remove the ice, it's too cold. Why can't they hear me? I'm speaking as loud as I can. Let me go!* His heart monitor jumped to and fro like a girl skipping through the park. His pupils dilated beneath his eyelids. *Don't let that man near me. He wants to kill me. Let me out of this ice cylinder. Is it ice or is it glass? Will it break or will it freeze me? Could someone please throw a stone, bring a heater inside my dream? I want to wake up. Nurse, please shake me!*

A signal went off at the nurses' station and a nurse ran to his bedside.

"Mr. Striker, can you hear me? Mr. Striker?" She placed her hand on his head.

I see the light through the ice. Why are all these prisms in my dream? I can see my hand- I can break through it with my hand! Striker's hands remained alongside his body. *Reach, Paul. You can get to it. Your heat will melt the surface and it'll fall away! That's it! Break the surface! Part the water and I'll be able to breathe!*

His head lurched back into his pillow, and slid to the side like a badly punted football. He inhaled deeply and his eyes shot open. They maniacally surveyed the white room as they darted in fear. His heart raced.

"Mr. Striker, Mr. Striker. You're in the hospital. Please relax," urged the nurse. "You've been in a coma, but you're OK."

He inhaled deeply again and again. He looked at the equipment attached to his body. "Where are they?" he asked groggily. "You've gotta find them!"

"You're delirious, Mr. Striker," the nurse told him. "Please calm down." She turned to the doorway and yelled to the nurses' station, "Call Lieutenant Cusick of the NYPD. Tell him Paul Striker's out of his coma!"

Striker grabbed her and said urgently, "You don't understand. He said he'd kill me and he walked off with the woman who was here. She's in danger too. He'll stop at nothing."

"Easy now. You've got to calm down, you're paranoid. You don't want a heart attack do you?" said the nurse.

Striker took a deep breath in, held it a second, then let go. "Nurse, the man who came in before was the man responsible for my shooting. He is hunting the man with me when I was shot." He ripped off his monitors and made an attempt to get up, but the nurse quickly restrained him.

"There's nowhere you're going tonight, Mr. Striker. The police are on their way. They've been anxious to talk to you and find out exactly what happened. You're lucky to be alive. You lost a lot of blood," said the nurse. "Be patient, the police will be here momentarily and they'll apprehend the culprits."

"There's not much time, Sid Barchetti said he'd kill me shortly. I also heard the woman speak to me."

"Why? Why would this man want to kill you?" she asked.

He refocused on his surroundings and calmed down. Again, he inhaled deeply then looked at his nurse. He gained his composure, "For a diamond."

Chapter 18
The Sting

Johnny ran across Madison Ave. and leaned on a building close by. He wandered to within 25 feet of Barchetti and Van Lowe, carefully watching his friend in the distance. Randall nodded his head.

Johnny lit a cigarette and began to smoke. He watched Randall walk close to their captive, as they edged their way up Madison Ave.

"Milly, if you wait a little longer, you'll be able to meet my best friend and associate," said Barchetti.

"I told you Sid, I don't want to meet your friend. I'm dating someone. I have no interest," said Milly. She went to walk away, but Barchetti's hand caught her arm.

"You're not going anywhere, sweet. Surprise," said Barchetti. Her eyebrows closed in and her face grew red with anger. She looked down at her stomach and found a gun pointed at her.

"I don't understand, I-

"I need your friend, Randall," said Barchetti. "He has something I want and to get it, I'll need you."

"Hey you ugly mother fucker!"

Sid turned to find Randall with a gun to Gino's ribs, "What the-

"Randall, thank the Lord you're all right!" yelled Van Lowe with excitement.

Barchetti stood in bewilderment. He watched Randall pull Gino closer.

Milly Van Lowe stood only feet from Barchetti, when she was airborne. Johnny's hand grabbed the girl with such velocity, he sent her through the air and into a spin. Her legs fell out and hit Barchetti, throwing him off balance. Johnny's hand fixed on her like the metal on a fresh weld. Before she had time to think, her legs moved in the same direction as Johnny's.

"Run Milly, run for your life!" shouted Randall.

Instantaneously, Barchetti snapped out of shock. His fingers clawed her arm to retain her, but he lost his grip and fell backwards.

Gino's reflexes sparked at Randall's distraction. He leapt, at Randall's right hand, grabbed the gun, and aimed it towards the sky. Both men wrestled for control. Randall head butted Gino, but his grip hadn't faltered. Gino jabbed Randall with his left hand, while Randall leaned all his weight forward into his knee. It connected with Gino's groin and the man fell over in pain.

Sid Barchetti had a split second to react to both situations. He saw Johnny and Milly run like a couple of cheetahs, moving faster each second and he saw his man fighting for control over the gun. He directed his attention to his comrade and decided to make his way across the busy thoroughfare. The cars honked in a mad hysteria, as he dodged the on coming traffic.

"Face it, Becks, you're caught," spouted Gino as he pulled Randall's legs out from his stance. The man threw all his weight into Beck's midsection. He fell and smashed his hand into the concrete. The force loosened his grip and bounced the gun on to the pavement. Gino kicked it from Beck's reach and pounded him into the concrete.

"Hang on to him, Gino! I'm almost there!" screamed Barchetti. The brakes of an on coming taxi sounded like a siren. The driver missed Barchetti by inches and Barchetti, hit the curb in a run.

Gino's strength and endurance overpowered Becks, as he desperately tried to free himself. He threw an elbow to Gino's face. *I've got to get clear of here!* He pushed Gino backwards to the cement and leapt to his feet. Sid Barchetti stood erect in front of him; his gun aimed at his heart.

"You're caught my friend. Now, I think we have some talking to do." He looked at Gino, "hail a cab, Gino, before the cops show."

Gino wiped his bloody nose, hailed a cab and disappeared with Becks and Barchetti.

Johnny and Milly took cover under the doorway of Saint Agnes Church. "Randall ordered me to get you out of there at all costs, so sit tight. I think we shook him. I'm gonna scout out the situation."

Johnny ran back from the church in time to see Barchetti, Gino and Randall disappear in a taxi. *God dammit! Where's Harry when ya need him!*

Johnny returned to the church, moments later. He moved like a sidewinder down the aisle, until he found Milly Van Lowe 6 pews from the front, bowed in prayer. He slid into the pew.

"Milly, they've got Randall. I saw them leave in a cab. Any idea where they might be going?"

"I have no clue, but I have the feeling Barchetti will visit Paul Striker again at the hospital. Maybe we should go there first."

"Good idea," said Johnny, "let's see Striker."

Chapter 19
The Confession

T he police arrived 15 minutes after the hospital's phone
call. Two officers stood next to Paul Striker's bed side.

"Lieutenant Cusick, we've known each other a long time.
I'm tellin you the truth!" said Striker.

"But this stone you're tellin me about would have international acclaim. It'd be known the world over."

"You don't understand. The guy who originally owned it
had millions of dollars worth of diamonds passing through
his hands constantly. He was the perfect diamond cutter; think
about it. If you handled diamonds all the time, wouldn't your
own diamond be just like any other object? Now, I'm sure he
understood the value behind such a stone, but maybe he was
more concerned with what he could make it, he was an old
man. If you were an artist and given a million dollars worth
of supplies, wouldn't you want to take your time to produce
the best possible piece of artwork you could? Besides, it's not
about the original owner anymore; it's about the guy who owns
it now. He has no clue what he's on to. I was shot trying to
explain this to him. The man who's after the diamond and shot
me is, Sid Barchetti."

"Sid Barchetti of Atari Gems? We know he's had his hands in dirty dealings, but no matter what we do, we can't make anything stick. He never gets caught with his hands in the pot."

"I know you can nail him this time. Barchetti has an insatiable appetite for gems. This diamond would make him one of the most powerful men in our trade. This guy, Randall Becks has it, and if I know Barchetti, he'll do anything to get it." Striker paused momentarily, "I'm willing to testify against Sid Barchetti."

"You know what that means."

He looked at the ceiling and inhaled deeply, he returned his glance to Lieutenant Cusick, "forgive me, my silence was to protect the family business. "

"What are you talking about?"

"I've been protected."

"Protected from what?" asked Cusick.

"Protected from the riffraff. He's in the protection racket."

"We've expected that for sometime, Paul. But we've never had anyone ready to testify against him," said Cusick. "Its dangerous."

"I'm ready," said Striker with confidence.

"You're ready to go to court? Why, now?"

Striker responded, "If I don't confess, I'll have to live with the agony and guilt of innocent deaths. I'm not going to hide my head in the sand the rest of my life. Randall Becks is a victim, with more at stake than he knows. I was shot over this, and that was the last straw. I love my business, I love my people, but there's a time you draw the line. Today's my day."

"Excuse me, excuse me," said a woman at the door. "Mr. Striker, you're awake! The nurse told me, but I refused to believe it. Thank, God."

"Who are you?" asked Striker.

"Well, you don't know me, but I'm a friend of Randall Becks- name is Milly Van Lowe. I spoke to you only hours ago when you were in a coma."

"You're the woman!"

"Yes, I'm Randall's girlfriend. I came here to pray for your recovery," she said. "We need your help."

"Come in, please come in. I heard you when I was under," Striker softly said.

Milly and Johnny walked into the room. Johnny cautiously eyed the policemen, who came to a stop at the end of the bed. "This is my friend Johnny. He protected me from a man named-

"Sid Barchetti," said Striker, interrupting. He turned to Van Lowe, "Barchetti threatened to kill me while I was in a coma."

"He threatened to kill you?" she asked.

"Yes, only a short time before you came here."

"He has Randall. Do you know where he might be?" asked Van Lowe.

"If he had to interrogate him, he'd probably take him to Atari Gems. I'm sure he has some hidden bunker in the back of his shop, where he can 'talk' to people. It's only a hunch."

"I think it's time to pay Atari Gems a visit." Cusick said. He turned to his assistant, "I wanta know everything about this guy before we raid his place. Get on the horn and see what you can find out. Look into what officers are in the area and send a couple to scout the place out. Don't tell 'em anything until we have a defined plan."

Cusick's assistant telephoned the station and the dispatcher put out the call.

Officer's Marrow and Lear were taking Harry "the Heckler"

into the squad car when they heard the APB, "any officers in the immediate vicinity of 48th and 6th Avenue, respond. We need a unit to Atari Gems on the northeast corner of 48th and 6th over."

Sal Marrow leaned into his open car window picked up the radio's mouthpiece, and spoke into it. "Marrow here. Nelson and I are practically in front of the place." He winked at Lear. "We got it covered."

The dispatcher replied, "Scout the place out and report back…If there's no trouble, wait for direction. Over."

"Got it," replied Marrow, "waiting."

Sal Marrow looked at Lear, then at Harry. He smiled. "This could be good for us Nelson. Let's sit tight before we trek over to Jersey."

"Lieutenant," said the dispatcher, "we have officers Marrow and Lear on the scene. How do you want me to advise?"

Cusick looked at Striker with a puzzled look. *Weren't those two guys being investigated by Internal Affairs? Seems awfully coincidental.* He spoke to the dispatcher, "Something's not right. Tell them to route around for a half-hour while I get my bearings. Tell'em not to alert anyone, until I say so."

"Roger," said the dispatcher.

Cusick hung up the line and picked up another. He dialed the phone.

"Internal Affairs, how may I direct your call?"

"This is Lt. Cusick of NYPD. I'm investigating a situation and I need the status of officers Sal Marrow and Nelson Lear. Can you tell me their allegations and a reason for their investigation?"

"One moment," said the clerk. "Your ID number please."

"645NY2112 Cusick."

"Thank you, one moment," replied the clerk. He came back a moment later, "they're under investigation for theft, blackmail, and suspicious activity. Anything else Lieutenant?"

"No," he responded, "that'll be it. Thanks." He hung up the phone and turned to his assistant. "I want a copter over 47th Street, and a squadron of police ready to dispatch when needed. We have to move on this," he ordered. "Milly and Johnny; I want you with me. We're gonna keep you safe. I know we'll need your help."

Chapter 20
The Proposal

The cab driver pulled his taxi to the curb in front of Atari Gems, "will this do it?" he asked.

"Perfect," replied Barchetti. He turned his head to Becks and sinisterly whispered, "Now, I don't want a word from you. If you give anyone so much as a hint about what's happening, I'll get your girlfriend back and make sure she dies a slow painful death."

Randall nodded and followed Gino out of the cab. They all looked at the squad car that the cab had pulled in front of. Nelson Lear leaned against it. Barchetti walked over.

"Nelson Lear," he said cheerfully, "it's been a long time, wonderful to see you again. I hope everything's in order."

Lear shook his hand, "Everything's fine. Your brother contacted me regarding some suspicious activity at the store." He pointed into the back of the police car, "when we arrived we found this biker who caused a little trouble with Bill rushing out. Bill and I made an agreement to his future. We're gonna take him out of the picture for ya."

Harry shifted his body close to the window and recognized his friend. His eyes opened wide with astonishment. Harry threw his shoulder into the car door in anger. It distracted all the men, except Randall who shook his head back and forth behind Sid's back. Randall quickly made a gun out of his hand and then a circle around the men, indicating all of them had guns.

Harry understood immediately. He nodded to Randall.

"He looks a little upset don't you think?" Lear said to the men, "But back to business. Dispatch contacted us moments ago. We think something's going on," said Lear.

"Let's not discuss it here. Why don't you gentlemen come in for a few minutes, so we can talk," Sid suggested. He turned his back on the police car and closely approached the officers. He whispered, "I have a second proposition for you I think you'll find," he stalled for a moment, "attractive."

"All right," said Lear. "Let me get Marrow and we'll talk. You have a private office we can talk in?"

"Yes, you'll be safe to speak." Barchetti nodded his head at Becks, "My proposition involves this man here. Can you cuff him and put him with the biker while we talk?"

Lear looked at Becks. Randall shrugged his shoulders, and then held out his hands. Officer Lear cuffed him and threw him in the car. The two officers walked with Sid Barchetti into Atari Gems.

"Nice mess, huh?" Randall said to Harry as he tried to get comfortable. "How'd you end up caught?"

Harry looked at Randall, "I was extracting information from Bill Barchetti inside the store. You know, about the stone?"

"Know about what?" asked Randall.

"You were right," Harry said pointedly.

"No," Randall looked incredulous, "you're not bullshitting me are you?"

"We're sittin here, in a cop car together. We're either going to prison or gonna die. Barchetti wants the diamond and they're gonna torture us for its whereabouts. The cops are on the take. They arranged a deal before you got here."

"What kind of deal?"

"A deal to dispose of me. Now, that you're here I'm not sure what they'll do," shrugged Harry.

"They'll want answers first, I'm sure of it. Is there a way outta here?"

"No," Harry guaranteed, "these babies are like Fort Knox. Once you're in, there's no gettin' out, unless they take ya out."

"There must be somethin we can do."

"Sit tight and if we're lucky, we'll get a chance to make a move later."

Randall looked doubtful, "Whatever you say."

Officers' Lear and Marrow followed Barchetti to the back of his empty shop, where they opened a private door. Inside the room was a corridor, then another locked door, and within that, another locked door. When he released the lock to the final door, Barchetti opened it to reveal a large padded room.

"Nice soundproofing," said Morrow.

"I don't like disruptions, I had the best installed," replied Barchetti. "Take a seat, gentlemen. Can I get you some coffee, maybe espresso?"

"I take it black," responded Morrow.

"Me too," said Lear.

"Two black coffees, it is. I'll be right back," he said.

Lear turned to Morrow, "this deal's getting sweeter by the second. We can't push Barchetti cause of what he has on us, so look at me and nod once if we gotta sweeten the deal more, nod twice if you're happy. Together our strength is best."

"Agreed," replied Morrow.

Barchetti returned, "It'll be a few minutes. Now, you said Bill already made a deal on the biker. The man I brought you has a stone I need, so he needs rigorous questioning. It's something for my private collection. As it stands, it's uncut and all I need to know is its location. I've invested a lot of time and money into it already, and I won't be happy until I get it. My deal- you bring me the stone and dispose of the two men. For that, I'll give you one million dollars each. You get a $100,000 cash advance, and the remainder will be paid into a Swiss bank account." Barchetti turned around, and ducked below his desk, removed a panel from the floor, and quickly worked the combination to his safe. When it clicked open, he pulled out a briefcase, which he threw on the table. He opened it in front of the two officers. "There's one hundred thousand dollars here, if you care to count it. All in $20.00 bills for easy spending. You have my word."

Both men sat dumbfounded. Lear looked to Morrow for approval and responded gleefully to his second nod. "Mr. Barchetti, both Sal and myself will be happy to do the job. We'll find you the stone and take care of the men."

"I want it in my hands for the balance to be paid. I also need proof of their death. Their heads should do the trick."

"You have our word," said Lear.

"Take the briefcase. I expect to hear from you in the next few days. Should you decide to take the money and run, I'll expose you both to the press and track you down no matter where you go. I don't have to tell you the consequences. If you do as I instructed, you can retire to South America. I think it's an easy choice," said Barchetti.

"Easy as pie," said Morrow.

Lear reached for the handle of the briefcase and pulled

it against his side. He looked at Morrow, "we should get to work."

"What about the APB?"

"We'll wing it. It'd be better to drop the briefcase off, shoot over to Jersey, and come back if anything creeps up. We can tell HQ we got a lead from Atari's and went in hot pursuit of Paul Striker's assailant," said Lear.

"Do you think they'll go for it?" asked Morrow.

"Definitely," Lear replied.

Chapter 21 '
Like the Wind

"This is the Bear. We're flying high over 47ᵗʰ. Car 62 is in our sights and we're waiting direction."

"Bear, this is Detective Cusick. We're in car 154 and plan to rendezvous with car 62 shortly. I need you to watch'em and keep me informed. Officers Lear and Morrow are shaking down a gem dealer, so if the car moves let me know."

"Bravo Cusick, we'll fly far above the building undercover. Be in touch," said the pilot.

Cusick turned to Van Lowe, "our pilot's got car 62, officers Lear and Marrow squad car in his sights. I have a good hunch your boyfriend's in the shop. If they're interrogating him, we could be awhile, but don't worry; we'll have it worked out soon."

"Can't you do anything, now?" she asked, "he could be getting hurt."

"We have to be optimists in this situation. They're not gonna kill him, cause he has information they need. They gotta protect their investment," replied Cusick.

She looked to the sky, "Please, let this end soon." She put her head in her hands and cried.

Johnny put his arm around her gently, "there, there. Everything's gonna be fine. I've known Randall for years and if there's a way out, he'll find it. He's resourceful; trust me. Before ya know it, we'll be lookin' back on this and laughing," he said. "He thinks the world of you, you know."

"I wonder if he knows how much I think of him."

Johnny replied, "I think he does."

"I wonder sometimes whether someone up there is leading me on. Everything seems to be going my way, when it always takes a turn for the worst," she said.

"Come on, Milly. We got three cop cars and a helicopter chasing down these guys. He might as well be the god damn, President!" spouted Johnny.

She smiled, sniffled and said with sarcasm, "I suppose he does have some importance, doesn't he?"

"He does to us, and that's what matters. Some of the best things come from patience. We'll be in the clear soon," Johnny said. He looked out the window lost in his thoughts.

Milly looked at the seriousness in the jokester's face, leaned over and kissed his cheek. He smiled, and then returned his gaze to the window.

"We're almost there," said Cusick.

The speaker in the squad car came to life, "Cusick, this is Bear, over."

Cusick grabbed the mike, "Cusick here, what da ya got?"

"They're movin."

"What da ya mean they're movin! They're suppose to wait for instruction."

"I saw the two officers get into the car, carrying a briefcase," said Bear.

"Was there only two?"

"As far as I saw, only two," said the pilot.

"What directions are they headed?"

"They're headed cross town towards the West Side."

"Keep on 'em," replied Cusick. He looked at the other detective, "get in touch with headquarters and have 'em contact car 62. Ask 'em if they found anything suspicious and if they need assistance."

"Yes, sir," he responded.

"So, where ya takin' us?" asked Randall.

"You'll see," said Morrow, "I understand you have something we need. I suggest you tell us where it is, so no one'll get hurt."

"We'll be damned if we're gonna tell you anything!" shouted Harry.

"It'll be an easy choice, live or die. You choose," said Lear.

"If we decide to give ya the info, what's to keep ya from killing us anyway," said Harry.

"We're cops, you'll have to trust us," said Morrow. He looked back at Lear and snickered. "If you hold out, you'll enjoy hours of pain and torture. Then again, if you don't like suffering, we can end it quickly." He turned to Lear again, "To the Warehouse, Jeeves."

Randall leaned over, "Harry?"

"I'm working on a plan," he replied. A large street sign grabbed his attention. "It looks like they're taking us to Jersey. They must rough people up at, 'The Warehouse'. My guess is it's somewhere over the border. They can't venture far from the city while they're on duty."

"Knock off the whispering back there!" yelled Lear.

Harry pulled away from Randall's ear and returned his face to the window. He watched the streets as they approached the tunnel.

"Cusick, it looks like they're headed for the Lincoln," said the pilot.

"Jersey? What the hell are they doin'?" Hey Tenskey, have you heard back from HQ on their car?"

"No, let me call back." He picked up the mike, "HQ, this is officer Tenskey car 154. We need info on car 62. What the hell's happening?"

"We'll get on it, now," said the dispatcher. The dispatcher turned the channel and dialed car 62.

"Car 62, any suspicious activity at Atari Gems?"

Morrow picked up the mike, "dispatch, this is Morrow. We checked out Atari Gems. After we talked with the owner, we were given a hot lead that's taking us to Jersey. We're in transit, now." He winked at Lear.

"You were supposed to wait instruction, 62."

"It was a timed lead. We only had a half an hour to respond, so we made the choice," replied Morrow.

"Do you need assistance?" asked the dispatcher.

"No. It's under control. We'll call if we need it, over."

"Ten-four," said dispatch.

The dispatcher changed to car 154, "Tenskey, dispatch. They informed us of a timed lead, they had to respond to. The lead's in Jersey and they had to respond within a half hour."

"Do you know where in Jersey?" asked Tenskey.

"No, they were vague. You need me to find out?"

"No, let it be. We'll take care of it. Thanks," said Tenskey. He turned to Cusick, "you heard that. What da ya think?"

"Something's strange. Give me a minute." Cusick stated. He sat back in his seat and rubbed his thumb and index finger across his chin. *Jersey, 45 minutes, something in his hand, and Atari. What information could provide such a hot lead? Let's say Paul's right about this guy Barchetti, and these guys were framed. The only way it could be covered up would be to kill Paul Striker and these men. Since they need the gem first, they'd have to find its location. That's it!* "Tenskey, I bet those officers have Becks in the back of their car! They need him to find the stone and I think they're gonna extract the info!" Cusick exclaimed.

He grabbed the mike, and contacted the pilot, "Bear, stay with 'em when they exit the Lincoln, and for God's sake, don't lose 'em!"

"Roger, Cusick," said Bear.

Chapter 22
The Chase

The propeller blades of the chopper thundered close to the ground over New Jersey, while car 62 whistled through the tunnel. When the police car unexpectedly burst from the tunnel, it spotted the low flying helicopter. The chopper took to the air.

"Sal, we've been tagged! We've got to lose them," said Lear.

"How in the hell can we shake a helicopter? Maybe they're after someone else."

"Like hell! I bet they've been on us. Do ya think they saw us load these guys?" asked Lear. "How much could they know?"

"Look at it this way, the only one they could have seen us load would be Becks. Our contact with HQ came after we loaded the biker. We gotta get rid of these guys, so we're in the clear. Any ideas?"

Randall responded from the back, "you can let us go, we'll keep quiet."

Morrow grabbed his pistol and cocked the trigger, "One more word outta you and we'll be cleaning your brains from the back seat."

Lear's voice erupted from silence, "we'll create a diversion."

"How da ya figure?" asked Morrow.

Lear's face ducked below the visor and looked up. His head rotated back and forth. He spotted a bridge in the distance, "Pulaski Skyway!"

"What da ya mean?"

"Here's the deal. We're gonna split up and reconvene later. I'm gonna lead 'em on a goose chase, while you take these guys to "the warehouse". Lock 'em up and we'll come back to 'em when we're outta the squeeze."

"Ok, what's the plan?" asked Morrow.

"I'm gonna slow the car down before we get to Pulaski Skyway. I'll turn, so we have it directly overhead. At that point, I want you to rush the guys out at gunpoint, heist a car and drive to "the warehouse". Make it 'official business'. In the meantime, I'll try and ditch the copter. Hopefully, I can find an open garage. It's now 2:45."

"I'll need two hours," said Morrow.

"Right. Meet me at the exact spot I drop you beneath the skyway," said Lear.

"I'll need an extra pistol and I should take the briefcase too. If they get you, we'd have a lot of explaining to do."

"Good idea. We're approaching the skyway," said Lear.

Morrow turned to his prisoners, "listen, this could be easy, or this could be hard. If you cooperate, it'll be a piece of cake. We're slowing the car to a crawl. At that point, I open the door, you guys jump and I'll be behind you with my finger on the trigger, so if you plan on doin' anything smart, don't! You'll meet fate and it'll be easy to explain your death."

"Seems easy enough," Randall said. He looked at Harry, whose misshapen face was unreadable. He turned back, "we'll do as we're told. You're the boss."

Harry nodded in agreement.

Lear watched the road carefully. He observed the skyway and its distance across Jersey City. The local roads criss-crossed beneath it. He saw an inconspicuous traffic light beneath a section of bridge in the distance.

"This is perfect, Morrow. When we're stopped at the traffic light, get out, but stay beneath the bridge. One wrong move and the pilot will know something's going on."

"Good, we're ready," said Morrow.

"Cusick, this is Bear. We still have 'em in our sights."

"You think they have any suspicions we're on them?" asked Cusick.

"Not sure, we were flying low to avoid losing him, when he surprised us coming out of the tunnel."

"You idiots, you think you're gonna lose a squad car with a number 62, so big on the god damn roof, a jet liner could read it? Has the car driven erratically since?" asked Cusick.

"No. He's going about his business. Nothin' strange," said Bear.

"When you were flying low, did you see the people in the car?"

"I couldn't see details, looked like there were four."

"Four? You sure about that?"

"Definitely four," said Bear.

The detective looked at the others in astonishment. "If there were four in the car who could the other person be? Do ya think they arrested someone prior to picking up Becks? What's the likelihood that they would have strange dealings with an additional witness?"

"Probably slim to none," said Johnny.

"Exactly," said Cusick.

"Maybe its Harry. Harry left us earlier; maybe they nailed him before they got Randall."

"If that's the case, then they're probably gonna extract the info, then knock 'em off."

"They can't do that!" screamed Van Lowe. "I can't let that happen."

"Don't worry, everything's gonna be fine," said Cusick. "Anyone familiar with Jersey City?"

Everyone replied unanimously, "No."

"Well, we gotta hope that Bear can lead us through this maze of streets. If we stay clear of the squad car, they should be okay for the time being."

"Now, get out! You only got about 30 seconds!" said Lear. Morrow jumped out and opened the rear door. He grabbed Randall's shoulder and pulled him out. He shoved his pistol into his back. He nodded at the biker. Harry exited the car beneath the shadow of the bridge. They ran to the black archway and blended into the sturdy beam of the 1930's bridge.

"You can hear the blades of the chopper if you listen closely," said Randall.

"Yea," said Morrow, "stay put." Morrow turned his attention to Lear, winked and the squad car made a right on High Street then sped up.

Morrow listened to the helicopter. The sound faded. "Don't fuck around with me boys or I'll kill ya right here. Biker, I wantcha to go into the middle of the street and wave down a car."

"What? The cars gotta be doin' at least 25mph, you've gotta be kiddin'. If I'm hit, I'm dead."

"If you don't, you will be. Just do it!" shouted Morrow. He turned the gun on "the Heckler".

"Harry, be careful," said Becks with concern.

Harry watched the quick pace of the cars. In between

traffic lights, he leapt to the center of the road. As he waved frantically, a 1986 blue Volvo came skidding to a stop.

"What the hell are ya doin'?" yelled the driver.

Morrow screamed from the curb, "we need your car," he flashed his NYPD badge at the driver, "it's official police business. I have two escaped convicts I gotta escort back to prison. You'll get your car back shortly."

"You can't take my car! I've gotta get to work-

-You're wrong. We can take your car and we will take your car. I'll get your address from your registration and you'll have it back tonight," said Morrow.

"I don't know, I-

"Hang on," said Morrow. He reached into the suitcase and grabbed a small stack of twenties wrapped in a rubber band. He threw the man the stack. "This should cover your expenses to work. Keep your mouth shut about this police business and buy yourself something nice. You'll have your car tonight."

"There's got to be a thousand dollars here! I don't need all that, I-

"Just take it. You hold the change till I bring your car back safely. Use $200.00 for yourself. We appreciate the use of it."

"Thanks," sputtered the driver, "I'll see you later then?"

"Yea," said Morrow. "Becks, you drive. Harry, you sit next to him and I'll be in back. No funny business."

Randall scooted in the driver's seat while Harry opened the passenger's door and sat down. Morrow jumped in the back with his revolver close to the back of Randall's ear. "Drive straight till I tell ya. Keep the speed limit and don't arouse suspicion."

"Bear, this is Cusick. We don't know Jersey City at all, so when you tell us where 62 is, use landmarks. We gotta pull off for a map."

"He's passing what looks like a statue. Could be a war memorial. My co-pilot's getting out a map now."

"We just pulled in a Wa-Wa, Bear. I'll be back in a minute," said Cusick. He turned to Milly and Johnny, "do ya want anything?"

"I can't eat," replied Johnny, "I'm scared whatever I put down, will end back up."

"Cup of coffee would be good," said Van Lowe.

"Coffee it is." Cusick exited the car and entered the Wa-Wa. He ran down the first aisle until he reached a small station for coffee and sandwiches. *Like a giant mall to a teenage kid or a toy to a child.* Cusick grabbed Milly's coffee and a Nestle Crunch and returned to the checkout counter. He spun the metal cage that held road maps until he found one labeled Jersey City. He pulled out his wallet to pay and as he looked out the window behind the clerk, he spotted a blue volvo stopped at the traffic light in the front of the store. He squinted.

Harry stared from his seat into the parking lot of a corner WaWa. He noticed a black unmarked police car, two people in its back. A man pointed to them from behind the store's counter.

"Jesus, it can't be! Hurry guy, hurry!"

The traffic was bumper to bumper. Officer Cusick threw down a $5.00 bill, "keep the change," he shouted, then he ran out the door. Johnny looked out the window of the car towards the highway.

Harry's eyes opened suddenly.

"I don't know Morrow, feels like the wrong way. You sure you know Jersey City?" asked Randall with sarcasm.

"You do?" he asked.

"About as well as Miami Beach," Randall said, "and I've never been to Florida."

Morrow smiled for the first time. Harry turned to Randall, "I'm getting kind of thirsty aren't you Randall." He nudged his leg.

Randall turned his head and noticed Harry point. He casually glanced over and saw a man running for his car. He turned to the driver's window, "Morrow, what the hell's that odd building over there." He directed his attention away from the Wa-wa when he pointed through his window. "You're not taking us to a slaughterhouse that looks like that, are you?"

"Come on, asshole! The light's green! What da ya waitin' for? An invitation?" said Morrow. "Jam the horn!"

Randall leaned his weight on the horn and the car in front took off. "You're the boss," said Randall. "Keep straight?"

"Yea."

Cusick jumped into the car. "It's them! I swear it's them! Give me that mike!"

"Bear, this is Cusick. Do you read?" He turned to the driver, "Move this car. Follow that Blue Volvo at a distance."

"Are you sure it's them?" shouted Milly.

"Ninety percent," said Cusick. "Bear, do you read?"

"This is Bear, what's happening?"

"Are you still with that squad car?"

"Yea. He started to speed up. He's turned back on his own tracks and looks like he's heading back for the tunnel."

"Can you get low enough to see the number of people in the car?"

"I don't know. There's a lot of overhead interference. If he heads back to the tunnel, I might be able to get the number before he enters, but he'll see me. Do you wanta risk it?"

"Hold off for now. Let me know when you're 100% sure he's heading for the tunnel," said Cusick. He turned to the driver, "trust my gut here and stay on the Volvo. I'm sure they've traded off somehow."

"Bear, at anytime during your tag, did you lose sight of them?"

"No. I've been on them the whole time. I only lose sight when they disappear beneath bridges."

"Have there been 'a lot' of disappearances?" asked Cusick.

"A few. Maybe 3, but not for more than 30 seconds."

Thirty seconds, that's an eternity! They could escape the car and transfer to another in that time. They must have seen the chopper when they emerged from the tunnel, Cusick thought. "I'll be in touch," he said to the pilot. He turned to Johnny, "is your friend cool and collected under pressure?"

"The coolest. Stone face."

"Do you think he'd tell the officer if he knew we were following him?"

"Not if he's in trouble. Besides isn't there an all points bulletin out for him anyway?" asked Johnny.

"Good point," said Cusick. "The problem here is that if the driver sees us tailing him, he's gonna want to lose us. The helicopter's trailing whoever's in car 62. I told him to try and see how many people are in the police car without being detected. If he can only see one, I'll feel 100% sure they split in two. If he sees at least three we can go back to follow the police car. I suppose it's true what they say about being in the right place at the right time. They must have figured out we were on them-

-But we're still trusting your gut," said Johnny. "You saw 'em from a distance."

"I actually think the biker tried to get my attention. Funny, eh?"

"I want ya to make a couple of quick turns, Becks. Follow Peach Street until you hit the third light, then make a right on Oak. When you hit the end, make a left on Roosevelt. Two blocks up you'll see an abandoned warehouse on the left. Pull into the shipping docks," said Morrow.

Becks adjusted the rearview mirror slightly. *Who are these guys following us? Maybe Harry knows. It must be an omen.* "Turn here, Morrow?"

"Yea."

Decrepit buildings were strewn down Peach Street and urban decay reduced strong brick walls to piles of rubble. Boarded up windows on abandoned buildings gave light to shadowed faces, which quickly darted back from the vision of the car. The police car moved behind an 18-wheeler, which separated the cars. The detective's car slowed to a stop when the Volvo turned on Oak. Tenskey edged up slightly to keep the Volvo in its sights. It disappeared at the street's end and the squad car cautiously made the turn to Oak.

"Good place for a homicide," said Johnny.

"They must have found this place that way." Cusick turned to the driver, "looks like we're practically on the water. There must be activity on the street cause the barbed wire fencing looks new. What better place then the waterfront to dispose of bodies quickly?"

Milly sobbed.

"Easy now," Johnny said, as he put his arm around her shoulder. He shot Cusick a nasty look.

"I'm sorry Ms. Van Lowe. We tend to look at worst case scenarios." The police car pulled to the curb. "It looks like

Roosevelt's a dead end. My guess is it stops at the river. I think we should go by foot from here," Cusick said. "What were the odds of seeing them after the switch?"

"Slim to none. Someone up there's lookin' out for us," said Johnny.

"Tenskey, we'll split up. You approach through the fence at the backside of the factory. I'll check the shipping docks, then the building floor by floor. It looks like an 8-story building, so it'll take some time. We could run into vagrants and squatters in our search. If we're lucky, we won't unearth a drug den. Got it?" asked Cusick. "Johnny, Milly, we can't risk your discovery, so I want you to stay here."

"I wanta go," said Johnny, "and I don't think you can stop me."

"We can't, but what about Van Lowe? You're gonna leave her alone?"

"I'll go with Johnny," said Van Lowe.

"I don't think that's a good idea, Milly. We don't know what this guy's planning. I'll stay with you and we'll let the police handle it."

Randall pulled through an open gate in the docking area, where they saw a large garage door. "I need you to open that, biker," Morrow yelled.

Harry exited the Volvo and opened the door. The car slowly pulled into an underground tunnel, which they followed to a private garage under the factory. Morrow unbuckled a small flashlight from his belt and waved the men at gunpoint up a single stairway into darkness.

"Couldn't you have found a cozier spot?" asked Randall.

"I suppose a bed with a pillow would be to your liking, Becks?"

"Yea, that'd be perfect."

"I'll make sure you sit in the interrogation chair, that way you can nap between beatings," said Morrow.

"So you mean, you're gonna beat us?" Harry asked sarcastically.

"It's a simple game, if you give me what I need, I won't beat you. You don't talk and you'll get the opposite."

"What if we give you a little information and keep our mouths shut about the whole thing?" Randall said.

"Not good enough. It's all or nothing," said Morrow.

"You know I have friends in high places," said Harry, "I'll keep your ass safe in the underworld. If you're put in the pen, you won't last a day."

"Who's to say they'd find me out?" asked Morrow.

"I'm just sayin'," said Harry.

The men walked at a snail's pace. Morrow held the barrel of the gun on Randall's head, while he lit the way. The hallway led into a large barren room with a 20-foot cathedral ceiling. The room was square with each wall approximately 40 feet long. A window overlooked the room from the fourth floor and another stood about 15 feet from the floor facing the outside. It let a miniscule amount of light into the room and what little light entered the room, made a crumpled paper, rope, and a grimy single mattress visible. A rat ran from behind the mattress, in front of Harry.

"God damn rats!" he yelled. He launched a kick that sent it across the room and into the cold hard wall. "I hate fucking rats!"

"You'll have plenty of 'em here, biker." He pointed to the corner of the room, "Get that rope, I want you to tie Randall's arms and legs to the chair tightly. I'll check the knots, and if I find them loose, I'll shoot your leg for starters," said Morrow. He pulled a device from his pocket and paced backwards.

"What's that?" asked Randall.

"A silencer." Harry whispered. He bent down and started to tie Randall to the chair. "Sorry to do this to you pal, but I don't think we have much of an option. If you speak, speak before me, cause I'm libel to say something to make him blow. Whatever route you choose to take, I'll follow ya, till the death."

Harry tightened the knot on Randall's hands, "I think we were followed."

"We were. I lost the car a couple of blocks back, but I trust my gut." whispered Randall. He looked over to the far corner and watched Morrow shining his gun. "I think they're here."

"Who, the cavalry?" asked Harry.

"The cops. The good ones."

"The ones from the Wa-wa?" asked Harry.

"They were cops?"

"Yea, I'm pretty sure. Believe it or not I think I saw Johnny in the back of their car."

"We can only hope," Randall replied.

"Real comforting," Harry said with sarcasm, "Hope."

Cusick and Tenskey sneaked away from the squad car and closed in on the warehouse. Tenskey crawled through a break in the wire fence, while Cusick followed the road to the docking area.

They must have pulled into a garage to hide the car from the road. Cusick walked over the oil stained concrete. The docking areas were closed and padlocked. He continued until he reached the end, where he saw another ramp that led to a garage. It had several smashed glass panes seven feet from the floor. He grabbed the frame and hauled himself up and through the window. He fell silent. A black cat crept deep in the darkness. *That's not a good sign!* The tunnel was long, with only enough space to fit a mid-sized car. Cusick pulled his flashlight out and followed the tunnel below the factory. He reached the underground lot and spied the Volvo parked in the first spot labeled President. *An executive lot.*

Cusick shined the light towards the stairway. He rubbed his finger on the wall. *Someone's scraped the dust from this recently.* He quietly ascended the stairs, listened carefully for sounds, but heard nothing.

"Aren't you done yet?" asked Morrow.

"Just about," replied Harry. "Wanted to make sure it's tight. Done."

"Alright, step back to the doorway and turn around."

"Which doorway?" asked Harry.

"The one we came through," he said.

Harry looked at him curiously. *I don't like where this is going.* "The one with the open door?" asked Harry.

Morrow nodded. "Do it now!" he yelled.

Harry backed towards the open doorway in a steady motion. He watched Morrow's finger on the trigger of his 45, the silencer attached. Within a yard of the door, Morrow clocked the trigger and shot Harry in the side. Harry was thrown backwards awkwardly through the doorway, holding it. Like a bolt of lightening, his adrenaline pumped through his stricken body. He sprinted through the darkness in the direction they came. Morrow anticipated the run and ground his feet in hot pursuit to the open doorway. He reached it and caught the biker's lumberjack shirt in distance. Blood puddles splattered the floor. Sal Morrow took position, aimed-

"Harry! Harry!" yelled Randall. Randall listened intently to the heel toe footsteps in the room next door. "God damn it, Harry!"

Morrow fired.

Cusick's ears pricked at the sound of Randall's voice and the quieted gun shot. It echoed down the corridors. *That's gotta be only a few floors up.* Cusick flew up an adjacent staircase.

Morrow approached the fallen man with his gun drawn. "Get up weakling!" he shouted. He kicked the ribcage not once, but twice. The biker remained motionless; his body, face down. A puddle began to form beneath. Morrow stood silent and watched him. *One less problem in the world.* He walked back towards the doorway, appearing seconds later in front of Randall, like a demon from hell.

"What did you do? What the fuck, did you do?" Randall said. He looked at the officer. His gun smoked and he noticed blood stains on his shoes.

"I don't think you'll need to worry about your friend any longer. He wasn't worth the effort. Frankly, I don't know what ya saw in him."

"He was my god damn friend! Suppose you never had one of them!" Randall yelled. He shook his head uncontrollably.

"Who needs friends when you've got money. That's all I need," said Morrow. "The way I see it, you have only one way of getting outta here alive, and that's if you tell me where the stone is. It's a simple question with a simple answer. When you tell me, I'll free you."

"Like hell you will! You'll kill me like you did Harry! There's nothing to keep you from doin' it. We're wanted criminals. Don't think I don't know your game. You can shoot us in 'pursuit'."

"Here's what I'm gonna do. I'm a gambling man." Morrow walked close to Randall. He opened the gun's chamber in front of Randall and dumped the bullets into his hand. He swirled them around, manipulating them between his fingers. "This gun has nine chambers. I'm gonna place one bullet in a chamber, and the others in my pocket. I'm gonna ask you the same question I've been asking you, and if you don't tell me or I don't believe what you tell me, I'm gonna pull the trigger. I'll start from your feet and move to your head, so when the bullet leaves the chamber it'll have plenty of places to hit you. After I pull the trigger for the third time, I'll add a bullet, two if I've already shot you, then I'll re-spin the chambers. We'll call it Randall roulette."

"How inspirational," Randall whispered sarcastically.

"What's that?" he asked, "I couldn't hear you." His face grew red with anger. He took his pistol across his left shoulder, and backhanded it across Randall's face. The backlash took Randall by surprise. He pushed himself backwards and tipped over his chair. He fell on to his hands and rolled over in pain.

Morrow placed him upright. "Wise ass." He placed a bullet in the gun and spun the chambers. "Round and round it goes, where it stops no one knows." The chambers came to a halt. "Ok, wise guy, where's the stone?" He pointed the gun at Randall's privates.

"If you think I'm gonna tell you-

"Bang!" shouted Morrow with all his might. Randall's face drained of blood until he was left with a sickly white complexion. Morrow crowed. "Funny how people lose screws when a loaded gun is ready to go off in their crotch."

Johnny sat quietly by the squad car until he heard a shout reverberate through the factory. "Milly, I gotta go, but it's not safe. Stay here."

"No, I want to go."

"Absolutely not- you need to be here when I bring him back. Please, just stay."

"You promise you'll bring him back?"

"You know I plan on it."

"Ok."

Quick Johnny sprinted in Tenskey's footsteps through the opening of the storm fence. He found an open door at the back of the warehouse and flew through. His head swiveled back and forth like an addict on speed. He located a fire exit at the end of the hall and slammed into the door. He hurled up four flights of stairs charged with adrenaline, before he stopped to rest and listen.

Officer Cusick climbed to the third floor, where he saw the biker's body sprawled on the floor. He crept closer and bent down to touch the man's jugular. *A faint pulse. If we don't get this guy attention quickly he's a goner.* He stood back in a crouched position and listened to muffles from a faint voice.

Tenskey had come to the same floor, from the opposite side. He closed in on the occupied room and noticed Cusick across the empty space. He nodded to his fellow officer.

Morrow took a dirty sock from the floor and shoved it in Randall's mouth. Randall hunched over the chair. He bit into the sock and breathed heavily through his nose.

"So, feel lucky today?" said Morrow. "Maybe this time you'll think twice about my question." He took the barrel of his gun and brushed it against Randall's bruised right cheek. It slid over Randall's slumped head to the back of his neck where he butted it in. "One shot in nine. What kind of chances does that give me? Pretty good for a gambling man." He walked in front of Randall and pulled up his chin. "One more time." He put the pistol between his eyes.

Randall stared down the barrel of the gun, the perspiration rolled down his forehead. His eyes blinked involuntarily,

"Fuck!" he yelled through the muffled cotton mouth rag.

Randall heard the trigger pulled, "click".

"Scared?" asked Morrow. He pulled the sock from his mouth.

The nerves throughout his body spasmed. He held his head up, composed himself and spouted, "Of your face."

Morrow's face squinted; he instantaneously pulled the trigger once again at his arm. It clicked. "It's your lucky day," replied Morrow.

Cusick moved closer to the doorway, and waved Tenskey from the other side. Both held their guns closely.

Johnny ran through the hallways of the fourth floor. "He's gotta be here, somewhere." He ran to the end of the hall where a window overlooked the interrogation room of the third floor. He caught a glimpse of his friend anchored to the chair. "That bastard!" He flew back from the direction he came, and sped down the stairs to the third floor. Guided by his instincts, he sprinted in the same direction as Tenskey took.

Tenskey held his position inside the door, watching Cusick's movements.

"I'm gonna kill that mother fucker," Johnny said to himself, as he sprinted full speed through the corridor towards Tenskey. He closed in quickly, not allowing Tenskey time to react. He pushed him to the side like a linebacker at full speed and barreled into the occupied room.

"Agghh!" Johnny yelled as he ran straight at Sal Morrow.

Startled, Morrow pulled his gun from his target and quickly pulled the trigger several times before he shot a single bullet into Johnny's shoulder. Johnny hit Morrow's arm and launched him towards the cement wall. Both police officers closed with their guns drawn.

"Drop it!" yelled Cusick. "Drop it, now!"

Johnny smashed Morrow's head into the ground and the

gun fell from his hand. It lay on the floor by him. "You fucking lunatic! I'm gonna kill you!" yelled Morrow. He looked at officers Cusick and Tenskey, "Aren't you gonna help me! The guy tied here's a crack dealer. I'm getting him to spill information. His bodyguard's down in the room next door. Damn near killed me!"

"Knock it off," said Cusick. "The gig's over."

Johnny got up, then kicked his side. Tenskey pulled him away, "Knock it off!"

Johnny turned to face his friend. Randall's head sunk low. He giggled madly. "You still around, buddy?" He picked up Randall's chin.

"That was a good joke Johnny, a good joke."

"What?"

"The bird shit. You really are the shit," he said.

"You're delirious."

"HQ, this is Cusick here. Get on the line with Jersey City Medical. I need 'em here yesterday! We got a man here with a lot of lost blood. He's critical. We're in a warehouse off the water, at the end of Oak Street."

"They're on their way," replied headquarters.

"Where's Harry?" Johnny asked.

"He's down the hallway. He was shot and in bad shape," replied Cusick.

Johnny walked around the corner to Harry's downed body. He walked up beside the behemoth, " Harry, you with us? Harry!" He slapped his cheek a couple of times. "Snap out of it. Don't you leave us!"

Cusick followed him in. "He's still got a slight pulse, but he's lost a lot of blood. Jersey City Medical should be here any minute. They'll take care of him."

Johnny shook his head in disbelief. He stood up and walked

to the nearest window. He smashed his fist through one of the windowpanes, then stuck his face into it, "Milly!" he yelled in a primal scream. "It's ok, come here quickly!"

Milly heard his yell and responded, she hurried through the broken fence and saw Johnny's head in the window of the third floor.

"Come through the broken door; go to the fire escape then to the third floor." Johnny said.

Milly followed his instructions and ran up the stairway until she found the third floor. She went through the door cautiously. Johnny appeared in the hallway, his hand held his shoulder tightly beneath his bloodstained shirt.

"I just saw the medics arrived, Milly. Randall's been beaten up pretty badly. Cusick said Harry's lost a lot of blood from a gunshot wound and we're not sure he'll pull through. The man's a warrior, so I feel confident every ounce of him will fight for survival. When you see Randall, take it easy. He's ok, but probably a little mentally unbalanced, right now," said Johnny.

Milly moved close to Johnny and kissed him. "Thanks for being here. You ok?"

"I'll be fine, once these guys are good," he said.

Milly breathed deeply and braced herself when she turned the corner. She saw Randall seated on the filthy mattress. "Randall," she said in a soft comforting voice.

Randall's eyes glazed over, "Milly! You're ok, thank God."

"Are you alright, sweet?" she said. She moved closer and stroked his face with her gentle touch.

"It's Harry. They're not sure if he'll make it. I owe my life to him, Milly. He's gotta pull through. I didn't think I'd see you again."

"I wondered that myself," she softly said. She gazed in his eyes, "I love you, ya know."

Randall's eyes filled with water, "I love you too, Milly.

Would you stay here with me? I don't want you out of my sight, even for a minute." he asked. He grabbed her hand and turned to Johnny, "Johnny?"

"Yea, Randall?"

"You think Harry'll make it?"

"He was shot twice, but you know he's got the strength of three elephants. The medics are working on him now."

"Johnny, could you make sure they give him all the help he needs?"

"Sure Randall." Randall walked to the window and looked across the garbage-strewn neighborhood. *I want outta here.*

"Cusick, this is Bear. Car 62 is definitely heading for the Lincoln. He'll be in the tunnel in a matter of minutes. How should I proceed?"

"We have the suspect's partner. They must have dodged you under an overhead. Proceed as follows, first – contact headquarters and tell them we have Nelson Lear under surveillance. He could be charged as an accessory to 1st degree assault. Second, make it a priority to have another set of officers' corner him as he exits the tunnel. If he's suspicious, he'll probably run. If we trap him at the tunnel, he won't have a chance. Third, have internal affairs contact me! I want to cut a deal for some information and I'll need their approval. Got it?"

"Understood," said Bear, "out."

Tenskey approached Cusick, "so what's the plan?"

"I'll talk to internal affairs about Sal Morrow and Nelson Lear. I want to arrange a reduced sentence for their cooperation in taking 'the big fish' Barchetti. If we can coerce them into cooperating with us, we could take him down on attempted murder, racketeering and probably even more charges."

"What if Lear and Morrow don't cooperate?" asked Tenskey.

"They'll pit themselves against each other. I hazard the thought of what prisoners would do to them in prison. Neither one of these guys want that and I'll bet one of them cracks. We just offer them decent deals. Capish?"

"You're a sly one."

"We need only one other thing," said Cusick, "the bait." He turned to Becks, "Randall, I want to apologize for all the trouble you've been through. I know it's been a horrible ordeal, but we have spoken with Paul Striker, who's emerged from a coma. He told us you and your friend are innocent of any wrongdoing and that Sid Barchetti tried to kill you. It's our mission to nail him, but we have to catch him in the act. He's been able to avoid the law for years and we can never get his charges to stick. I finally have a plan to catch him, but we need to use your diamond as bait-

"I don't know-

"It's yours and will remain yours. We need it to lure him in and without it, I'm afraid we won't get anywhere. We can't substitute another stone because of his expertise in the field. NYPD will send you with armed guards to recover the stone and protect you. If you bring it back with them to headquarters, not only will you be rich, but you'll be famous for your assistance in bringing in Sid "The Big Fish" Barchetti."

Randall paused for a moment, "I'll let you use my stone to sink Barchetti, but I want total anonymity. I want to return to a normal living," replied Randall.

"That's understood. We'll use the stone but we'll take total responsibility for his apprehension. The stone will be returned to you once we have him in custody," replied Cusick.

"Fair enough," said Randall.

"Tenskey, have two of our best men escort Mr. Becks and his friends to pick up the stone, then return to headquarters."

"Yes, sir," he replied.

"At the request of internal affairs, Officer Nelson Lear is to be apprehended. Car 62 is in transit from the Lincoln tunnel back into Manhattan from Jersey City. Those in the vicinity of the Lincoln tunnel, please report immediately to the tunnel opening."

Two cars near 34th St. proceeded to the tunnel prior to Lear's exit. They set up their cars as a roadblock. Nelson Lear's car came out of the tunnel. *What the hell's going on, thought Lear.* He watched a helicopter fly low above the tunnel opening. Two patrol cars had their pistols drawn on him.

Lear pulled his patrol car to the side, stepped out with his hands raised. "What's the problem?"

"We've been asked to take you in for questioning."

"Who asked?" screamed Lear.

"Internal affairs," said the officer.

Nelson Lear looked at the cars that boxed him in, and the unsurpassable high walls. He nodded his head in defeat, "let's go then." He got in the back of his fellow officer's car and was led back to headquarters.

Chapter 23
The Net

Lieutenant Cusick and Officer Tenskey walked through the curious and angry stares at 77th. Precinct with Sal Morrow cuffed. As they shuffled him through, they saw Nelson Lear seated beside his arresting officers. Morrow winked at Lear before Officer Tenskey shoved him into Interrogation Room I, and then closely followed him in. Cusick returned to Nelson Lear, who sat casually in front of a paper-covered desk, grabbed his arm, pulled him up and escorted him to Interrogation Room III, just opposite Morrow's room. A representative from Internal Affairs sat in the back of Room III.

"Officer Nelson Lear, do you know the trouble you're in?"

"I don't know what you're talking about," said Lear.

"Well, your partner was captured with the two suspects in the Central Park shooting. One, Randall Becks, and a biker named Harry X, both accused of attempted murder. Your partner shot the biker twice and left him for dead. At the time, he was caught interrogating Becks, who was tied to a chair and brutally beaten. You know anything about this?"

"No."

"Well, he must have gotten there somehow. You sure?"

"I drove Morrow to Jersey City to pursue a lead in that case. I dropped him there, so I could pursue another," said Lear.

"And that was?"

"That was to come from the jeweler, Paul Striker. I needed to fill in details on our suspects."

"Well, I have news for you, Paul Striker's out of a coma. He told us the two men that were our prime suspects were entirely innocent. In fact, he tried to protect Becks, from another jeweler named Sid Barchetti. Evidently, he was behind the whole thing. Striker said it had to do with a diamond the size of a baseball."

A diamond! That crook! Probably worth a fortune. "That's news to me."

"Well that's strange," Cusick said with astonishment. "You see, your partner was caught with a briefcase full of money. $98,000 dollars to be exact. We tracked you by helicopter from Atari Gems and the pilot saw you leave with the briefcase."

"We stopped by Atari Gems as a result of an APB. While we were there we established the lead that took us to Jersey City. Barchetti offered us a good deal on jewelry if we deposited the large amount of cash you found. You don't just walk out the door with that kind of money."

Cusick yelled, "So, the money ends up in a warehouse with your partner, whose beatin' the hell out of these guys!"

"Safekeeping," Lear replied.

"Sounds shabby to me. Face it, you were paid $100,000 to extract information and keep your mouths shut. If convicted, you get a mandatory 5-10 years in prison. If you lived through the first year, because of a boyfriend named Bubba, you'd have your self-esteem, your money, and your retirement shot to shit.

I don't need to fill you in on prison, in fact, I could find your worst enemy and make sure he's transferred to the same cell. I'm gonna to let you think about that for a minute."

Christ, he couldn't do that! He wouldn't. Lear broke out in a sweat.

"I'm gonna make you a sweet offer, for helpin' us nail Sid Barchetti. If you help us take him down, we'll put you in the witness protection program. It's a good deal, after all, who knows what kind of deal your partner will work out. We need only one of you, so whoever clucks first…" he paused, "I'll give ya an hour to think it over. Cigarette?"

"Yea," said Lear.

Cusick exited the guarded room and walked across the hall to Room I, where he found Sal Morrow in a cold sweat. His hand twitched as it lay across the table.

"How's it going guys?"

"Piss off," yelled Morrow.

"Look a little tense Morrow, thinkin' bout your new boy-friend?" Cusick said.

The man behind the table stood up, "Lieutenant Cusick, I'm Bruno McCormick of Internal affairs, pleasure to meet you. We were just filling our friend in on the charges we have on him. For some strange reason," he said sarcastically, "he's been a little, irate. I suppose since he was caught red-handed with a briefcase full of money, a man practically dead and another severely beaten, he's in denial. Can't be put in a hotter seat, I'd say."

"I'd say, you're right! Don't suppose he'd wanta work a deal out, would he?" asked Cusick.

"What kind of deal?" asked Morrow impatiently.

"Easy there bucko," said Cusick. "Let's suppose you help us get Sid Barchetti. We could reduce your sentence. Instead of 10-15 mandatory, we could get you five, with the ability of parole after three. I think that's fair, don't you?"

"Give me a break. They'd kill me in the first 6 months! You'd have to get me off, for us to work together. I got too many enemies."

"Let's face it Morrow, we gotcha by the balls. Ballistics will match those slugs from Harry X to your gun, and that damn briefcase filled with money is undeniable. We know Sid Barchetti's operated a fence and a protection racket. Obviously, he's had people on the outside lookin' out for him," said Cusick. "We need someone on the inside."

"Freedom or nothing," said Morrow.

"Your partner seemed ready to cooperate. He's in a better position for us to make a deal. He wasn't caught spillin' the ink, if ya know what I mean."

That bastard! He's going to turn on me after all this? "I've known Officer Lear for 15 years." *This guy's bluffing!* "You may have to work out a deal with him," said Morrow.

Detective Cusick leaned over Morrow, who didn't flinch. An eternity passed before Morrow's eyes dodged his penetrating stare.

"We'll see," replied Cusick. He stood up and walked out of the room with Officer Tenskey.

"So do ya think one of 'em will break?"

"We got Morrow, but I'm not sure about Lear. I'd rather use Lear. According to Morrow's record, he's unpredictable. He may warn Barchetti," said Cusick. "Keep 'em isolated. I don't want 'em speaking to each other."

Chapter 24
Sealing Loose Ends

S id Barchetti carefully examined his 1.5-millimeter platinum and iridium pellet under his electron microscope. He placed his assortment of jeweler's tools next to him and carefully manipulated the minuscule mass. *These holes look about right to hold my poison.* He looked up again and blinked a few times before he returned his eye to the microscope. *Two milligrams of ricin should put Mr. Striker out of commission. They'll never detect this baby.* He loaded the metal ball, only about the size of a pinhead, with the ricin and then into a miniature gas gun designed with velcro arm straps. He took the gun and strapped to his right wrist. *If only you'd kept your mouth shut.* He pulled his long sleeve down over the device and buttoned his cuff. He casually walked over to his suit and slipped it on. He walked out the door.

Ten minutes later, he arrived at the hospital. He followed the winding hall until he reached the elevator and went to Striker's floor. He approached the nurse's station when he overheard some talk evolve from the man's room. He stopped to listen.

"So you're telling me this guy Barchetti operates a protection racket? How long's he been controlling it?" asked the officer.

"Over 10 years."

"God, how could he keep it quiet so long?"

"Too much money at stake. That street's a literal gold mine. If you make three times the amount you have tied up in inventory and you have millions of dollars in inventory; hell, you do the math. I worry though, cause all he has to do is snap his fingers and he could destroy my whole business. My family's been at the same location since 1878. I'm the third generation. It's not about the inventory per say, it's the people whose grandmothers and grandfathers came to visit mine. Their families have become mine over the years and people don't take to change easily. That's why I paid him. I wanted my customers, my business and me, of course, to be safe," said Striker.

"So why the change in heart?" asked the guard.

"Well, something happened to me the day Becks came in with that diamond. Here's an innocent guy, with no clue what he's got. I knew Barchetti would kill him if he couldn't buy the diamond cheap. So he had his thugs follow the guy into my shop. I looked into Beck's eyes, and I don't know, he looked pained- I saw sorrow, some of myself," said Striker. "It's funny how strangers can step into your life for only minutes and have a profound change in your direction on life. It's like God issued Becks this mission, unbeknownst to him, and my change was the byproduct of it."

"I know what you're saying," said the guard. "I think we've all had that kind of thing happen to us at one time or another."

Sid Barchetti stood motionless. *It's Bala Bala Diamonds, I need to destroy. The destruction of his shop would be the death of his soul. I've gotta hurt that guy and no better way than to destroy his shop.* Sid Barchetti turned around and slid away quietly. He left the hospital unnoticed.

Chapter 25
The Discovery

August 17ᵗʰ 5:15 pm:

An unbearably humid day gave way to rain, which poured from the dark skies over Manhattan. He popped his automatic umbrella open and walked west towards 6ᵗʰ Ave, the main thoroughfare. Paul Striker was inside the front window of Bala Bala Diamonds dismantling a window display. Henry stopped momentarily and peered through the glass. He pointed to a ring.

"Paul, is this your work? It's fantastic!"

Striker's face edged close to the window, "Did it myself. Fifteen VS1 diamonds mounted to form an Egyptian scarab. Its eyes are Ceylon sapphires. If you like it, I'll give you an exceptional deal."

"Your designs get better and better every time I see you, Paul. Keep up the good work; if you get anything worth cutting, see me."

"If I had diamonds worth cutting, you'd be the first one I'd see. But how could you possibly squeeze me into your busy schedule?"

"Paul, you're a good friend. It's hectic, but I'd always make time for you. When you're ready for some more pointers, stop up."

"Thanks, Henry." Striker responded. "You're walking home tonight?"

"No, the heat's too much. Doctor says I should watch the ticker and I shouldn't smoke." Henry pulled out a cigar, bit off the end, spit it in the street, and torched the other. He took a long drag, "so I switched from cigarettes to cigars. It's not like I listen to him anyway. What the hell do they know!"

Striker laughed, "Goodnight, Henry. I'll see you tomorrow."

"Goodnight, Paul."

On 6th Avenue, Henry hailed a cab.

Every hour on the hour Cusick questioned Morrow and Lear. He consistently drilled the consequences into both men and after 6 pm, Morrow broke into a plea for mercy. A half-hour later, Lear broke with an offer of the witness protection program and a few concessions. Cusick took advantage of the opportunity and arranged for a private consultation one-on-one between the two men.

"I need you to meet Sid Barchetti. We need motive for Paul Striker's attempted murder, and we prefer to catch him red handed with the diamond. We've obtained permission from Randall Becks to use the stone as bait. When you get to Atari's you can tell him your mission was successful. We'll wire you with a miniature microphone beneath your shirt, so we can listen in. Once the stone's traded and in his possession, say the word coal, and we'll converge on the shop."

"Sounds easy enough," replied Lear.

"What time were you suppose to meet with him?" asked Cusick.

"I had to have the stone by tomorrow morning. When I had it, I had to call him to establish a time. He's flexible, with this kind of deal," said Lear. "He'll meet anytime."

"I wanta meet tomorrow morning at 7:00 am, by then we should be situated. Why don't you call him now?" asked Cusick. He handed the phone to him. Lear picked up the receiver and dialed Barchetti's number.

"Atari Gems, can I help you?"

"Sid, it's Lear."

"Lear, I've been waiting to hear from you. What's happening? Have you made progress?"

"We've made progress. The biker's dead and Becks is wearing down. I'm convinced we'll have the information and stone by tomorrow morning. Why don't we meet at 7 am. I'm 90% sure we'll have the stone by then. You'll have the money?"

"Of course, how often have I let you down?"

"You've always been reliable. 7:00 am," Lear confirmed.

"7:00 am it is. I look forward to it." Sid said. He hung up the phone and picked it back up immediately. He dialed his brother.

"Bill, I need your help."

"What is it Sid?"

"I need you to plant a well concealed bomb. It has to be fast with lot's of damage."

"I could use plastic explosives," Bill said.

"Sounds like a good choice. Can you set it for a particular time?"

"Shouldn't be a problem. What's the target?"

"Bala Bala Diamonds."

"Paul Striker finally got to you, eh?" asked Bill.

"More then you know."

"Ok, consider it done."

"Be clean about it, and then take a trip to Jamaica, on me. I'll join you there and we'll comb the beach for awhile," Sid said.

"That's incentive!"

"Take a flight out tomorrow afternoon, while I tie up loose ends. I'll book mine for tomorrow night. The day after, I'll meet you at the Pink Flamingo Club, at noon."

"Can I presume you'll have the diamond there?"

"Yes, it's practically in my hands as we speak. The deal should be sealed by tomorrow morning. I'm going to fly out of Newark. Take care of this business and I'll take care of you."

"You got it!" exclaimed Bill.

He hung up the phone.

Chapter 26
The Day

H enry Hillerman eyed the plump lips of a gorgeous In-
dian woman on the jewelry calendar above his desk. The
brightly colored sari she wore emphasized her cleavage and
drew the yellow of a 22 karat gold necklace from her brown
skin. His finger drifted from her breast to the numbers below.

*Another two months, October 18ᵗʰ and my goal will be met. The
D-day of Henry Hillerman. I'll have the world stage just in time for the
holidays. What more exposure could I get?*

The motor of an ancient air conditioner vibrated at full
steam and gave off a droning hum. It did little more than
provide white noise in the oppressive summer heat. The overhead lamp, held by two flimsy chains, drifted lightly across the
grooves of his workbench. Each one, glistened with years'
worth of embedded gold dust. It cast reflections around the
room, like miniature embers popped from an invisible fire.

Henry wiped his hairy arm across his forehead, and lathered
it in perspiration. He pried the soiled white shirt from his puny
body, and then looked at the annoyance mounted in the 10ᵗʰ story

window. *If only I'd bought a fan!* He pulled his magnification glasses down from his forehead and sharpened his focus on the stone.

The intense gaze left no room for error between him and his subject. The mallet poised in his hand with the stillness of a Remington Bronze and in an instant, every nerve channeled into action as he brought the mallet down with the precision of a German engineer. Henry's ears pricked at the noise. He smiled.

Three-quarters complete! Henry picked his large velvet pouch from the bench, puffed it out, and tucked away his stone. He looked around and as anticipated, saw no one. *Retirement, here I come!*

Lena, when I finish this stone, I'll buy you the largest tombstone in Mountainside Cemetery. It'll be larger than the Pyramid of Giza and more beautiful than the Mona Lisa. It'll be the finest Italian marble.

He approached the alarm, typed in his code and exited onto the quiet street.

=•((•))•=

The following day, Sid Barchetti's alarm woke him with the sound of soft jazz. It echoed through his enormous luxury bedroom like a symphony at Carnegie Hall. His body lay comfortably beneath a canopy with drawn drapes on a thick down mattress. His head was buried in soft feather pillows when he decided it was time to turn over, and shut off the alarm. He looked at his clock, *5:30 am, I should get down to it. It's going to be a long day.* He stood up and walked across the floor to the plush velvet drapes that hung over the window. He opened them and looked out. He watched strangers walk in slow motion on the street below, scattered. On the horizon, the sun rose over the trees in Central Park and broadcast shadows over green grass.

It's so easy to disappear in this city if you need to. A blend of the right clothes, the right glasses, the right hat and you could be someone's father, someone's brother, someone else- a complete foreigner. It's amazing to watch these people, each one rides an independent merry-go-round that runs by itself, but interconnects with New York City and forms a whole. He pointed out the window. *When I return, I'll disappear like you- a faceless human with no history.* Sid Barchetti closed the curtains, and then set the coffee machine. *That's the way it'll have to be.*

He picked up the phone from his marble tiled wall and dialed Nelson Lear's cellular.

"Hello?" answered Lear.

"Lear, it's Barchetti. We're still on for 7:00, no?" he asked.

"Yep. Getting' myself together now."

"You have the stone?" asked Barchetti.

"Yep. I'm looking at it as we speak." He winked at the detective.

"Good. My store, 7:00 am prompt."

"We'll be there," said Lear. He hung up the phone and turned to detective Cusick, "He's not gonna like the fact Morrow isn't there."

"I'm glad you said we. What can you convince him with as an excuse?"

"Sid knows Morrow's mother's been ill. I could tell him his mother passed away. It'd probably be the only excuse he'd except," said Lear.

"You should have mentioned it while you spoke to him. What are the odds Morrow received the phone call this morning before you spoke to him, for God sakes it's 5:30 am," Cusick exclaimed.

"I could tell him he received the call last night, and he thought he could make it back here for the deal. He contacted me via cellular to let me know he was running late. Sid knows how close we are, so that might hold him for the time being."

"It'll have to do. We'll stick with that pretext and roll with it. We'll have to be quick on our feet, if something comes up. Keep your thinkin' cap on and don't let the lack of sleep get to you."

"Na, I've lived on less sleep before," Lear replied. "Just another day, another task at hand."

Barchetti entered the bathroom. He put on the speaker-phone and hit automatic redial, as he hopped in the shower. The phone rang.

"Hello?"

He talked over the rushing water, "Bill, its Sid."

"Thought it might be you. Everything's set, and the ticket's booked. It's gonna be a fine time, Caribbean way."

"Just get there safely. Have a good trip, and I'll see you, tomorrow."

"Take it easy, brother. You be safe too. Ciao."

"Ciao," Sid said.

He sang Ave Maria as he lathered the soap on his hairy chest. He scrubbed himself down with a loofa before he shut off the water. He stepped on to the slick tile floor and looked into the steamy mirror. He wiped it with a cloth so he could see his face. *Handsome devil.* He opened the bathroom cabinet and pulled out an old mahogany box, a shaving mug and brush. He lathered up his face, and carefully took the old ivory straight edge from the box. The blade flashed under the lights in the bathroom as it caressed his chin.

When he cleaned the foam from his face, he finished with a splash of Eternity for Men, winked at himself, and proceeded to his bed. He grabbed a foldout suitcase from his closet and pulled 4 Armani suits, 5 Donna Karan slacks and an assortment of casual polo wear from his hangers: every item, completely wrinkle-free and perfectly dry-cleaned. *Now, I'm ready, for some relaxation!* "Anything I miss, I'll buy. It shouldn't take more than 3 days to finish the facets in the islands. Once that's complete, I'll fly to Amsterdam and speak with some people. What better place to fence a diamond than Holland," he said to himself. He got to his doorway, turned around and blew his place a kiss. "Good bye, home sweet home."

Nelson Lear turned the ignition of his police car at 6:45 am. He scratched at the wires hidden beneath his uniform, and then toyed with the stone in his pocket.

"Remember, Lear we've got men everywhere including an outta sight chopper. It'll move on my command, so don't think of anything stupid. It'll screw your platinum parachute," said Cusick.

"I know," he replied.

"Coal's the key word, you know the drill. We'll watch your back."

Lear's police car pulled away. He turned on the radio and began to think. It was the first time alone since his capture. *What better way to appreciate the essence of this city than an early morning drive.* He rolled his window down. *I hope to God other cities have this wonderful smell that escapes delis and restaurants every morning. I'm gonna be transplanted like an immigrant- a forced migrant, without a choice. If they transplant me to the Midwest, I'm sure to go crazy. I can't live without the hustle and bustle, the unpredictability, and the pure adrenaline high of these streets. Where will my life begin?* He took a deep breath of fresh air and looked at the images of stores lined back to back. *Amazing how strange immigrants are. They have this grandiose image of prosperity and this image becomes so realistic, it takes over their mind. They get here, squeeze 2 people to a room, the size of a single bed, and proceed to work 14-hour days. Many never make it, but I suppose it's the hope they live for, maybe it's better than from where they came. Once the board is scratched clean, I'm gonna make it work. I'll bury this whole ordeal, get a wife, start a family, and live the right way. This is my wake up call, baby.* He took a gigantic inhale of fresh air. *Ah, that wonderful smell.* "New York, New York a wonderful town, the Bronx is up and the Battery's down."

Cusick looked curiously at his follow officers, "Is he singing?"

"Sounds like it," said Tenskey. "Who'd a thought a guy going into such a dangerous situation would sing?"

"I guess you'd sing too if you were about to go to prison, and you got a second chance. I know I certainly would," said Cusick.

Sid Barchetti arrived at Atari's at 6:40. He deactivated the alarm, re-locked the door and turned on a single bench light. He went through the doors that lead to his soundproof room in the back of the store, lifted the carpet under his chair, and shuffled it to the side. He grabbed the edge of a large tile and lifted it to reveal a small trap door. He reached in, twisted the combination until the safe popped open. He loaded stacks of $50.00 bills into a duffle bag and put four bundles of $50.00's in his own pocket.

"That should do it," Barchetti said. "Now, when I have that stone, I'll be scot free, but I can't forget to confirm my flight." He sat down on his chair, picked up his cellular and dialed 411.

"Operator, I need the number for Continental Airlines. Reservations, please."

"One moment." She returned graciously, "that number is 1-800-Cont-Air. Have a good day."

"You too." He hung it up then dialed, "Good morning, my name's Sid Barchetti. I'd like to confirm my flight to Kingston, Jamaica tonight on flight 1867."

"One moment, Mr. Barchetti." He heard her fingers tap her keyboard. "Here it is Mr. Barchetti, Flight 1867 departs Newark at 6:45 pm. and arrives in Kingston, Jamaica at 11 pm. If you're checking any luggage, please arrive an hour before departure time. Thank you for flying Continental."

"Thank you," said Barchetti. He rubbed his hands together and surveyed the room. A red light lit in the upper right corner of the room. "He's here."

Sid Barchetti walked from his back office to find Nelson Lear inside the front door. "Glad to see you still have a key."

"How'd you know I was here," asked Lear.

"We all have secrets, mine's a little red light that glows when someone opens the door. Come with me. I bought us some coffee and donuts. You do like Duncan Donuts don't you?" asked Barchetti.

"I'm a policeman aren't I? Of course I love 'em."

"Where's Sal?"

"His mother passed away during the night. He contacted me this morning before I left to tell me he's running late."

"You didn't knock him off for the money, did ya?" Barchetti asked sarcastically. "I could see you doing that."

"You kidding? He's my partner and friend, I couldn't."

"You'd knock off your own Mother for the right price."

"Not a chance."

"Come on, have a seat in my office. I want to get down to business. Let me reset the alarm," said Barchetti.

"Who's going to disturb us this time of morning?" asked Lear.

Barchetti looked at Lear carefully, "you're not nervous are you?"

"Sid, you know me better than that. I was worried about Marrow setting it off. I did what has to be done and to be honest, I'll be glad to get this weight off my shoulders. I need a small advance in cash that I'd like to hide away before work."

"That's not a problem, I'll deduct it from the amount I wire into your account," he looked at Lear again, "I don't know, Nelson. I know Sal's mother has been sick, but it seems awfully coincidental she died last night of all nights. I don't feel comfortable talking without Sal here. Can I see the stone?"

Nelson Lear reached in his pocket and pulled out the stone. He held it out to Barchetti. The light twinkled in its cut facets.

"Yes, that's it. It's even more beautiful then when I first saw it." He reached down for the briefcase of money, hypnotized by the diamond. He pulled it on to his desk and faced the briefcase to Lear. He released the locks with his free hand. "That enough of an advance?"

Lear reached in and grabbed a stack of money. He fanned the cash into his face, smelling the fresh bills. "Yea, that'll be fine. It's amazing what we do for this green stuff. Money's such a beautiful thing. Can you tell me one thing, Sid, I'm curious."

"What?"

"Is coal where diamonds come from?"

Sid watched a trickle of perspiration drop down his forehead. The red light lit on the wall.

"What did you do?" Barchetti screamed.

Nelson Lear's smile lit from ear to ear, "Nothing personal, Sid."

"You're wired!" In an explosion of anger, Sid Barchetti whipped out the revolver from his shoulder holster. Lear stared down the barrel of the gun.

"Nothing personal, Nelson," he said. Barchetti pulled the trigger and Lear's head exploded on the wall. His body crashed to the ground. *That's first degree, and life behind bars. Gotta move.*

He leapt across his desk and opened a small camouflaged panel in the wall. Inside was a button, he immediately pushed. It opened another large hidden panel towards the floor of the room. Sid pushed over his desk, and angled it towards the main door. He quickly crawled through the escape hatch, which led to a concrete corridor. He returned the panel to its original position and locked it with two push locks. He crawled deep into the passageway and down the stairs till he reached another hallway at the bottom. He followed this beneath 47th Street. He looked at his watch, it was 7:07 am.

The police force jimmied the lock of Atari's front door when they heard the password. Cusick and Tenskey led five policemen into the store with their guns drawn.

"What the hell's going on?" Cusick screamed at the surveillance van. "What was that shot?"

"I think Lear's down, he was found out!" yelled the operator from the van, "Get in there!"

"Officer down!" yelled Cusick to the others. "We gotta get in through those doors! I'm not sure how this guy's set up, but watch for traps!"

The officers filed in one after another door after door. They approached a large oak one at the back of the store.

"Locked," Tenskey said. He took his gun and blew the door handle off. They tried to push the door in, but the door held tight.

"Detective, the door's secured by dead bolts. What should we do?" asked a policeman.

"We don't know if Lear is alive or dead, and we don't have time to wait. Blow the deadbolts!"

The officers blew numerous gunshots through the frame of the door. They heard the blunt shattering of metal on metal as each of 3 dead bolts were blown away. Two men threw their shoulders into the door and the door broke free. It revealed another steel clad door.

"Same thing, boys." Cusick edged closer to the door. "Nelson! Can you hear me? Nelson!" he yelled. He patiently waited for a response, but heard nothing. "Clear the door if you can hear me." Cusick waited 15 seconds. "Go ahead, guys."

First they blew off the doorknob, "another dead bolt, sir."

"Go ahead and do it but be prepared for return fire. He'll have one of two things prepared, A, he's going to be holding Lear hostage or B, he'll be ready to shoot till his death. I'm bettin' he's shot Lear and is hunkered down. Cover each other, and go in cautiously," he said. "Now."

The officer shot twice predicting where the dead bolts were. They heard the devices fly from the door. The men went to each side of the door, as the door slowly creaked open. A dead silence overcame the room. Cusick popped his head in and out cautiously. He saw Nelson Lear hunched over in a puddle of blood on the floor. The desk lay on its side like a barricade.

"Barchetti, the games over, hands in the air! If you don't get up nice and easy, we'll shoot ya in cold blood. Don't make us do that!" He paused for a response. "Ya hear me Barchetti? If ya don't speak up we're gonna blow your desk to pieces, one bullet at a time." He paused, and then looked at his squad. He nodded his head at two officers, who went inside the doorway and jointly fired a set of rounds into the desk. They stopped and returned to safety behind the door.

"Barchetti?" said Cusick. He looked at his men, "something's strange here." He stepped into the doorway, his gun pointed directly at the desk. He heard no sound, "Cover me."

He crept along the wall, like a shadow without a blink or a breath. His pistol aimed at the center of the desk until he was in range to kick it. He pulled back his leg and threw it at the wood. Immediately, he expected a gun to emerge, but nothing came.

"What the- He's not here! Surveillance, get the medics in!" He went to Lear and found a mass of bone and flesh where the bullet entered his head and shattered his skull. He closed the icy stare of Nelson Lear and radioed back, "No need for the medics, call the coroner, he's dead," Cusick said "Where the hell's Barchetti! He couldn't have gotten outta here." He surveyed the soundproof walls and started to tap them with his knuckle. He walked around the room, until he heard a hollow thud. "Here, I think somethin's here. Look for a release! We've lost a lot time! Everyone hurry, and find any kind of button or trigger to release this panel.

"I found it!" yelled a policeman. He pulled open the panel and released the door, which only opened a quarter of an inch.

"It's locked from the inside. Get your guns out, we'll have to knock out these locks too. It's like Fort fucking Knox in here." Two of the men pulled their guns and shot out the panel. "I want three officers down that passage. I'm heading out the front to talk with Becks!" He picked up the cellular and contacted HQ. "It's a massacre in here. Nelson Lear was shot point blank between the eyes. It looks like Sid Barchetti's on the run with the diamond. He disappeared through an underground passage. I got three men down the hole."

Cusick exited the store when a large explosion suddenly ripped through the neighborhood. Debris flew everywhere down the block. Screams and hollers came from people hit by falling glass and debris. "Jesus!" he screamed. He stopped in his tracks and watched a plume of smoke rise above the stores. He returned to his microphone, "I'm gonna need more paramedics, and more police. We gotta a situation out of control. I'm sending my officers to the explosion area to help the injured and wounded. I'll leave the men down the hole, to chase Barchetti. This is Cusick, out."

Randall and Johnny saw the explosion from the surveillance van. They stepped outside the van.

"Johnny, this isn't fun any more."

"Yea, I'm wonderin when it's gonna end."

"This guy's like god damn, Al Capone! My luck to walk in the guy's shop with a fuckin diamond the size of a baseball. Man, my diamond!" His head turned erratically on his shoulders looking for a place to run. He saw a man emerge from a doorway opposite Atari Gems. Randall watched the man take a few steps towards a Kawasaki 500. He was the same build as Sid Barchetti.

"Johnny, it's him. I don't know how, but he came out a doorway on the opposite side of the street. It's him!" Randall yelled. He turned to face the villain, "Barchetti! I know it's you!"

Immediately, Barchetti hopped on the Kawasaki, revved the throttle and took off.

Randall and Johnny ran to a nearby Harley and hot-wired the cycle. Johnny hopped in back of Randall and they both took off in hot pursuit of the criminal.

Cusick overheard Randall's scream, but was too late to respond. "Bear, are you there? Bear, God dammit, answer me!" he yelled from inside a police car.

"Yea, Cusick, I'm here."

"We got a cop killer, one Sid Barchetti, on motorcycle haulin down 47th Street. He's got Randall Becks in pursuit on motorcycle also. Can you see 'em? They should be obvious."

"Got'em," said Bear. "They're passin' Madison, now Lex."

"I want an update every couple of blocks, so we can head 'em off. We just started our vehicle," shouted Cusick.

Randall and Johnny rode within 50 yards of Barchetti, but as the traffic backed up at a light, Barchetti took to the sidewalk.

"Hang on, Johnny. It's going to be a rough ride," said Randall. He heaved the heavy motorcycle on to the sidewalk like a paperweight.

Barchetti weaved in and out of the pedestrians on the walkway. People dropped bags and belongings that complicated the Harley's ride. The obstacles littered the sidewalk and despite Randall's maneuvering of the large bike, he hit a grocery bag, which splattered, on a nearby wall.

Barchetti launched himself back to the empty street, with help from an avoided stoplight. He gunned the Kawasaki and did a belligerent wheelie in a blatant distaste of riding. On the straightaway, Randall and Johnny again closed the distance.

"Cusick, this is Bear. I've got'em going downtown on Lex. Wait, they've just turned East towards First Avenue, to avoid the congested area. This guy's gotta be a New Yorker."

"Hang in there, Bear. I'm gonna try and get a road block!" He switched channels. "Dispatch, dispatch, this is Cusick. I need several roadblocks set up immediately. We got an extremely dangerous cop killer on motorcycle. He's probably headin' out of the city. I want blocks set up at the Midtown tunnel, the Brooklyn Bridge and the Holland."

"Yes, sir," said dispatch.

Barchetti eased the throttle as the traffic backed up once again. *These Goddamn fools are ruining my plan. I'll die before giving this diamond up!*

"We're getting' closer Randall! Stay with him. I taste success!" yelled Johnny.

Barchetti moved the motorcycle back to the sidewalk and again rode the busy walkway.

"Cusick, Bear. He's still on first and definitely going downtown. The guy's insane. He goes from riding the street to riding the sidewalk."

"You better believe the guy's crazy! I think he's a pipe bomb ready to explode."

"He made a right on 35th, back towards the West Side and through the center of town."

"Don't tell me that, Bear. That leaves the Lincoln wide open."

"Come on you fucks!" Barchetti screamed. *I'm gonna kill both of your families with a snap of my fingers when I'm free and clear! You have no idea who you're dealing with.*

"What'd he say?" Randall asked Johnny as the air buzzed in his ears.

"He said something about ducks. Where da ya think the guy's goin'?"

"Beats me, but we'll follow him to the end of the earth if we gotta!" Randall said.

The thunderous Harley echoed down the corridors off 35th Street, between city buildings. It's screaming machine-gun sound made pedestrians in the distance watch for the oncoming bikes. Foot traffic parted like the Red Sea, as the bikes barreled towards Herald Square.

"I've got open visibility Cusick! I can bring the copter down for a closer look. The first motorcycle just entered Herald Square and stopped. He's positioned his motorcycle perpendicular to the on coming one. He's aiming his gun towards the other riders. Jesus, Cusick! He's shootin' at 'em! The motorcycle's veered off the park towards 32nd Street, away from Barchetti."

"Is anyone hit?" yelled Cusick.

"I can't tell. Wait, he's aiming the pistol at us! I gotta take it up! Cusick!" yelled Bear. The helicopter started its ascent when a slight popping sound cracked the windshield. The bullet pierced Bear's chest and rendered his hands helpless. The steering column fell forward and sent the helicopter in a dive towards the ground.

People scattered like ants from the falling piece of machinery. The helicopter blades cut into the bronze and stone bell built in 1877. Its body crashed into the cement sending Bear's lifeless body half way through the cockpit.

"Bear, Bear!" yelled Cusick. Static filled the other end of the microphone. He turned to the other officer, "I gotta bad feeling about this." He pushed the intercom speaker. "Anyone in pursuit of the Kawasaki that started on 47th Street, please beware. The man's armed and dangerous."

A reply came from the broadband, "detective, the suspect just shot a fuckin' helicopter out of the sky. What kind of firepower does he have?"

Cusick looked at Tenskey in disbelief. He sat momentarily in silence, "we don't know what kind of firepower the suspect has. Where's he, now?"

"At the time the chopper was crashing down, he had already returned to his bike and was heading further towards the West Side."

"Do you know if another motorcycle was in pursuit?" asked Cusick.

"We saw a Harley, return to follow from a distance. The motorcycle's sound must have alerted the suspect. I don't think there's any safe distance with that bike."

"Thank you, officer," said Cusick. He looked at Tenskey, "I'd bet my right ball he's goin' for the Lincoln." He looked down at his watch. "It's rush hour. He's gonna get caught up at the tunnel. Do you think we can get some cars there in time?"

"Gonna be tough, but you'll have to do it now. It's easier for them cause they're on motorcycle."

Cusick sent out the A.P.B.

"Hang in there, Johnny. How's the shoulder?"

"It's only a nick. Couple of inches closer, and my ass would have been grass. Good thing I got my lucky rabbit's foot."

"What? You got a rabbit's foot?"

"It keeps me safe, Randall. Sometimes, you need all the help you can get. So far, it's been pretty good to me. You might want to think about getting one!" he yelled.

"Maybe after this whole thing's over, I will! Can you believe this guy? A Goddamn helicopter! I thought that only happened in movies!" exclaimed Randall.

"Just don't ride his ass. I don't want to end up like that pilot," cried Johnny.

"But you got your lucky rabbit's foot. We really have the chance to test it out. Hang on!" shouted Randall. He gunned the throttle and closed some distance. "The traffic's backing up, Johnny."

"Doesn't seem to be slowin' him down. He's headin' for the Lincoln, but it's gotta be jammed by now. He's one crazy asshole."

The motorcycles weaved their way in and around traffic. When they arrived at the mouth of the tunnel, no police cars were in sight.

Sid Barchetti's mind worked like a machine at full steam. *There's no way I can weave in and out of traffic through the tunnel like this! If I ride the walking ledge, I'll be home free, but I'm gonna kill these pests first.* Barchetti pulled his motorcycle to the edge of the tunnel's walkway. He stopped, threw down the kickstand and stood off his bike. He watched the men weave in and around cars towards him. Barchetti pulled his pistol, aimed and shot.

The first bullet Barchetti fired ricocheted from a car hood and sent the men for cover. They ducked below a stopped car.

"You think he has enough ammo to keep this up?" asked Johnny.

"I don't know. He must have used quite a bit already. Maybe, we can get him to pop a couple more bullets. Traffic's at a stand still. Let's split up while he looks for us. Pop your head up and down like one of those whack-a-mole games, and wait until he fires four shots. We'll meet back here. Break!"

Both men hunched over and ran in different directions around the stopped traffic, stopping on occasion to crawl.

Barchetti's vantage point was above the cars. *Trying to trap me, amateurs? Come on, sneak in, so I can nail you.* He took a shot at Johnny's back creeping below a car hood. The bullet bounced from the car. Randall crept in the opposite direction, closing in on the man. In a fit of fury, Sid Barchetti started to blast the hell out of his gun. Both men lay down on the street as bullet after bullet pierced the cars that kept them covered. Barchetti laid down 10 rounds before he stopped. Tucked his gun back in his holster, hopped back on the motorcycle and entered the tunnel via the walkway.

"Randall, you there?" yelled Johnny. "You OK?"

"Yea, I'm all right. You?"

"Good. You think that was enough rounds?"

"More than enough! He's entered the tunnel. Head for the bike," shouted Randall.

Both returned to their standing positions and ran for the Harley. They sparked up the bike and drove on to the walkway.

"Johnny, this is gonna be tight. There's no room for error." Randall maneuvered the motorcycle till it was the dead center of the pathway. "We have less than a foot on each side to maneuver. Whatever you do, don't shift your weight. I don't have room to compensate for your movement at high speeds."

"High speeds?" said Johnny.

Randall gunned the Harley and sped up to 25 mph. *I've got to close the gap. If he's too far ahead he'll have time to stop and kill us in our tracks. Gotta keep the pressure on.*

"Is anyone at the Lincoln? Did anyone get there?" yelled Cusick into the intercom.

"The traffic's at a stop all around the vicinity, detective. Very little room to move," spoke an anonymous voice.

"He's probably in the tunnel already. For God sakes they're on motorcycle!"

"This is an APB on gunfire at the Lincoln Tunnel. Three men on motorcycle are reportedly involved. One man fired on two men from a Kawasaki. No pedestrians injured. From reports, the men have ridden into the tunnel. Anyone in the area, please report."

Cusick grabbed the microphone, "HQ, get Jersey on the phone. Let'em know what's happening." *Crazed psychopath. Where you gonna hide? Where are you going to hide?*

Sid Barchetti moved cautiously through the tunnel. *I wish I could avoid the long loop outside the Lincoln! I'm vulnerable there. If they bring in another helicopter, they'll shoot me by air.* Barchetti watched the path, careful not to slip either way. He ignored the loud sound of the Harley in the distance. He swayed his head to watch the traffic slowly move towards the end of the tunnel. *They'll expect me to appear from the tunnel on motorcycle, but not in a car. If I hijack a car, to cover myself, they'll lose me in the traffic, I'll need a roof overhead and a hostage. It's too soon for them to set up a detection system.*

Sid Barchetti closed in on the end of the tunnel, knowing every moment was critical to his success. He stopped his motorcycle 100 yards from the exit, and catty-cornered it to obstruct the path. He jumped over the guardrail and panned his eyes across the rows of cars. He targeted a green Honda Civic. The alarmed driver locked the doors, but at the sight of Sid's gun, quickly released the locks. Barchetti opened the rear door and shut it behind him. He faced the driver.

"My gun's pointed at your back, so don't think of anything funny, or you won't be alive tomorrow. You're going to get me out of here. I'm going to lay back in your seats and I want you to pretend I'm not here. If you see two men in your rearview mirror approach your car, let me know. Capish?"

The man shuddered, "Yes, sir."

"Lower the rear passenger window!"

The window descended and Sid lay back behind the driver's seat. He arched his knees and put his forearms over them pointing the gun directly at the open window.

The Harley came upon the empty motorcycle. "We got a problem Johnny, me boy," said Randall. "He must have hopped in a car to escape the tunnel."

"But that could be any car!"

"The traffic hasn't moved much since we've been down here. He has to be close. Get down between the lines of traffic and search the cars."

"Well… do I have a choice?"

"No, but don't worry. I'll take care of you, man."

Johnny jumped down and began walking forward peeking in people's cars. He heard car locks slam shut. He started to worry as he neared the mouth of the tunnel. He edged up to the Civic's trunk and ran forward until he stood in the center of the passenger window. He turned and faced Barchetti.

"Shit!" he yelled.

Sid pulled the trigger of his gun and the gun jammed. "Fuck!" he yelled.

Johnny ducked and quickly ran back towards Randall. "He's in the green Honda!" He mounted the Kawasaki in front of Randall's Harley.

By this time, the car exited the tunnel and Barchetti stayed down to reload.

"This is New Jersey State police Chopper 192. I'm over the exit to the Lincoln Tunnel awaiting two motorcycles to emerge. It looks like I have the first exiting, now. He's speeding along between cars. Wait, the other motorcycle just emerged, but it doesn't look like he's chasing the other bike, in fact, he's fanned out to the opposite lane of traffic. What the hell's goin' on down there?" asked the pilot.

"This is detective Cusick of NYPD, how many riders do you have on the second bike?"

"One."

"There were two going into the tunnel," He responded.

"We lost a rider, Cusick," said the pilot.

"Do we have cars arriving at the scene?"

"They're on their way. They're gonna form a road block at the top of the hill."

"Will they make it in time?" asked Cusick.

"They're arriving now."

"How far up the hill are the motorcycles?"

"About half way. It looks like both motorcycles have united to the sides of a green car. One's riding the left of the trunk, the other the right. One's pointing to the car. Jesus! It looks like the back window just exploded! Both motorcycles scattered. I'm not sure if we have a motorcycle down. They were quick to move. One's moved behind an SUV towards the guardrail. The other came to a stop. What am I looking at chief?" asked the pilot.

"There's a wanted criminal in the green car. He shot a policeman and did some extensive damage in the city. He's very dangerous and highly intelligent, so I'm sure he knows we're close to the end. He's got firepower," said Cusick.

"Well, I think the other drivers figured that 'cause the cars behind him stopped, when they saw the rear window explode."

"Is the motorcycle behind the truck a Harley?" asked Cusick.

"Hard to say, but it doesn't look like one of those neon Japanese bikes."

One of those guy's must be on the ditched motorcycle. "The two bikers chased our criminal, Sid Barchetti, into the tunnel and it looks like he found a car inside. Tell your friends at the roadblock to let neighboring cars through, until they get somewhere close to the green car. We have a potential hostage situation, so be prepared with a marksman, anchored high at the helix for a shot. We're entering the tunnel now, so it's all you. Don't take this guy likely. We don't know what he's packing," said Cusick.

"Understood," said the pilot.

Randall held the Harley behind the SUV. Sid Barchetti watched him swerve into the shadow of the vehicle. *If I'm going to hell, I'm taking Becks.* He took careful aim at the SUV's back tire then fired. It was only seconds when the truck swerved to the left cutting Randall off.

Randall swerved towards the railing as the truck gunned the gas to avoid him. Randall, with little time to react, skid the back out and went into a slide. His right leg got pinned beneath the motorcycle and broke on impact. The thick blue jeans slid up his right leg, twisting it beneath the motorcycle. The Harley came to a halt.

"Stop the car! Stop the God damn car!" Barchetti yelled.

The car came to an abrupt halt. Sid watched Randall slap the pavement in pain and struggle to move himself. "Driver, I don't want you going anywhere, you're with me. If you move the wrong way, I'll bury you. There's something I have to take care of before I leave here, and that something is lying over there, pinned under a motorcycle. Out!"

Barchetti aimed the pistol at the driver's head as he exited the car. He pulled the man close with his left arm and proceeded to take baby steps beneath policemen's astonished eyes. Sid's head dodged left and right as he heard the thundering blades of the helicopter overhead.

Randall watched helplessly as Barchetti approached with his hostage. *God Dammit! Randall, you gotta move, cause this fuck's coming for you!"* He jolted forward and backwards, crying in pain, while his arms worked frantically to move the Harley from his shattered leg. Sid slowly neared.

Johnny, reluctant to move from his unknown position, watched with patience. He silently revved the Japanese bike. *Damn you! You won't take him today or ever, asshole.*

Barchetti edged closer and closer to his fallen foe. He laughed with excitement, closing the distance. He pulled his hand quickly from the hostage to pat his pocket. When he felt the stone secure, he held the hostage tightly to his body.

Randall's hope diminished along with his struggle, *Lord, please take me quickly. If by some miracle you allow me to live, I'll be eternally grateful. I give of myself completely.*

Barchetti approached Becks until he towered over him. He looked down.

"Mr. Randall Becks, you've been quite the adversary and nothing but a sore on my ass since we met. But thanks to you, I'll be a few million richer."

"If you ever escape," Randall said through gritted teeth.

"I'll do better than escape, I'll get off. My friend here will make sure of that. You wouldn't be a worthwhile hostage; you're like an injured horse, which needs to be put out of his misery."

"Fuck you!"

"No, fuck you my friend. Did you ever think it would end like this? Certainly, I didn't expect to have the whole NYPD and New Jersey state troopers on me. Thanks to you, I'm in deeper than ever, but I finally have the stone. With the stone comes the ultimate power, and you know I enjoy power. Unfortunately for you, you've reached the end of your rope."

"Have mercy on me, Sid. Obviously, you've fought as hard for that diamond, as I did to keep it. You've won. I only wanted a break in life, nothing more. I was stupid to think I could outsmart you for the price of this simple stone. My life's worth more and I should have known this," plead Randall.

"Shut it. You should have realized, but it's too late. You can't change what I'm gonna do, but don't worry, I'll do it quickly. Between the eyes good for you?" asked Barchetti.

"Please, I'm begging you! Have mercy! At least let me see the diamond once more before I die. All the trouble, the pain, the suffering, my dying wish."

Barchetti looked into Beck's pathetic face. The hostage's uncontrollable shake annoyed him, so in an instant, he released the prisoner from his left hand, but pointed the pistol close to the man's head. His loose hand grabbed the stone from his pocket, pulled it out, and held it towards the sun.

The light cast a bouquet of colors through the prisms of the diamond. He manipulated it between his fingers and watched the twinkles of light dance on the street. Mesmerized by the rainbow, he felt a sudden jerk and flash of pain down his arm. He turned to see a slight movement of a rifle in the rocks. He refocused on the Kawasaki rider whose hand knocked the diamond into the air. He aimed the pistol at Johnny's back.

The impact of Johnny's hand from his moving motorcycle popped the diamond high. Its movement was surprisingly slow, as all eyes turned to the brilliant gem. The sunlight flashed into and out of the gem like a disco ball rotating in a dark nightclub. Johnny hadn't lost sight of it for one second, but he lost the location of his motorcycle.

Sid pushed his hostage loose as he positioned both hands on his gun. The hostage, in a panic, sprinted in the opposite direction.

"No!" yelled Randall. His head mixed with emotions. *Don't let this innocent bystander die, Lord. Please don't let the diamond smash to the ground! My goddamn leg,* "Arrghhh."

It was then, that Randall heard the thud. A loud thud, like a 2 x 4 cracked across a pillow. He wiped his hand across his moist face to reveal a handful of blood. He saw Sid Barchetti's body wobble, and then he heard the second thud. He heard Barchetti's pistol fire as his body fell back towards him. He held his hands high to catch the falling torso.

Quick Johnny's eyes worked feverishly, as he leapt from the moving motorcycle. *Daddy don't speed, the rain's too hard. Not around the corner Daddy, Mommy don't let him speed around the corner. It's raining too hard. We're gonna crash Mommy, Daddy. I love you.* Then Johnny remembered how his baby seat crashed through the window of their car and how his parent's hit the telephone pole. The sunlight cast its rays through evil gray clouds when he awoke as a child. He was alone. The light warmed him and his hands stretched out to touch his parents, but they were too far. *The diamond, the lights, they're too far.*

He stretched with all his might and like that lonely child; the time seemed an eternity before his fingertips touched the smooth facets of the stone. With the excitement of his first touch, his torso stretched an extra inch enabling him to capture the whole stone.

He tucked his arm into his stomach and crossed it securely with his other as his body now arched towards the ground like a cannonball. His thick leather wallet was the first thing to impact with the ground. His jeans tore in the thigh as they met the tar. The sharp pain escalated at an unbearable pace. His body thrown violently until it silently came to a rest 25 feet later.

"Johnny! Johnny! Can you hear me?" yelled Randall. Desperate to see his friend, he tossed Sid Barchetti's body to the side, with a shot of adrenaline. He used all his remaining strength, to pry his leg from the wreck. His nails dug into the street and pulled him to the middle. He could see Johnny's curled torso. "Johnny, answer me God dammit!"

The thundering pain bounced in Johnny's body. He heard Randall's faint screams as they echoed like a soft voice in the distance. He looked at the diamond tucked in his hand; its weight like a 50lb. barbell. He strained every tendon and every nerve to move it.

Randall saw Johnny's elbow move in the distance. His jagged forearm raised parallel to the street for a number of seconds, as it hit an invisible force field. Then like a flag hoisted up a pole, the backside of his hand appeared. It stood erect, like a steel pole in the distance. Johnny's hand rotated until he held between his fingers the undamaged gem. It was more radiant and powerful then he ever imagined.

I'm free. I'm finally free, Randall thought. He collapsed.

The helicopter hovered over the scene. "Headquarters, we need a Medivac here immediately," the pilot screamed.

Chapter 27
Epilogue

One Year Later

"Hey guy, how much is the huge glass water bottle? I need something for my change."

"Well my friend, that's no ordinary bottle. I bought it from an estate sale with ten others, all filled with sour wine. The bottles dated 1926 to 1932."

"Ain't that during prohibition?"

"Yea, I hadn't thought about it, till I dumped the sour wine they contained, probably from rum running days. I bet they belonged to a gangster, but since this is the last bottle I have, I'll take $25.00 on it- a bargain."

The stranger looked at him in doubt. "That's a wild story. Kinda, like the story of that guy who bought a safe and discovered the world's largest diamond. I read in the paper this guy Hillerman discovered it over 5 years ago after his wife passed. I don't know why some idiot couldn't get past the emotions and not cut it immediately - he was a damn diamond cutter! That's just stupidity. I heard the guy who recovered it just sold it for 50 million yesterday. Can you imagine?"

"Hard to believe," he said. He turned and yelled, "Johnny, did you hear the headlines this morning?"

"No, Randall, what's goin' on?"

"Those clowns who found the world's largest diamond sold it for 50 mil! I think the whole things a ploy. Before you know it, the flea market will be a place to visit the social elite! It's all a sham!" yelled Randall.

"Hey, don't complain, guy. If that happens, we'll get better prices for our stuff!" Johnny said. He turned to look at a woman in front of his table, "Lady, if you buy that for $50.00, the guy over there will do a dance for you."

She looked over at Randall, "he will now? That might be interesting."

Randall laughed. "Hey, Harry! Did ya hear?"

"Of course I heard! All I can hear is your big mouth! I knew a guy once who made birds shit all over that guy. Sometimes I wish he'd do it again! Funniest thing you ever knew."

The stranger looked back at the intimidating biker, "you mean you actually knew the guy?" he yelled.

"Yea, saved my life once," Harry replied.

"No kiddin'," said the stranger.

"Truth's stranger than fiction," said Randall.

The stranger turned back to the assorted merchandise on Randall's table. He surveyed the unusual items when his interest closed in on his ring. "What an incredible ring! That's not a real diamond, is it? It's huge!"

Randall smiled. "It's genuine. As a matter of fact, its part of the Hillerman diamond, but behind this diamond ring, is a story itself."

LaVergne, TN USA
09 January 2011
211719LV00002B/84/P